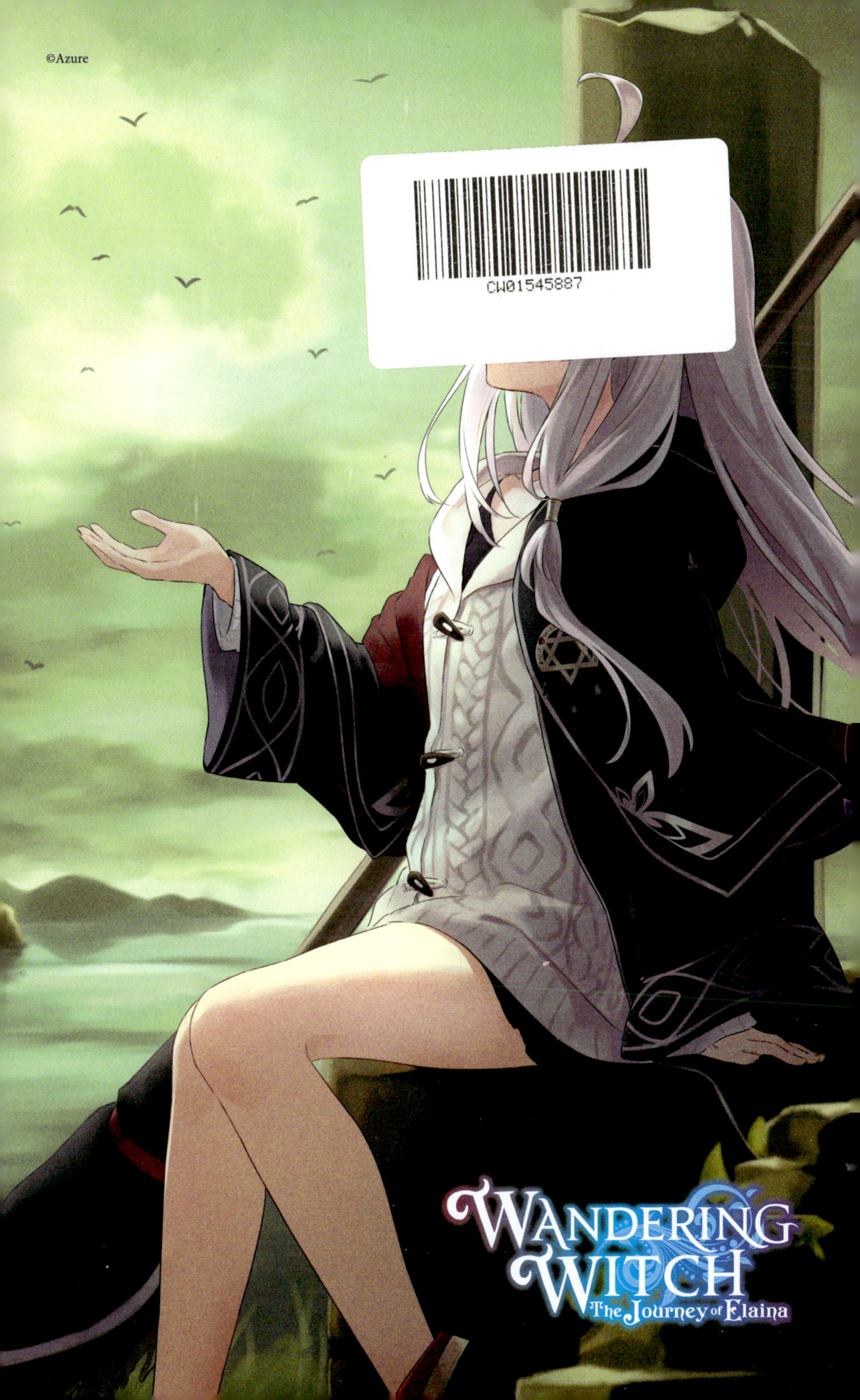
©Azure
CW01545887
WANDERING WITCH
The Journey of Elaina

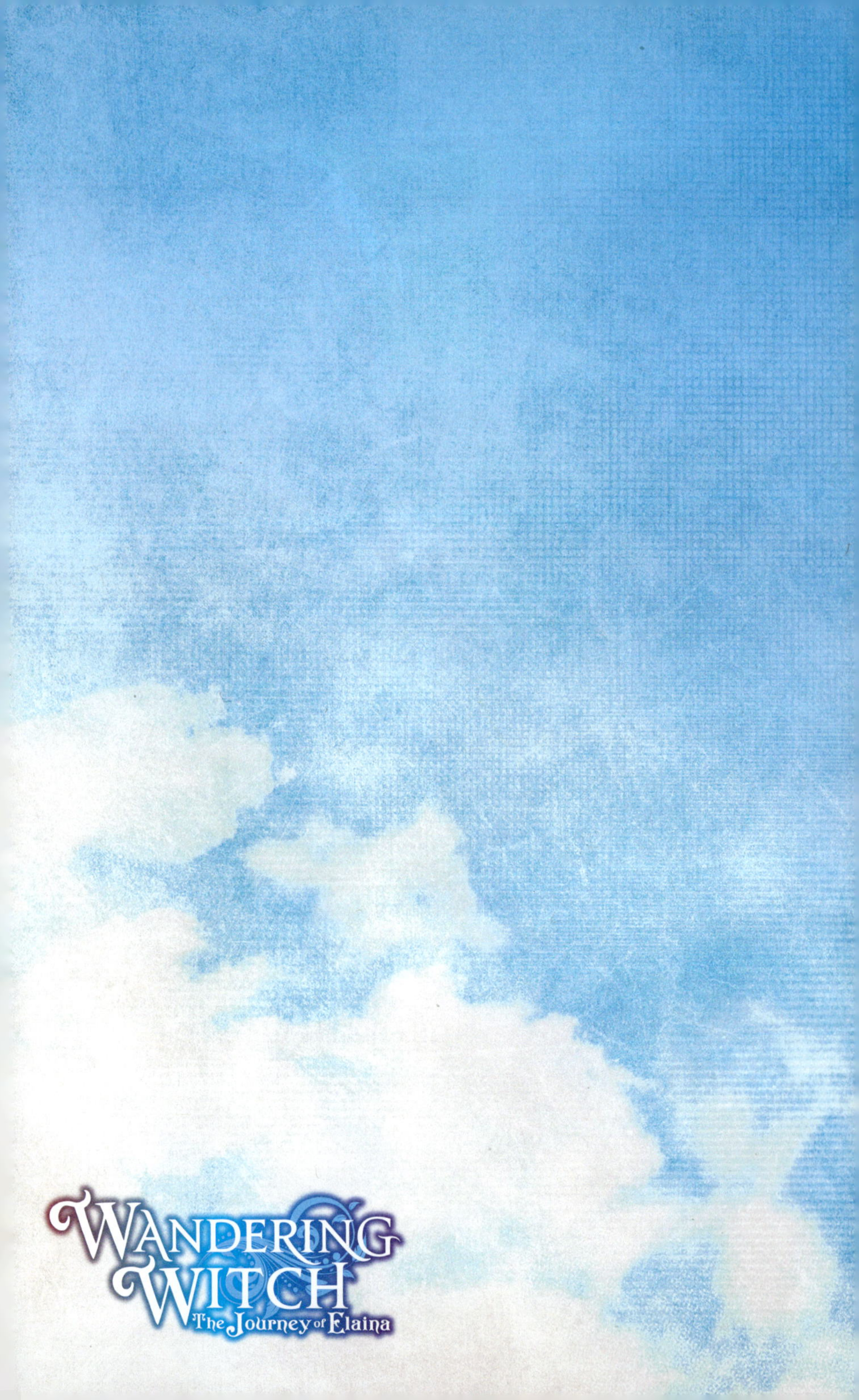
WANDERING WITCH
The Journey of Elaina

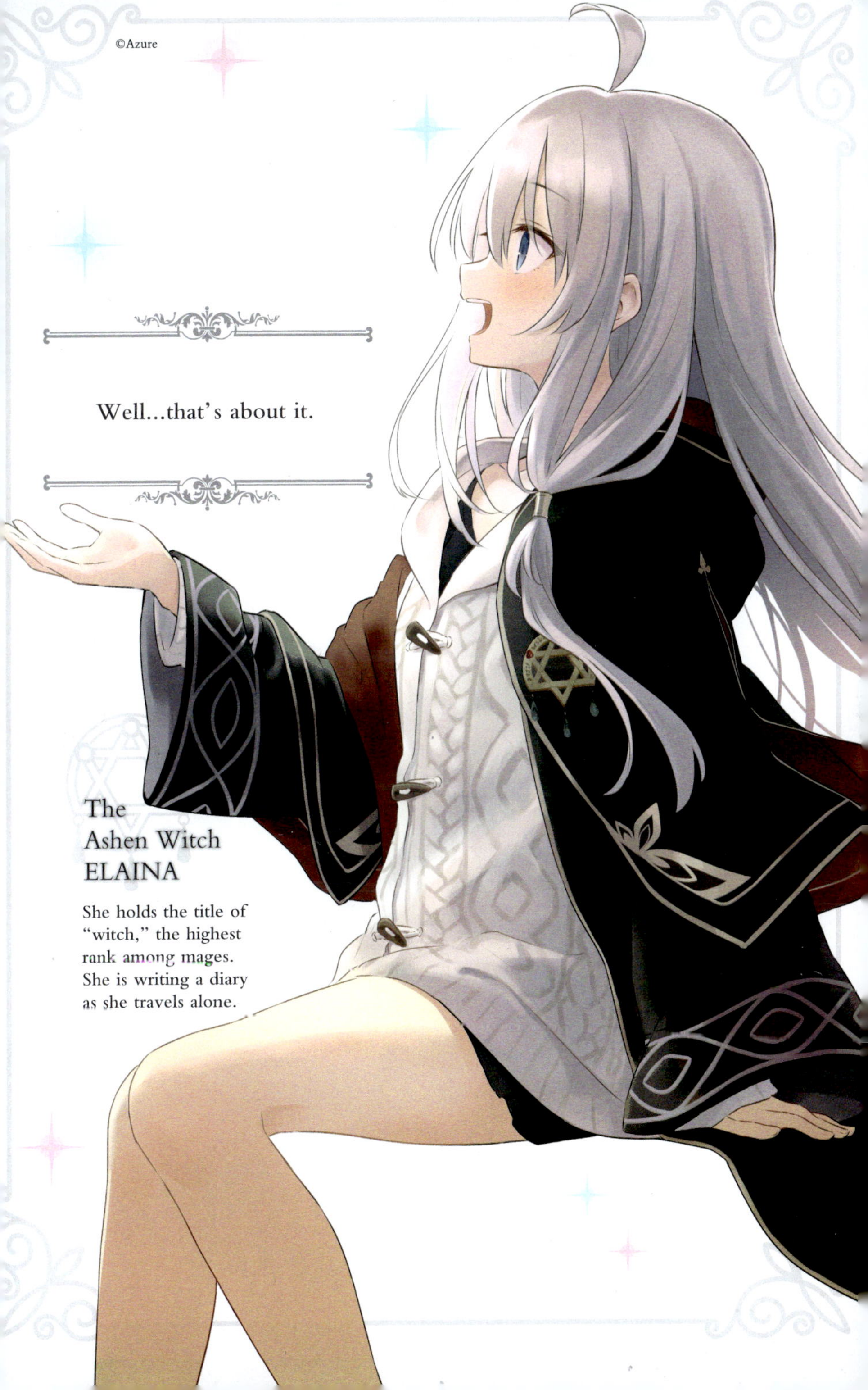
©Azure
Well...that's about it.
The Ashen Witch ELAINA
She holds the title of "witch," the highest rank among mages. She is writing a diary as she travels alone.

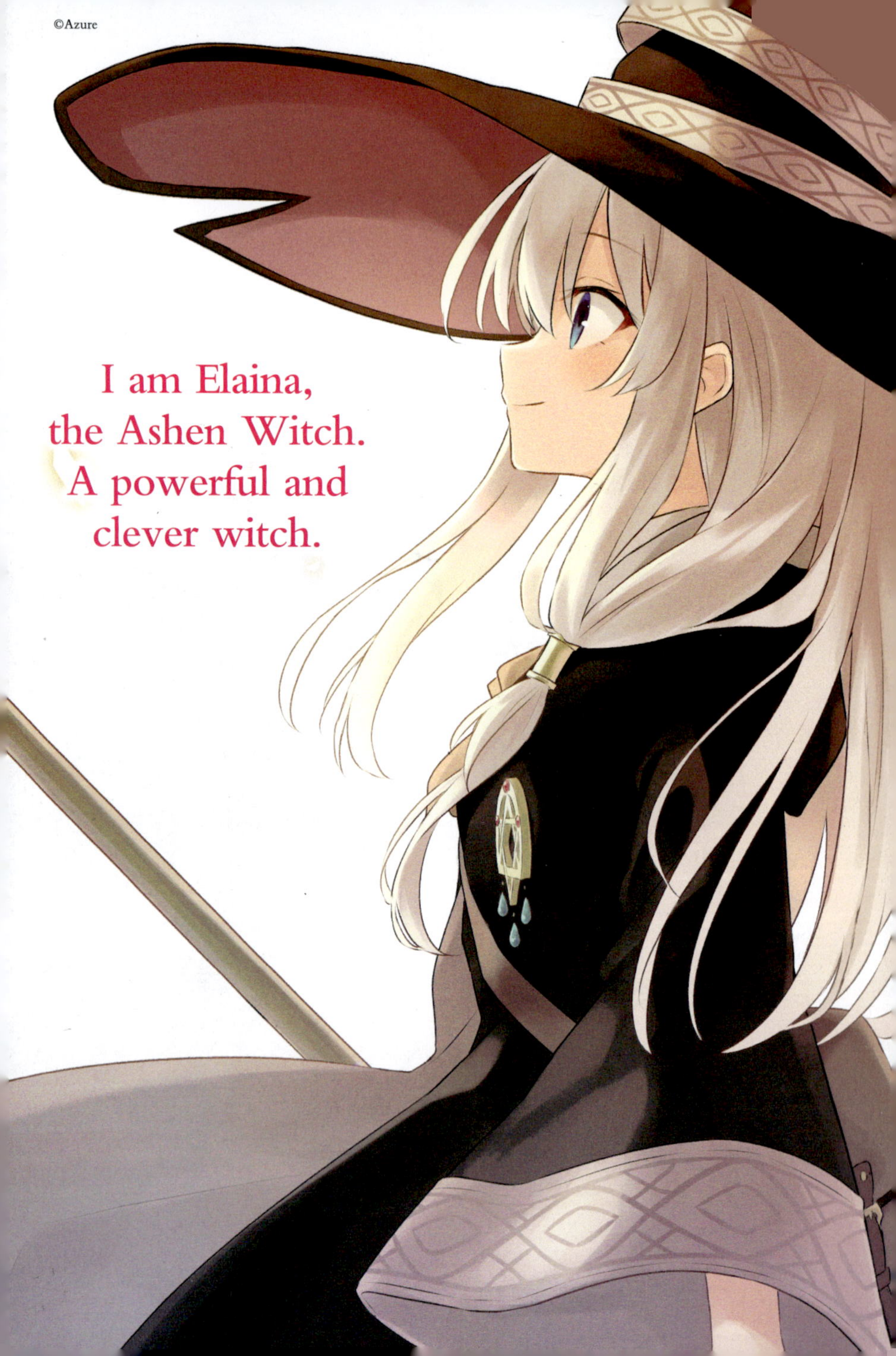
I am Elaina,
the Ashen Witch.
A powerful and
clever witch.

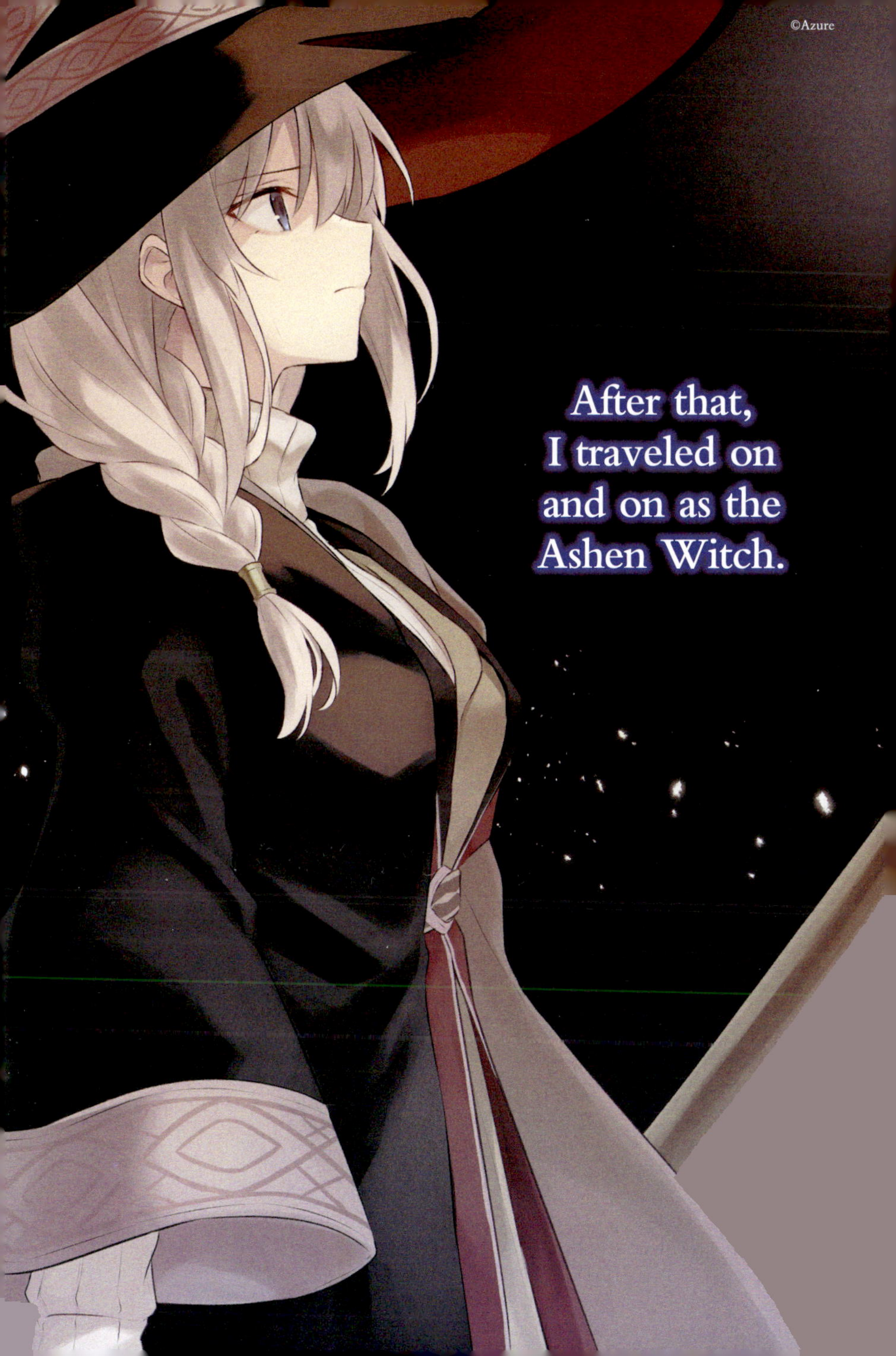
After that,
I traveled on
and on as the
Ashen Witch.

WANDERING WITCH 15
The Journey of Elaina

CONTENTS

CHAPTER 1   Complete Bonus Stories Collection   001

CHAPTER 1 STORY 1 A Scary Story 001	**CHAPTER 1 STORY 12** The Snowman and the Witch 067
CHAPTER 1 STORY 2 Miss Fran's Maxim 005	**CHAPTER 1 STORY 13** Little Witch 071
CHAPTER 1 STORY 3 The Finest Food 009	**CHAPTER 1 STORY 14** An Academic Anecdote 075
CHAPTER 1 STORY 4 The Witch's Magic Trick 015	**CHAPTER 1 STORY 15** Pumpkin Festival 079
CHAPTER 1 STORY 5 A Story Worth Celebrating 021	**CHAPTER 1 STORY 16** And So Miss Sharon Is At It Again Today 091
CHAPTER 1 STORY 6 Elaina's Scam Course 025	**CHAPTER 1 STORY 17** The Selfishness of the Ancient Dragon Luciella 095
CHAPTER 1 STORY 7 The Center of Food Culture Exchange 029	**CHAPTER 1 STORY 18** Plaster Repair Specialist (Charcoal Witch) 099
CHAPTER 1 STORY 8 The Harmful Results of Being Unable to Lie 035	**CHAPTER 1 STORY 19** The World Through His Eyes 103
CHAPTER 1 STORY 9 There's No Way My Little Sister Could Be So Cruel 039	**CHAPTER 1 STORY 20** Avelia's Secret 119
CHAPTER 1 STORY 10 Surprise 043	**CHAPTER 1 STORY 21** Amnesia's Anguish 121
CHAPTER 1 STORY 11 The Country of Birthdays 051	**CHAPTER 1 STORY 22** Saya's Daily Routine 125

©Azure

CHAPTER 1 STORY 23	Elaina's Birthday 129	CHAPTER 1 STORY 34	A Story About a Psychological Test 189
CHAPTER 1 STORY 24	A Mysterious Phrase 135	CHAPTER 1 STORY 35	Am I Pretty? 191
CHAPTER 1 STORY 25	Mirror, Oh Mirror 137	CHAPTER 1 STORY 36	Amnesia and Avelia 197
CHAPTER 1 STORY 26	Alte and Linaria's History Hunt: A Traditional Statue 147	CHAPTER 1 STORY 37	The Cursed Box 199
CHAPTER 1 STORY 27	Hot and Cold Elaina 151	CHAPTER 1 STORY 38	A Scam Story 203
CHAPTER 1 STORY 28	The Tale of the Sweets Shop and the Witch 155	CHAPTER 1 STORY 39	A Story of Staple Foods 207
CHAPTER 1 STORY 29	The Tale of the Sweets Shop and the Master and Student 159	CHAPTER 1 STORY 40	The Ghost in the Teapot 211
CHAPTER 1 STORY 30	Miss Fran's Culinary Awakening 165	CHAPTER 1 STORY 41	A Strange Presence 215
CHAPTER 1 STORY 31	Leveling the Playing Field 169	CHAPTER 1 STORY 42	A Certain Country's Specialty 219
CHAPTER 1 STORY 32	A Tale of Teachers and Students 173	CHAPTER 1 STORY 43	A Story of the Country of Stories 223
CHAPTER 1 STORY 33	Another Scary Story 185		

CHAPTER 2   The Cursed Doll That Always Comes Back No Matter How Many Times You Get Rid of It   227

CHAPTER 3   A Story of Saya and Sheila's Tobacco   235

CHAPTER 4   The Tale of a Certain Traveler   249

©Azure

WANDERING WITCH
The Journey of Elaina

JOUGI SHIRAISHI

Illustration
AZURE

15

New York

Wandering Witch
The Journey of Elaina

JOUGI SHIRAISHI

Translation by Nicole Wilder

Cover art by Azure

This book is a work of fiction. Names, characters, places, and incidents are the product of the author's imagination or are used fictitiously. Any resemblance to actual events, locales, or persons, living or dead, is coincidental.

MAJO NO TABITABI vol. 15
Copyright © 2020 Jougi Shiraishi
Illustrations copyright © 2020 Azure
All rights reserved.
Original Japanese edition published in 2020 by SB Creative Corp.
This English edition is published by arrangement with SB Creative Corp., Tokyo, in care of Tuttle-Mori Agency, Inc., Tokyo.

English translation © 2025 by Yen Press, LLC

Yen Press, LLC supports the right to free expression and the value of copyright. The purpose of copyright is to encourage writers and artists to produce the creative works that enrich our culture.

The scanning, uploading, and distribution of this book without permission is a theft of the author's intellectual property. If you would like permission to use material from the book (other than for review purposes), please contact the publisher. Thank you for your support of the author's rights.

Yen On
150 West 30th Street, 6th Floor
New York, NY 10001

Visit us at yenpress.com ✶ facebook.com/yenpress ✶ twitter.com/yenpress ✶ yenpress.tumblr.com ✶ instagram.com/yenpress

First Yen On Edition: March 2025
Edited by Yen On Editorial: Payton Campbell
Designed by Yen Press Design: Wendy Chan

Yen On is an imprint of Yen Press, LLC.
The Yen On name and logo are trademarks of Yen Press, LLC.

The publisher is not responsible for websites (or their content) that are not owned by the publisher.

Library of Congress Cataloging-in-Publication Data
Names: Shiraishi, Jougi, author. | Azure, illustrator. | Wilder, Nicole, translator.
Title: Wandering Witch : the journey of Elaina / Jougi Shiraishi ; illustration by Azure ; translation by Nicole Wilder.
Other titles: Majo no tabitabi. English
Description: First Yen On edition. | New York, NY : Yen On, 2020–
Identifiers: LCCN 2019052222 | ISBN 9781975332952 (volume 1 ; trade paperback)
Subjects: CYAC: Fantasy. | Witches—Fiction. | Voyages and travels—Fiction.
Classification: LCC PZ7.1.S517725 Wan 2020 | DDC [Fic]—dc23
LC record available at https://lccn.loc.gov/2019052222

ISBNs: 978-1-9753-6871-5 (paperback)
       978-1-9753-6872-2 (ebook)

10 9 8 7 6 5 4 3 2 1

LSC-C

Printed in the United States of America

WANDERING WITCH
The Journey of Elaina

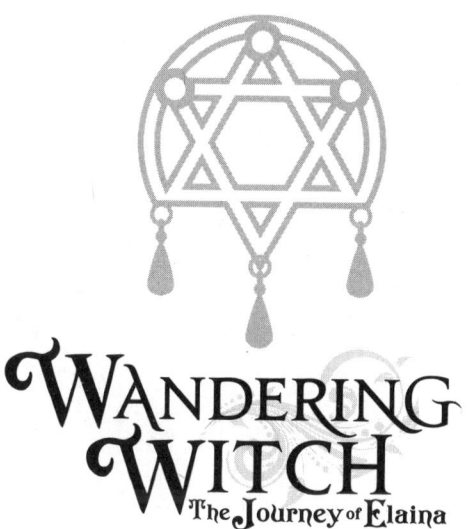

CHAPTER 1 STORY 1
A Scary Story

"And so after that man gobbled up every last one of the *manjuu*, he said this: 'Ah, I'm scared. Now hot tea is scary.'"

There was a lovely crescent moon hanging in the night sky over the Country of Mages. Beneath the moon, at an inn, Saya told me the story as she took a seat on the bed, wearing a look of total terror.

"…I'm sorry, you said this was a scary story, right? Where are the scary elements in the story you just told me?"

"Whaaat? I can't believe what I'm hearing. You're a boor, Elaina. Think about it on your own."

"…………"

I had only asked because I was disappointed by the contents of her story. This was after Saya had barged into my room suddenly in the middle of the night, going on about "Let's tell scary stories!" and whatnot. Still, for some reason, I was the one being scolded.

"Okay, next it's your turn, Elaina. Come on, try and scare me!"

"Sure."

"Oh, but I can't really handle scary stories! So I request the kind of story that is just a little tiny bit scary but ultimately has a happy ending!"

"That's a tall order."

I was even more puzzled as to why I was now being forced into telling her a scary story. And she had set the bar quite high.

But unfortunately, I had no shortage of material for that sort of story.

"I see. Very well, then, I'll give you one of my spare stories."
Then I told it to her.

Somewhere out there was a traveler.
Upon arriving at a certain country, the traveler took a room in an inn as always and stayed the night. However, the room the traveler rented was terribly strange. Night after night, some unfamiliar stranger came in and invited the traveler, "Eh-heh-heh…let's sleep together…heh-heh…"
The traveler, fearing for her safety, barricaded her room so that no one could come in. She felt safe, sure that now no one could enter.
However, the unfamiliar stranger, in a dreadful turn of events, broke down the door.

"No one knows what happened to the traveler that night—"
When I finished telling my story, Saya shuddered dramatically and said, "Eeek…that's so scary. That unfamiliar stranger was definitely a stalker! Poor traveler!"
"By the way, the story I just told is true."
"A t-true story…? Eeeek… I'm scared. Elaina, let me sleep with you, please."
"I figured that was your intention in coming here from the start, but I absolutely refuse."
"Oh, come on! Now I'm going to be too scared to sleep! It might even affect my training tomorrow."
"That's not my problem. Please go shiver yourself to sleep."
Then I glared at her while sighing. "And hurry up and fix the door, will you?"

[Publication Information] Volume 1
Melonbooks Buyer's Bonus

[Author Comments]
    This story is based on the very famous rakugo bit "Scary *Manjuu*." I wasn't really aware of it, but I wrote another bonus story for Volume 10, which was a turning point in this series, using the same themes. Moreover, it has exactly the same title! You never think anything through, do you, Shiraishi?!

CHAPTER 1 STORY 2
Miss Fran's Maxim

"Elaina, everything we cultivate over the course of our lives becomes a foundation for living, you know."

One day in the middle of my training, Miss Fran suddenly said something strange that sounded like an aphorism of some sort.

You reeeally get to know someone after being with them for a long time, so I had long since accepted that when she said things like that, it usually just meant she was hungry.

So I didn't disguise my grimace as I answered, "*Sigh...* Is that so?"

"Yes—everyone has things in their past that make them blush to think about, or an experience that was so difficult, it made them want to die, don't you think? But by no means should we try to erase those things from our pasts."

"By the way, do you have any such past experiences, teacher?"

"Of course. Even at my age, I've gotten lost because I was chasing a butterfly and found myself on the verge of tears. That is my past, so painful, I could die…"

"Wow…"

I didn't need to hear that…

"Do you have any, Elaina?"

"I had one just now, when I asked you that question, Miss Fran."

"……"

"Right, so in the end, what are you trying to say?"

"……"

Suddenly, my teacher's lips curved into a smile, and she said, "Even when we make mistakes, it's precisely because of those mistakes that humans grow, bit by bit. Past mistakes become our foundation for moving forward. So it's important not to fear them and to try all sorts of different things."

"By the way, what did you learn from the mistake you just told me about?"

"I learned that butterflies are fickle, so I will get lost if I follow one."

"But, Miss, weren't you chasing butterflies when I first met you?"

"...Ah."

I see. It looks like your foundations are still quite shaky—

Instead of saying that, I asked, "But if that's the case, couldn't you sometimes do the cooking instead of me?"

"No, no. I don't do such things."

"Your words and actions contradict each other..."

"What are you talking about? I am performing the action of 'I don't cook.' By no means am I avoiding cooking because it is a big hassle. I'm someone who can do anything, if I try."

"...So then, what have you learned from performing the action of 'I don't cook'?"

"The unshakable fact that even if I don't make anything, with my pupil here, who is good at cooking, it's possible to live a rich life."

"......"

"Thank you for everything you do."

Her foundations are not only shaky, they're sinking as we speak.

It was a maxim I couldn't help but question. But when she thanked me to my face, it gave me a strange feeling, part joy and part embarrassment.

...But anyway, those feelings shored up my own foundations.

"Should we go ahead and eat already?"

[Publication Information]   Volume 1
Toranoana Buyer's Bonus
[Author Comments]
  This is a bonus original story I wrote to go with Volume 1 of *The Journey of Elaina*. Since the page count of the bonus stories that go out to the stores is limited, I often had to work hard to make everything fit, and it makes me smile to see evidence that I was already struggling when I wrote Volume 1.

CHAPTER 1 STORY 3
The Finest Food

Deep in a particular forest, an apprentice witch who dreamed of traveling on her own was undergoing training with a senior witch.

The apprentice's name was Elaina. She was a young woman whose most striking features were her ash-gray hair and her lapis-blue eyes.

By the way, she was also a genius.

And who exactly do you think that genius was?

That's right, it's me.

"……"

Well, I'm just kidding, but…

"Take a look at this, Elaina. I made some amazing food."

I couldn't help but hope that Miss Fran was making some sort of joke when she said that.

"Elaina, from time to time, I would like to eat something more delicious," my teacher had grumbled just the other day.

Since she always made me do all the cooking by myself, I'd wondered what on earth she was saying. I'd gotten angry. I had run entirely out of patience.

"No way. You need to cook sometimes, Miss. This is really starting to make me angry. Until you do some cooking, I'm not making a thing. I'm refusing to budge on this. I'm really serious, okay?"

Like I said, I was very upset.

Still, she must have felt remorseful, for the very next day, sure enough, my teacher made some food for me.

She cooked for me…I guess I could say, but…

Now, how exactly do I explain this? Spread across the table was a truly tragic tableau.

"…So this is your fine food, is it…? Hmm, your eyes are getting dull, Miss."

I let out a sigh.

However, apparently my sigh of grief sounded like a sigh of admiration to my teacher, because she smiled again and chuckled as she said, "Now look here, Elaina. Can you tell what ingredients this dish uses?"

"Is that squid ink pasta?"

"No, it's peperoncino."

"I see, so modern peperoncino noodles are pitch-black? Very enlightening."

"By the way, I used the highest grade of noodles I could get." Miss Fran was calm. Apparently, my frank opinion had passed right in one ear and out the other. "All right, next. Can you tell what ingredients are in this soup?"

"Huh? Sorry, I don't see any liquids."

"You see, for this, I used the highest grade of lobster!"

"…All I see is a lobster that's been stuck in some mud…"

"This is soup."

"Soup, is it?"

Well, if my teacher says so, I suppose it must be true.

"Okay, can you tell what I used to make this dish?"

"Weeds?"

"This is top-grade salad."

"What is top-grade salad…?"

I no longer had any idea what she meant.

But at this juncture, I was finally able to catch on to what my teacher was trying to say.

"Um, Miss?" I asked, pretending to be timid. "Are you by any chance trying to say that this is the finest food because you used the highest-quality ingredients?"

"Yes, I am. What of it?"

"......If you could make fine dishes just by using high-quality ingredients, then we wouldn't have anything to worry about. But I'm pretty sure the fact that we're complete amateurs is what's going to determine whether we can actually make delicious food out of those particular ingredients."

Many people who deal in fine dining draw mysterious patterns on the white part of plates with sauce or arrange the food so beautifully that it seems like a waste to mess it up, but I think that's probably something born out of the playful nature of chefs who have too much time and energy to spare, and think like *Ah, oh no, shoot. The flavors are perfect, but there's just something missing here. I want to add something a little more artistic!*

I think it's only fitting that the type of people who handle the finest ingredients are that fastidious about their work.

But as I narrowed my eyes, Miss Fran said to me, with plenty of confidence, "Elaina. I find it unacceptable that you reject my cooking before eating any of it. Doesn't it look absolutely splendid in appearance? I can guarantee the flavor, too. It's to die for."

Uh-oh.

Is she saying that the dishes before my eyes also have an artistic quality to them?

"......"

It's rather avant-garde.

So I actually tried eating them.

The proof is in the pudding.

She was right that until I tried it, I wouldn't know whether or not my teacher's cooking was any good.

I was immediately assaulted with waves of regret from the bottom of my stomach.

"......Bleeehhh!"

I'll go ahead and refrain from describing here what happened next.

○

"How was it? My cooking was just supreme, wasn't it?"

"Yes. The most supremely disgusting thing I've ever eaten in my life. I can't believe how full of confidence you were presenting something like that. What is the matter with your tongue, teacher?"

I spit abusive language at her, and my teacher answered in an aloof manner. "Oh my, what are you talking about, Elaina? I said that food was of the finest quality, but I never said a word about it tasting good, you know."

"……Huh?"

What does that mean?

"Incidentally, I also tasted it earlier and briefly lost consciousness. My cooking is awful after all, huh? It's supremely disgusting. No matter what kind of ingredients I use, it seems they turn to garbage as soon as I lay my hands on them."

"If you knew the dishes were garbage, then why did you make me eat them…?"

"Well, now you understand just how abysmal I am at cooking, right?"

"……"

"But your cooking is just wonderful, Elaina. It's got real flavor; it's the finest of food. Rather than cooking for myself, I prefer to eat your cooking."

"……"

"Which is to say, please cook for us again today."

So that's what it comes down to, huh?

As I let out a sigh, I headed for the kitchen. Thankfully, since we had an astonishing array of ingredients acquired by my teacher, flavoring was no problem.

On the contrary, since the place was overflowing with the highest-quality ingredients, I was able to flex my culinary skills more than usual.

I realized I had been successfully played only after I had drawn patterns with the sauce.

[**Publication Information**]   GA Books Official Blog
[**Author Comments**]
　　Similar to how the *yakisoba* you eat from a food stall at a summer festival or at a house by the sea is so delicious that you can't believe it's of this world, I think the flavor of a dish can change dramatically based on the environment that surrounds it, even when it's the same old food. When eating delicious food, an environment that enhances its deliciousness is also important. Mysterious patterns drawn on ridiculously large plates are also necessary for that type of presentation.

CHAPTER 1 STORY 4
The Witch's Magic Trick

"Elaina. The fact is, you know, about me…is that I can use magic."

This happened during my training days.

Deep in the forest, in a little house that stood quietly at the top of a tree.

My teacher, Miss Fran, said something very strange.

"What's the matter, teacher? Did you finally lose your mind?"

My teacher, who went by the name of the Stardust Witch, appeared to have forgotten who she was. Nothing could be more awful, right?

"Ah, sorry, my mistake. Wait just a moment, please. Ummm…"

After flipping frantically through a book that had the title *Weekly Publication: Magic Tricks for Dummies* written on it, my teacher seemed pleased to say, "Now I've done it. So that was the line for people who can't use magic, huh…? I'm sorry, please let me start over again from the beginning."

……

Apparently, my teacher is interested in magic tricks or something like that.

"Do you have a lot of free time on your hands, teacher?"

"I do not. I just wasn't doing anything, so I thought, 'Oh, that's an idea. It might be nice if I could do magic tricks.' There's not really any reason beyond that."

"That situation is called having a lot of free time."

"By the way, Elaina, would you like to make a little wager with me?"

"A wager?"

My teacher nodded as she set a deck of cards on the table.

"I'll ask you now to take one card of your choosing from this deck.

After you've memorized the number that is written on that card, please return it to the pile. In a splendid feat, I will find the card you chose and hold it up," my teacher said, holding *Weekly Publication: Magic Tricks for Dummies* in one hand.

Incidentally, the first issue of that publication apparently cost one copper coin. However, subsequent issues cost one gold coin each. A real rip-off, huh?

"…So what about this wager?"

I could more or less see what was about to happen, but just in case, I went ahead and asked. Anyway, I had no doubt she was going to say something like "*If I win, I want you to swap dish washing duty with me.*"

"In the event that I correctly guess the card you chose, I win. You'll take over dish washing duty, please."

See?

In the kitchen, a huge number of plates and utensils had piled up and overflowed. I had unintentionally gotten carried away and cooked too much food, so the number of used dishes had grown to ridiculous levels. Add the fact that the dishes containing the dark matter Miss Fran had created were in there with mine, and the kitchen was an absolute picture of chaos.

She was probably fed up with the overwhelming number of them.

So this was her giving in to temptation, I suppose.

"Heh-heh-heh… As long as I have this book, it's an easy feat to fool Elaina's eyes…"

Miss Fran was buzzing in anticipation of tricking me.

"Well then, if you fail, you wash the dishes instead of me for a week, please."

I was buzzing with the excitement of seeing through her plot.

○

"All right, go ahead."

My teacher fanned out the deck of cards and said this as she held them out to me. The red patterns drawn on them spread out in an elliptical shape, like so many flower petals.

"Okay."

I pulled one card out from around the center of the deck. It was the joker.

While I was doing so, my teacher was glancing down at her copy of *Weekly Publication: Magic Tricks for Dummies*. By the way, it looked like the first issue came with a free gift.

When I replaced the joker back into the center of the deck of cards, my teacher said with a gasp, "You returned your card, yes? Well then, now let's bring the card you drew up to the top of the deck." She gathered the cards with a couple of taps.

Then she held her hand over the top of the deck and said something that sounded like a kind of incantation. "...Hi-yah..."

She looked a little embarrassed.

Then she turned over the very top card.

It was a joker.

"The card that you drew was this joker, right, Elaina?" My teacher wore a self-satisfied look. "Heh-heh-heh. I am your teacher, after all, Elaina. I have insight into everything you do!"

"......"

"Well, all right then, Elaina. As promised, I think I'll have you take over washing the dishes for me."

She sounded incredibly self-satisfied.

In response, I let out a deep sigh.

"Completely wrong. The card I drew was not that card at all."

"Oh my, you mustn't lie, Elaina. I am your teacher, you know? I have insight into everything you do. The card you pulled was, without a doubt, this joker."

"No. It wasn't *that* joker."

"...What did you say?"

I spoke plainly to my teacher, who wore a puzzled and somewhat apprehensive expression.

"Those cards—they're all jokers, right?"

"……………………Whatever are you talking about? Of course not. That's silly."

"Okay, turn over the second one and show me."

"I would rather—"

"Miss."

"I refuse."

"Not allowed. Flip it over, please."

"I would rather—"

"Quickly."

"I decline."

Since I was getting nowhere, I snatched the cards away forcibly.

When I spread the cards I had taken from my teacher's hands out on top of the table, I covered it in clowns. It was truly a magnificent display, nothing but clowns. Smiling at me with the petty smiles of those intent on making a fool of me.

They were jokers. All of them.

"It looks like I win."

I flashed the most satisfied expression I could muster, and my teacher made a truly disappointed face.

"…Tch. How did you know…? My magic trick ought to have been perfect…"

My teacher was glaring bitterly at *Weekly Publication: Magic Tricks for Dummies*.

"I am your pupil, you know? I have insight into everything you do!" I replied.

○

Weekly Publication: Magic Tricks for Dummies

Every week, in exchange for its high sales price, that book apparently came with a free gift item that supposedly helped the user perform the trick inside. It was written right there on the cover.

Incidentally, Miss Fran's copy had written on it: COMES WITH A PACK OF ALL-JOKER CARDS THIS WEEK! USE IT, AND YOU, TOO, CAN BE A FIRST-RATE MAGICIAN!

Since she had been reading it right in front of my eyes, that meant both the secret of the trick and the means of her trickery were completely visible. To put it another way, it meant it was a magic trick even a moron would understand.

"I have to do all of these all by myself...? Ahh...I can feel my heart breaking."

Miss Fran's head drooped as she beheld the terrible spectacle spread across the kitchen.

So far, I haven't revealed to her how I had seen through her magic trick. I probably never will.

After all, my teacher has insight into everything I do, right?

[Publication Information]   GA Books Official Blog
[Author Comments]

When I told the editorial department they would be fools to present the above bonus story in order to advertise my books, they said, "Fine, but we're putting it up on the GA Books blog!" This was the second story that was published that way. There actually was one more, but that one got stuck into the main books.

CHAPTER 1 STORY 5
A Story Worth Celebrating

That day, we arrived in a country that seemed to be having some sort of peculiar festival. The main avenue was decorated with showy arches and other ornaments, and the people manning the street stalls that lined the road were strangely excited.

It didn't take much time before I realized they were apparently conducting some sort of celebration.

But, well…

"Um, excuse me?" I grabbed a girl who was walking down the street and tilted my head as I asked, "What exactly are you celebrating today?"

The girl's eyes instantly lit up as she said, "Well! You must be a traveler, hm? Welcome to our country!" and grasped both of my hands, pumping them up and down. It was much too intense for a greeting.

After swinging my arms about for a while, she continued, "Today, you see, is the Anniversary of the Day When One Hundred Travelers Came to Our Country at Once! It must be fate that your journey brought you here on this very day!"

"Huh."

"By the way, yesterday was the Anniversary of the Day When Our Country Quit Taking State Administration Seriously, and tomorrow is the Anniversary of the Day When the Number of Anniversary Days in Our Country Exceeded Three Hundred!"

Somehow, just hearing about those three occasions was more than enough for me to feel like I understood what kind of place this country was.

"By any chance, do you have these types of festivities all year round?"

"Of course! Every day is an anniversary day! …Except for the day after tomorrow, that is."

"Which means the day after tomorrow, you take a break from the celebrations?"

"Not at all. The day after tomorrow is the one day when there's nothing specific that we need to commemorate. So we can't have a festival. And in our country, being unable to celebrate is akin to death… Ohhh, I start getting depressed about it two days in advance!"

And yet you seem to have an abundance of energy, so maybe it would be a good idea for you to look up the definition of depressed *in the dictionary? I mean…*

"In that case, couldn't you just have the Anniversary of the Day When There Was Nothing to Commemorate?"

"That's brilliant!"

Her eyes opened wide, and she once again grasped both of my hands and pumped them up and down. As before, her response was much too intense.

In the coming days, the country's cycle of anniversary days would be successfully completed, creating a wonderful place where every day was a celebration. Even now, as this wonderful country held festivals almost every day, they seemed to be entertaining their travelers and sightseers.

But what a happy country it must be, celebrating every day of the year!

Being able to hold a festival every day is certainly something worth celebrating.

[**Publication Information**]   GA Novels Launch First Anniversary Buyer's Bonus

[**Author Comments**]

This is the bonus story I wrote for the first anniversary of the launch of GA Novels.

I'm a light novel author who wrote a bonus story that had absolutely nothing to do with a first anniversary…

CHAPTER 1 STORY 6

Elaina's Scam Course

"The reason why we have called you here today, Lady Witch, is none other than this: Recently, a gang of fraudsters in our country have started employing more advanced methods, and we would absolutely love to receive your counsel on this matter."

Finding myself suddenly summoned by a government official of a certain country, I received this earnest request.

What can they possibly be expecting from a traveling witch? I'm just out here traveling. It's not like I'm an authority on different scamming methods or anything like that, but—

"Ah, Lady Witch, we've heard the rumors about you. Recently, you've been earning money by palming off suspicious items to the residents in neighboring countries, isn't that right?"

"……"

"We can expect your cooperation, yes?"

I see, so he's trying to say they'll throw me in jail if I don't cooperate.

…So that means this is less of an appeal for my cooperation and more like simple blackmail?

"We've taken the liberty of looking into several of the fraudulent business practices you have been conducting in neighboring countries, Lady Witch."

"Um, okay… You have, have you…?"

"For some reason, it seems you've been pushing sales of these sorts of documents at a high price, yes?"

The official placed a magazine on the table in between us. Written in large letters on the cover was the title *Methods Even Idiots Can Use to Easily Make Big Profits!* The handwriting was familiar. Because it was mine.

"Ah yes…I did distribute…such things… That's right…" I averted my eyes.

"It seems you've made quite a tidy sum. About how much would you say you've made?"

"Um…I'm sorry, but I've forgotten the exact figure…"

"Oh! Then you've made so much, you can't even remember? I see, I see." For some reason, the official was scribbling away on a memo pad with a pen. "Ah, right, right. This is a change of subject, but these materials—how did you sell them? It couldn't have been an easy feat to sell ordinary sheaves of paper for such a high price, could it?"

This has turned into some kind of interrogation…

"Um…that's kind of a trade secret, you could say…"

I continued averting my eyes. All I could do was stay quiet about the things I couldn't say. However—

"Oh, is that so?" The official cast a sharp glance in my direction. "We heard this by way of another rumor, but apparently, when you were selling these booklets, you were telling people, 'If you can't buy it for such a high price, no problem! There's an arrangement where you get ten percent cash back if you get another person to buy one. In other words, if ten people buy this from you, you get all your money back,' and other such things as you went around selling them everywhere."

"……"

"In other words, the people who bought these from you had to get a further ten people to buy one from them, and then each of those ten people had to get more people to buy them, but…Lady Witch, do you have any comments regarding this situation?"

"…………Um, by any chance, is this an interrogation…?"

"Lady Witch." The official looked at me with a broad smile on his face. "I can count on your cooperation in resolving this situation, yes?"

......

As I suspected, he seems to be trying to say they'll throw me in jail if I don't cooperate.

[**Publication Information**] Volume 6
Gamers Buyer's Bonus
[**Author Comments**]

Seriously, isn't that fraud?! I thought when I read back through this. The Elaina in this story is probably the version of her that is rotten to the core and appeared in the last chapter of Volume 3…probably… Around the time I was writing Volume 6, I wrote a fair number of stories in that vein, so I feel like I've gone all in on the fraud angle. Just like Elaina in this bonus story, I've come to feel a little bit embarrassed about the blunders made by my former self.

CHAPTER 1 STORY 7
The Center of Food Culture Exchange

It was midday when I finally arrived in that particular country.

I had heard secondhand rumors about it in other neighboring countries. This was a major country that was known as the center of food culture exchange. Apparently, it was a wonderful place where the food cultures from all the surrounding countries blended together in a pleasant way.

"Welcome, Miss Traveler," a soldier said to me in front of the gate as he bowed. "This is the country of Evifurya."

"Evi…? Huh, what's that?"

"Evifurya."

"What is that?"

"Ha-ha-ha. What strange things you say, Miss Traveler. Evifurya is exactly that—it's Evifurya."

"…No, but what I'm asking here is what is that Evi-whatever you're talking about—?"

"Evifurya is Evifurya."

Apparently, he's not going to give me any more details.

Ultimately, I wound up entering that country of Evi-whatever while still racking my brain over what it might be.

○

Apparently, the Evi-whatever this country had taken its name from was a kind of soul food, the most popular and delicious dish they had, and the pride of the country.

I see. Very interesting. I'm curious to see just what kind of food it is.

And so, to that end, I visited a nearby café and immediately ordered some.

"Excuse me. Give me one order of the most highly recommended dish in the whole country."

But unfortunately, by this time, I had completely forgotten the name *Evifurya*, so I ended up ordering it in this incredibly roundabout way. But I figured that if it was really the most prominent dish in the country, well, then I wouldn't need any detailed explanations, would I?

"Right away!"

And in fact, the employee nodded in understanding and went into the back of the shop, so I figured they had probably understood me.

Before too long, they came back.

"Here you are."

And what they set down on my table was—well, how do I describe this? It was a puzzling pancake with a huge amount of cream piled on top of it.

"…Um, this is the Evi-whatever?"

At my words, the employee tilted their head. "No, it's not? Did you want to eat Evifurya, miss?"

"Uhhh…yes. I did, but…isn't this country the country of that Evi-whatever?"

"Oh-hoh-hoh. Not at all. This is the country of the Shi◯Whirl."

"I'm sorry, I couldn't hear part of what you said."

"I said, this is the country of the Shi◯Whirl."

"……"

I was bewildered by the appearance of yet another new word. And then—

"Oh, now, I just can't let that fly! This is the country of the Shi◯Whirl, you say? Pshaw! This is the land of Miso Stew Udon!"

At the adjacent table was a manly looking man, clambering out of his seat as he made this assertion.

"To start with, could this ever play the role of a staple food? This here's a dessert. It could never be the leading part!"

The employee raised their eyebrows at the manly man. "Well! How can you possibly say such a thing?! Miso Stew Udon can only play the leading role during the winter season, surely! Why don't you realize that it's the ShiOWhirl, which can play the leading role year in and year out, that reigns supreme?"

"......"

My head was getting more and more turned around with the appearance of yet more new words.

The two of them left me alone with my headache as their argument heated up.

"I'm telling you, the ShiOWhirl is the best—"

"No, it's Miso Ste—"

"You two. Don't you think you could leave things there? Aren't you embarrassed to be fighting in front of a customer?"

Just as I was getting the feeling that things were getting out of hand, the soldier who had been on gate duty earlier stepped in to mediate.

"The best food is Evifurya."

Nope, I was wrong, he just came to pour oil on the flames.

"Huuuh?"

"What are you saying, you jerk?!"

"I should ask you! What are you two saying?! You're a couple of brats who don't even know how superior Evifurya is!"

Can we not agree that they're all delicious?

"Hoh-hoh-hoh…at it again?"

I was determined to remain a bystander, but appearing suddenly by my side was a mysterious old man wearing a know-it-all look.

Often, when trouble breaks out, such an old man with a know-it-all look will suddenly appear and explain the situation to you. It's part of being a traveler. Make sure you remember that.

"Young lady. Look around you. Everyone has their favorite dish, and they quarrel about them, you see?" Apparently, he was in the mood to explain things to me.

"In other words, this place is the battleground of food culture, young lady."

"Sorry, I kind of don't really understand what you're saying."

Unfortunately, I felt like I didn't understand the situation, even with the help of a know-it-all old man.

What exactly is a battleground of food culture?

"Hoh-hoh-hoh…well, just look."

"…*Sigh*." As I was urged to do, I watched their movements carefully.

The people who had been quarreling eventually came to a point where one of them said, "Fine, let's try them and compare to see which is the most delicious."

After that, they started praising one another's dishes.

"So tasty…"

"It's the flavor of home…"

"What in the…? This is really good, huh…?!"

Ultimately, they took each other's hands and reconciled.

Through this turn of events, I finally understood.

This country, which had many different food cultures, had probably seen many clashes like this one before, between the many culinary traditions and their different dishes. Whenever that happened, they each accepted the other, and in that way this place became the center of food culture.

I was deeply moved.

"So when cultures clash with each other, that's where the exchange happens, right, old man?"

In response to my words, the old man broke into a smile.

"Sorry, I don't really understand what you're saying."

"……"

At any rate, the food in that country was super delicious.

[Publication Information]   Volume 6
Animate Tokai Region Limited Bonus Story
[Author Comments]
    This is a bonus story limited to Animate Nagoya. Since parody routines narrow the scope of a story's humor, I try not to overuse them, but this was a bonus story, so I figured what the heck? This bonus story is chock-full of parody items.

◀ CHAPTER 1 STORY 8 ▶

The Harmful Results of Being Unable to Lie

"Elaina, Elaina, what do you think of me?"

"……"

This was the Country of Truth Tellers. An extremely annoying place, where no one was permitted to lie, or rather, no one was able to lie in the first place.

While there, I was having some difficulties.

"What do you think of me? But first, why have you been keeping quiet?"

For the last little while, Saya had been repeating the same question over and over again.

"……"

I had been staying quiet.

For a person whose words were full of lies (in short: me), the enchantment applied over this country did nothing but harm.

I'm sure the king of the country thought it would become a lovely, honest place because no one could lie, but sometimes, the thing called the truth can become more of a nuisance and more difficult to deal with than a lie.

After letting out a deep, deep sigh, I said, "Saya. Stop asking me that question. I don't know how to answer."

"Huuuh? Why would you have trouble answering? Tell me the reason, please, clearly and concisely, and specifically."

"……"

I was in a bind.

I had no doubt I would suffer the consequences if I thought or acted carelessly in this country.

And that was why I was cautiously, cowardly keeping my mouth shut. Nevertheless, when it came to Saya, she was still hanging around me as always, and she kept on asking questions.

"Elaina. You know, for my part, that I trust you so much, Elaina. You're more important to me than anybody else—"

"Hyah!"

I squeezed a piece of cloth into her mouth and wound it right around to the back of her head, where I tied it in a knot.

Now you can't talk anymore.

"Whhrrdyumydsh?" She seemed to be trying to ask where I had bought the cloth.

"I knew your mouth would get you into trouble, so I bought it in secret a little while ago."

"Sowwerbwebayed!" So well-prepared…she seemed to be trying to say.

"If you keep on saying things you shouldn't, next time I'll wrap your whole head up in cloth, so brace yourself for that."

"Mww…"

That shut her up.

Then, after I could finally speak safely, I let out a single sigh of relief.

Since I wanted to be my usual lovely, honest self, and suffer no consequences, I didn't want to say anything uncalled-for.

Or rather, there was no reason why I should have to go out of my way to say anything to validate her.

It wasn't like I would be enjoying a sightseeing trip with a person I hated in the first place.

"……"

Well.

I could never say such a thing in front of her, no matter what.

[Publication Information]   Volume 2
Melonbooks Buyer's Bonus

[Author Comments]

This was a story about a country of honest people. Even Saya couldn't possibly have thought that by showing no affection, Elaina was being incredibly affectionate.

I'm changing the subject here, but in the anime, Eihemia looked supercute, didn't she? Shiraishi here really likes girls in glasses. So I also liked the levelheaded girls who appeared in the episode about Royal Celestelia. Also, I was surprised to hear that the voice actor for the prince was Katsuyuki Konishi. The prince was so cool…he was holding a super-lame sword, though.

CHAPTER 1 STORY 9

There's No Way My Little Sister Could Be So Cruel

Elaina, can I talk to you about something...? Recently, my little sister has been super mean to me. She's always been a cruel girl, but recently I feel like it's gotten more obvious, or at least more frequent. As her big sister, I'm very unhappy about her rebellious phase.

Today, I was arranging my things to get ready to go back to work, but as I was doing so, my sister came to me and said, "Huh? What's with that filthy towel? You'd actually use something like that? Big Sis, you're a girl, so why don't you take a little more care with your grooming?"

She said that, and then she confiscated my towel! Isn't that awful? Even though I had only used it a few times! I mean, it wasn't even that dirty!

What's more, she had the nerve to say, "Big Sister, this one suits you well," and threw a new towel at me! Moreover, it smells great! I love it!

Huh? Isn't her behavior adorable, you ask? No, no, listen, Elaina. As a matter of fact, my sister's acts of savagery didn't stop there.

"Big Sister. What do you usually eat? Bread that you bought at a street stall? Oh no. That sort of thing is why you're still a little shrimp, no matter how much time passes. Eat things that are better for your body!"

She had the nerve to say that, and then she dragged me out to a nearby high-class restaurant against my will! Isn't that just awful? First she abused me, calling me a shrimp, and then she exposed me to public scorn by taking me to a restaurant that was a complete mismatch for a shrimp like me! What's more, after we got there, she said, "Okay, open up!" and fed me my food! Isn't that cruel?! She wasn't satisfied just making me a laughingstock, she went so far as to treat me like a child! It's the first time I've ever received such treatment!

Eh-heh-heh...but I did like that part, too.

Ah, even though I say I liked it, it wasn't like that, you know? She's a far cry from you, Elaina. I mean, I like her in a totally different way—

"I didn't really ask."

Who on earth was the witch who interrupted Saya's lovestruck boasting?

That's right, it was me.

I'm sure I was probably making a very annoyed face.

"...So Saya came to me yesterday to discuss that with me. What do you think?"

"I don't really care much."

"Is that so? ...By the way, what is that thing you're clutching so dearly right now?"

"Huh? My big sister's towel."

"......"

"It smells like my sister."

"...Oh, I didn't really ask."

"I'm not giving it to you."

"I don't want it! What's wrong with you?"

I'm sure I was probably making a very annoyed face at this time, too.

"Oh-hoh-hoh... I love my big sister."

At any rate, I felt that at this point, there was only one thing I could say.

There was no way Saya's little sister could be this cruel.

[Publication Information] Volume 5
Toranoana Buyer's Bonus

[Author Comments]
  This story makes you think that Saya is just bragging, even as she calls her sister cruel, but as a matter of fact, she was in a different sense being awesome (that's a compliment) all along.

By the way, these bonus special stories jumped straight from Volume 2 to Volume 5, so you're probably wondering, "Hey, hey, what happened to the bonus stories for the volumes in between?" but since there weren't really any requests for bonus stories to go with Volumes 3 and 4, I never wrote any. Incidentally, some of the bonus stories from Volumes 1 and 2 were recycled into the main storyline, so the spread of bonus stories from Volumes 1 through 5 that made it into Volume 15 is quite sparse.

CHAPTER 1 STORY 10
Surprise

My heart was leaping with joy at the prospect of being reunited with Elaina after so long in Qunorts, the Free City, when suddenly, I was struck with an idea.

"Wouldn't Elaina be happy if I brought her a surprise present or something?"

The present I prepared for her was some ordinary bread.

If I were to list Elaina's favorite foods, bread would be the only thing on the list. It was a cheap gift, but the requirement for a present isn't to spend a lot of money, it's the thought behind it! The best gifts are gifts that will make the recipient happy, rather than gifts that are merely expensive.

And so I had decided to give her a present, but...

"The timing is tricky..."

What timing would make Elaina the happiest? After all, Elaina was a person who ate bread when she was hungry. She also ate bread when she had free time. As if bread was her first priority, it was in her nature to attract bread to her around the clock. It seemed like, no matter when I handed her my gift, she'd say, "*Oh, thanks,*" as she added it to the bread she'd already bought for herself. Then my present wouldn't have any meaning.

This is a real head-scratcher...

"I overheard your dilemma."

As I was puzzling over this problem, my little sister, Mina, suddenly appeared without any warning. I was a little bit startled.

"…Where did you come from, Mina?"

"I am always watching over you, Big Sister."

"…Ah, I…see…"

"Stop making that face."

"What kind of face am I making?"

"An openly disgusted face." Then Mina deliberately cleared her throat and looked down at me. "You seem to be troubled, Big Sister. May I assume you can't figure out when to give Elaina her present?"

"Huh, you know about that?"

"Yes. I always know what's going on inside your head, Big Sis."

"…Ah, I…see…"

"Stop making that face."

"What kind of face am I making?"

"An emotionless face." Then Mina turned away from me a little bit and said, "If you're having trouble giving her your present, I could offer you some help. I've got a good strategy."

Oh-hoh!

"A strategy?"

I asked again with tactless frankness, and Mina chuckled and tossed her hair proudly, then said, "Do you know what it is that brings someone the most joy when they're given a present, Big Sister?"

"What?"

"Try thinking about how you would feel if you got a present from me."

"I would generally be pretty happy about getting something from you, Mina."

"……" Mina suddenly turned her face away. "That's not what we're talking about right now."

"Huh…?"

But when I thought about it again, I still couldn't quite pinpoint what it was that made someone happy when they got a present. I ended up puzzling over it for a while.

"Hmm…?"

I don't catch on quickly.

After watching me think for as long as she could stand, Mina finally shrugged, and with open disappointment, she let out a single sigh, then said, "You're hopeless, Big Sister."

After a generous pause, with a very self-satisfied expression, she said, "It's the surprise."

○

"What exactly is a surprise?"

Once again, I demonstrated my ignorance as I asked Mina that question, but my little sister readily explained, "People are usually happy when they get a surprise, Big Sister. You need to sneak up on her, and after you surprise her, give her the present."

"...Sneak up, and then hand over the present..."

Oh-hoh!

...Sounds perfect!

So to that end—

"She doesn't look busy..."

I had set my sights on Elaina, who was loitering aimlessly in a café. I was approaching from behind. If you're going to surprise someone, I believe this is the most standard method.

As I crouched down and slowly crept toward her, I recalled my conversation with Mina.

"Big Sister. When it comes to surprises, if you want the most effective method, there's nothing better than this," she told me.

"You approach from behind and go, 'Guess who?' right?" I replied. *"I see, that makes sense. You used to do that to me all the time, Mina, until just a little while ago."*

"That's not what we're talking about right now."

"You stopped doing that recently, didn't you? Why?"

"Shut up."

At any rate, there could be no doubt that using this method was the best way to make the other person happy. I crept up unnoticed and approached Elaina's defenseless back.

Slowly, so slowly.

And then—

—when I had only one step left to go—

"For some reason, I can smell bread."

"……!"

—Elaina suddenly turned around.

Well!

I hid myself in a panic. I'd been planning to surprise her, but I'd gotten surprised myself, losing everything. The operation was a failure.

"…Huh? Must have been my imagination…"

Ultimately, Elaina then started reading or something.

But there was no way I could give her the bread once things had turned out that way, right?

So I decided to try again on another day.

The following day, I prepared some different bread and gave it another go.

This time, I decided on a different strategy. Instead of approaching from behind, I was going to leap out from a hiding place to surprise her.

But—

"Huh…? I can smell some sort of…mellow aroma coming from over here…"

Why on earth was this happening? Elaina immediately reacted to any person carrying bread. She quickly approached the hiding spot where I was concealing myself.

This plan was a failure, too.

"……"

There were a few things I think I more or less managed to figure out after failing twice, but even after that, all my tactics ended in utter defeat.

Whether I tried hiding behind something, or approaching from behind, or watching her from a distance, no matter what I did, Elaina got wind of me, just because I was holding bread.

"Huh? I sense there's bread in this area..."

Consequently, no matter how well I hid myself, she immediately suspected something. She never discovered me, because every time, I just narrowly managed to escape, but even so, I was never once able to give her the bread.

Elaina noticed me every time I was already holding bread.

What in the world is going on here...?

"Uuugh...this is never gonna work, is it...?"

Eventually, I was at a loss for what to do, and I sat on a bench and let out a sigh.

I can't keep doing this!

I sat there sulking.

"It's rare to hear you sighing. Did something happen?"

Just then, Elaina suddenly appeared from somewhere. As she did, she broke into a grin. "Something smells awfully good, huh?"

"Where did you come from, Elaina?"

"I always appear wherever there is bread."

"......"

What does that mean...?

"Is something bothering you?"

Well, now that you ask, there is something...

"Ah, well, you see, I—"

I was about to run my mouth and tell her that I was greatly perplexed because I had decided to give her some bread as a present but couldn't find the chance to give it to her, when I stopped myself.

After all that sneaking around trying to give her a surprise, if I disclosed my plans to the target now, it would lose all meaning, wouldn't it?

Even worse than that...

...it turned out that...

"By the way, Saya, do you think I could have a piece of that bread?"

...I was exposed.

Elaina just chuckled as she stared intently at the bread. As I wondered how on earth Elaina had developed her sense of smell, she pointed at the bread in my hand and tilted her head again as she asked, "Just one. Would that be all right?"

"……"

Well, it wouldn't be a surprise anymore, but I figured, since I was originally planning to give them to Elaina anyway, it was fine, really.

"Go ahead, please. Never mind just one—have them all."

In the end, I didn't pull any little tricks or anything; I simply handed the bread over to Elaina.

"Thank you very much."

Elaina broke into a smile again. I had wanted to make her happy and had devised a clever little surprise, but as long as Elaina received bread, she was happy anyway.

After that, Elaina and I ate the bread together and enjoyed a brief rest.

Well, I guess I didn't need to surprise her after all!

Shortly thereafter—

As we were stuffing our cheeks with bread, Elaina frowned and screwed her face up as if she was hesitating to say something.

She mumbled, "That reminds me, recently, I've been getting the feeling that someone has been watching me…"

"That was probably me."

"Huh?"

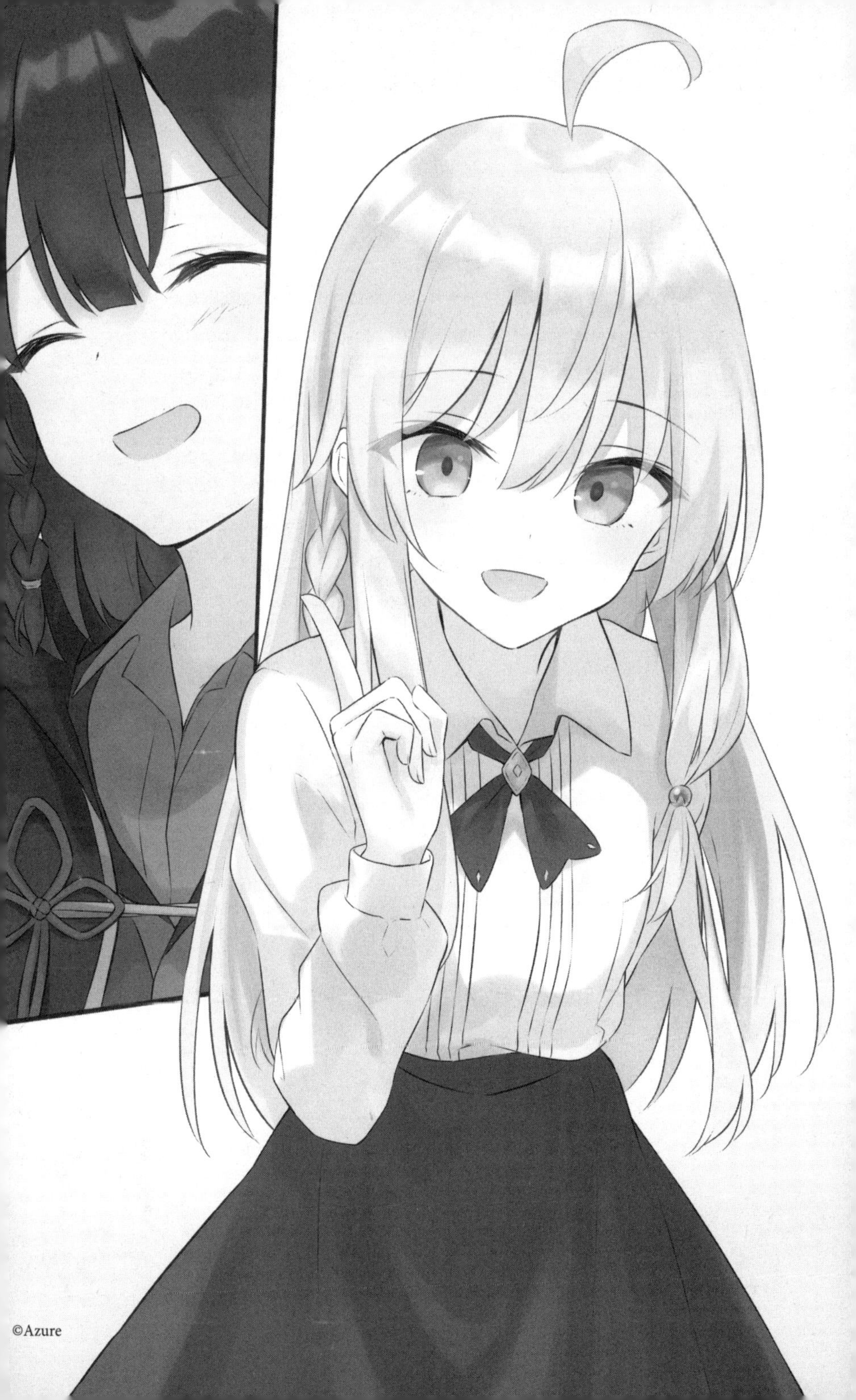

[**Publication Information**]   Twitter Post Story
[**Author Comments**]

This is a bonus story I posted on Twitter, and in terms of chronology, it fits somewhere around Volume 5.

Off-topic, but Tomoyo Kurosawa, who plays the role of Saya in the anime and drama CDs, is such a perfect match for the freewheeling Saya that sometimes I feel certain Saya herself is in the room with us. Really, whenever I hear her work, I enjoy Miss Kurosawa's voice acting so much that when I'm writing the manuscripts for the drama CDs, my pen often produces scenes where Saya appears.

CHAPTER 1 STORY 11
The Country of Birthdays

"Welcome, Lady Witch! Welcome to our country!"

The country I arrived at that day seemed like a perfectly ordinary place. Honestly, if I were to try to explain why I went there, I'd have to admit I had absolutely no clue where that place was or what kind of country it was. In a word, I just simply found my way there on a whim during a spare moment in my travels, and that's where I wound up.

Since it was a very special anniversary, I had thought that if possible, I would like to make it to an interesting destination, but the region I was traveling through didn't seem to have that many interesting places, and ultimately, I sort of drifted my way to this one.

After bowing to me, the soldier at the gate said, "Now then, there are a number of things I would like to ask you, Lady Witch, upon your entry."

He held a sheet of paper and a pen in his hand and started. "First, please tell me your name—"

What began from there was the usual entry examination.

Name. Occupation. Purpose for entry. I was asked a number of such simple questions.

Elaina. Witch. Sightseeing. I took it upon myself to answer his various questions with simple words.

Then the gate guard said, "I see, very well... Now, when is your birthday?" He tilted his head as he asked.

It was a question often asked as part of immigration inspections, but I didn't really want to answer.

But if I didn't tell him honestly, I wouldn't be able to progress beyond the gate, and so I answered, "...October seventeenth."

…That was how I answered.
That's right.
It's today.
Today is my birthday.

That was exactly why I hadn't been too keen on answering and why I had wanted to go someplace interesting in celebration if I could.

Besides, I just knew when he learned my birthday was that day, the gate guard would grin and ask, "Oh! Happy birthday. How old are you turning?" I really hated when that happened, but there was no avoiding it, so I answered him, a little reluctantly.

"…Mm-hmm, October seventeenth…"

Contrary to my expectations, the guard's response was indifferent.

"…Hmm? October…seventeenth…?"

At least I thought so, but his real reaction came a moment later.

"October seventeenth…? That's today, isn't it?! Today! It's your birthday, isn't it?! My word! What a day! This is serious!"

Considering how late it came, I thought his reaction was fairly overblown.

"Oh noooooooooooo! Everyone, come quiiiiiiiiiiick!"

…Oh, come on, that's just excessive.

"The witch! This one! This witch! It's her biiirthdaaaaaaaayyy!"

Wait, wait, you don't have to make such a big fuss over something like a birthday.

Ignoring me and my thoughts on the matter, the guard yelled out earnestly, screaming until his throat was hoarse, and because of that, people began to gather around us, looking surprised.

"What did he say?"

"It's this witch's birthday?"

"This is serious!"

"Everyone! Prepare the party!"

"And make it snappyyy!"

"Um…huh?"

I was confused.

"Okay then, Miss Witch! Come over here!"

"Since it's your precious birthday, it would be terrible if you didn't enjoy it!"

"Come on, then, right over here!"

"Um…uhhh…?"

I really was confused.

Ultimately, the impromptu crowd led me away, and I wound up being forced through the gates and into the country.

What on earth…is going on here…?

○

"All right then, I'd like to go ahead and introduce the people who have birthdays today."

A nonsensical scene spread out before my eyes.

It had to be some sort of party venue. Everything I could see was colored white, and there was a chandelier hanging from the ceiling. Round tables were placed here and there, with all sorts of people sitting at them.

All of them were strangers to me. I did not know a single person, including the master of ceremonies.

And speaking of me, for some reason, I had ended up changing into a dress.

What on earth is this about?

"The name of today's birthday witch is Elaina. She is an esteemed witch who travels the world as the Ashen Witch."

"Um."

"Today is October the seventeenth. It is the witch's birthday. Everyone, give her a big round of applause!"

"Um…"

The MC ignored me and plowed ahead. Maybe he couldn't hear my voice because I was being showered with applause.

Maybe I ought to smile. Actually, wait, what is going on here? Is this a wedding? Who am I marrying?

"By the way, this is not a wedding."

What now? Is he reading my mind?

"This is a birthday party."

Do people really have such extremely gaudy birthday parties?

"From today's leading lady, Miss Elaina, please, let's have a word of greeting."

What? Why?

But sure enough, the birthday party proceeded apace, ignoring my bewilderment, and suddenly I was forced to stand in front of the great crowd of people.

"Um…thank you very much…?"

When I gave a sharp little bow, applause rose from the tables here and there, along with some voices.

"She's cute!"

"The cutest in the whole world!"

"Huh? That might be going a bit far."

"Huh? A bit far is just far enough, surely?"

What is this, a humiliation exercise?

"Thank you, Miss Elaina."

The MC dutifully kept the festivities moving forward in a detached voice. "Next, I would like to propose a toast to wish for Miss Elaina's continued happiness. To lead us in the toast, I invite Miss Elaina's lover to the stage. Saya, please come forward."

……

Huh?

How can this MC say something so strange without any hesitation?

I was still puzzling over this when a black-haired young woman stepped up onto the stage, looking like she had every right to be there. For some reason, this woman, who I was sure was part of the organization known as the United Magic Association, was on this day dressed up in a fancy dress.

"Hi, everyone! I'm Elaina's girlfriend, Saya!"

She gave the worst self-introduction.

"What are you doing, Saya?"
Aha, so then this must be a dream, yes?
This was about the time that it started to dawn on me.

First of all, there's no way Saya, who should have been wandering through the world as a traveler just as I was, would be in a place like this. If she was, that would make her a stalker, a stalker for sure.

"Elaina...happy birthday..."

For some reason, her eyes were wet with tears. "I...I'm very honored to be able to attend your birthday party, Elaina...as any lover would..."

"No, we're not lov—"

"Cheeeeeeeeeeers!"

She evaded the issue.

She did her very best to evade it. In the worst way. The very worst ever, just like her awful self-introduction.

After the toast, it was time for chatting and eating. Incidentally, there were all sorts of things I wanted to ask Saya, but she blew me a kiss, and after giggling bashfully, she returned to one of the circular tables.

What is going on here? Well, it's just a dream, so whatever.

"And as for today's menu, we've used plenty of the rabbits hunted down by Elise the beast girl."

I see, I see. This is a dream, right. So even Elise is here. I suppose she would be.

Once the toast was over, dishes began to be carried out one after another, and we entered the conversation hour. Although, when it came to me, I was alone on stage in my fancy dress, so I honestly didn't have anything to do.

And because I had nothing to do, I started nibbling away at Elise's rabbit dishes.

After a short while, the MC appeared holding a bundle of papers and said, "Everyone, I'm sorry to interrupt your conversations, but in keeping with this auspicious day, we've received many congratulatory addresses and communications, so I'd like to take this opportunity to present some of them."

It seemed like the best way to kill time. By the way, at this point, I was no longer surprised by anything that was going on. I was ready for whatever came next.

"We received this from Lady Fran, the Stardust Witch."

I was at the ready, when a felicitation came in suddenly from someone I never expected. It was from my teacher.

"'Elaina, best wishes on your birthday. By the way, do you know how old I am? Oh-hoh-hoh, it's a secret!'"

I'm sorry, I don't get it.

"Moving right along, this came from Lady Sheila, the Midnight Witch. 'Elaina, did you know this? When you quit smoking, your mind starts working way faster! Isn't that amazing?'"

That makes sense. Please stop smoking, then.

"Next up, we received this note from Lady Riviere, proprietor of Riviere Antiques. 'Happy birthday. By the way, I wonder when I can expect you to return the money you borrowed from me?'"

You're quite petty, aren't you?

"And next, we have this, from Lady MacMillia, employee at Riviere's Antiques. 'Elaina. I haven't gotten my money back from you either.'"

You didn't even loan me anything, did you? What are you doing jumping on her bandwagon?

"Up next, notes we received from the informant twins. 'Happiest of birthdays.' 'Many happy returns.'"

Wishes for the coming year? Get serious.

"Continuing along…uh, we got this from a ghoul. 'Gruel…taste good…' The entry ends there."

Please don't send me your journal entries.

"And next, this comes from a couple in Windmill City. 'Happy birthday, traveler. By the way, we got married. We're going on our honeymoon soon. Oh-hoh-hoh, aren't you jealous?'"

Please don't use your congratulatory message to brag.

"This next one comes from a (self-proclaimed) hard-boiled female mage. 'I'm hard-boiled, so I won't give you my name! After all, that's the hard-boiled way! Anyway, happy birthday! For your present, I'm gifting you with coffeeeeeeeeehhh...' Huh, the paper's all dirty, so I can't read any further."

Disgusting.

"And next, this, from Lady Atolie. 'A very happy birthday to you. I'm sorry that I cannot participate on this day when we should be celebrating you. I hope that you enjoy the rest of your travels, with memories of this day in your heart.'"

Somehow, I felt strangely moved, even though she was just saying normal things.

"Next, we received this from Lady Viola. 'Atolie is so adorable, writing a proper note even while she curses your name! She punched me for saying that!'"

I bet she did.

"Moving along, we got this from a muscleman. 'The thing about marriage is that it's like muscles! Whether they shrink or expand, they're always together! Also, sometimes, just like muscles, it will tear to pieces and start to hurt! That's right! Muscle pain and the unpleasant moments in a marriage are very similar! But never fear. No matter how many times it tears, no matter how many times it causes you pain, so long as you can just withstand that pain, there's always tomorrow. If you can overcome muscle pain, your muscles will develop even firmer bonds and grow strong and sturdy. Do you understand what I'm trying to say? That's right, weight lifting is the very essence of marriage. In other words, I want to marry muscles.'"

That's not marriage. Please don't get the wrong idea. Also, get a life and forget about muscles already.

"Next up, the representative for about fifteen different versions of Elaina, this came in from Foreign Affectation Elaina. '*Khorosho!*'"

Yes, yes, khorosho, khorosho.

"Next, we received this note from your broom. 'Recently, my split ends have gotten really terrible. Please consider doing some maintenance.'"

This is not a suggestion box. And besides, you're with me twenty-four-seven anyway.

"This next one comes from Lady Avelia. 'Elaina, my big sister recently went off somewhere. Do you have any clue where she might be?'"

I do not.

Hang on, what? She's missing?

"Aaand so on and so forth, we got lots of well-wishes, but reading all the rest would be a real pain, so I'll leave them out."

The MC brought things to a close with these incredibly concerning words, and the curtain fell on what had been nothing more than self-introduction time masquerading as well-wishing.

…Amnesia is missing?

How?

○

Once the presentation of well-wishes was over, and after everyone had eaten and chatted for a little while, then it was apparently time to cut the cake.

A woman in a suit brought a cake over near me.

What's going on? Is this a wedding cake?

"Now then, I'd like to move us along to the birthday cake cutting ceremony."

I was wrong, it's a birthday cake cutting. Wait, what exactly is a birthday cake cutting ceremony?

"Uh, so does that mean I cut it by myself?"

If this were a wedding cake cutting, the bride and groom would chatter and giggle as they cut slices from the cake, right? The MC would egg them on by saying things like "*This is their first task as a couple!*" and "*Spoon-feed your partner, show the hugeness of your love with the huge size of the spoon!*" as the bride thrust a sickly sweet clump of sugar into the groom's mouth. That's how things generally went. That was about the time the MC would typically chime in with some not very clever comment like *"What's this? That's an awful big bite! She might turn out to be a real ogre of a wife!"*

However, for a birthday, wasn't I on my own?

…Wasn't I all alone?

"Since we are now holding the cake cutting, I will introduce the individual who is taking on the special role of cutting the cake with our guest of honor! Everyone, please welcome her with a round of applause!"

Apparently, this was where things differed from a typical wedding ceremony.

Greeted by applause, a certain young woman stepped up on the stage, holding a saber in her hand.

The woman, with short white hair, swung her saber around vigorously and said, "Hyah!"

"……………………What are you doing, Amnesia?"

Standing right there was Avelia's older sister, who had been missing.

But I wasn't all that surprised. After all, she had been glancing over at me for a while. From just off stage, she had been looking at me with a sparkle in her eye, as if to say, *"Am I on yet? Am I on yet?"*

"Well, I heard it was your birthday, huh, Elaina? And so here I am."

"Are you my girlfriend or something?"

"Of course not!"

"Thought so."

"I'm your lover!"

"……"

Seems like all my friends have been transformed into lovers in this dream…

"Yes, and considering that this is your birthday, we've enlisted the help of Lady Amnesia." The MC interrupted my thoughts.

"Ready?" Amnesia took me by the hand and made me grip the hilt of her saber.

"……"

Somehow, it didn't look entirely unlike a real wedding cake cutting.

…Well, it's just a dream, so I don't really care, I guess.

With that thought, I wrapped my fingers around the hilt of the sword.

"W-wait, stopppppppppppp!"

As I did, a scream rang out. The saber, which was headed straight for the birthday cake, stopped in its tracks.

"Huh? Um? What? I'm sorry, I don't really understand. E-Elaina, that girl, wh-who is she?"

It was Saya.

Saya leaped out in front of us in a panic. In her dismay, she didn't seem to be able to express herself in words anymore. She seemed to be laughing and crying at the same time, but in the end, no matter how I looked at her, she was definitely upset.

"Heeey! You've got me right here, so who is that person?! Why do you look like you're getting along a little too well?!"

"Oh, we're not really getting along all that well…"

"Huh? But, Elaina, you don't seem like you mind her company!" Beside me, Amnesia giggled. It was kind of a scary laugh. "By the way, who is she?"

How can you even ask that…?

"This is my friend Saya—"

"I am Elaina's lover, Saya! Who are you, Miss White Hair?!"

"I am Amnesia. Elaina's lover."

"No, neither of you is my lover."

Please don't talk like either of you is my one and only.

"Hang on, I really don't understand what you're saying here! I mean, Elaina's lover? That's me!"

"You're the one who's talking crazy! That's *my* role!"

No, like I said, neither of you is my lover. In fact, I don't even have a lover. What's more, this reality doesn't even exist. It's a dream, after all.

"Huuuh? Just tell me what's going on here. What is your relation to Elaina? Have you two slept together? By the way, I've slept with her, you know!"

What are you doing stirring things up like that?

"I—I have, in fact! We've slept together! Actually, when we were traveling together, we slept together almost every night, you know?"

You mean in the same room? What are you bragging about? We did that because you're a terrible sleeper.

"A-almost every...night...? And you traveled...together...?"

But apparently, Amnesia's fib had, strangely enough, given Saya a lethal mental image.

Saya hung her head. "I-it can't be... My Elaina has been stained a filthy gray..."

She started crying. I felt bad that she was sinking into despair, but I had always been gray.

"Heh-heh...looks like I win this one! All right then, Elaina, shall we cut the cake?"

Amnesia whirled around to face me, then made me take hold of the saber again, and guided it toward the cake.

Thinking that I didn't really care, about whatever just happened, I pushed the sword down into the birthday cake—or was about to.

But just before I could—

Wham—the cake exploded, and pieces went flying everywhere.

Bits of sponge cake, cream, and strawberries splattered onto me and Amnesia.

No one told me this cake would explode when we cut it. What's going on here?

I was just about to raise my voice in protest, but this was a dream.

In a dream, anything can happen, so surely even a cake could explode.

"Heh-heh-heh... If the cake you're cutting is no more, then the cake cutting itself can't happen, can it?!"

In a dream, anything can happen, so surely even Saya could lose her mind.

"My Elaina belongs to me! Give her back!"

Gripping her wand, Saya glared at Amnesia.

I see, so the one who exploded the cake was you?

"All right, then—this suits me just fine. Bring it on!"

Then Amnesia turned her saber on Saya.

In a dream, anything can happen, so surely even Amnesia could start acting strange.

Then Amnesia and Saya ignored me entirely as they battled it out across the birthday party hall. They slashed at the round tables, scattering them, and sent all sorts of things flying with spells, and the party room instantly became so chaotic that it made my head spin just to look at.

But it's okay!

This is just a dream, after all!

"……"

But even considering that I was in a dream, I wondered if it wasn't really too chaotic. If it wasn't indeed getting out of hand.

"Uh… The cake cutting is over now, so allow me to announce performances by friends…"

The MC started to smooth things over.

Is that what it's time for?

"……"

I looked down at the birthday party space, which was caught up in a great clamor of merrymaking.

This is my dream.

At first, I had thought all the people seated around the party room were unfamiliar strangers, but—looking more closely, I recognized each and every one of them.

For example, there was a man there as fat and round as a barrel and two twins who closely resembled him. There was a man who had sat endlessly on a bench in between two countries and a girl I had met in a country where they persecuted the ugly. I saw a young man who had aspired to become a detective and a young woman who had done nothing but vomit near him. There was also a girl who loved apples, a cat, and a mage I had seen in the Country of Truth Tellers—

This was my dream, so all the characters were made up of all the people I had met up to now.

"......"

I wondered whether, if I was to continue my travels from that point onward and then have a similar dream the following year, if at that time I would spend my birthday surrounded by even more people?

With my fingers, I scooped the wreckage of the cake off my cheek where it had splattered and stuck, and as I licked it off, I vacantly considered such matters.

○

"........................"

My awakening was summarized in a single word: awful.

First of all, that was not the kind of dream you want to have on your birthday.

What was all that, seriously?

When I forced my heavy body to rise against its will, the world outside my inn was still shrouded in the darkness of night.

Apparently, I had experienced some strange dream, perhaps out of excitement that the following day was my birthday. I felt like the loud revelry that had been going on until just a moment earlier was still echoing through my mind.

The hands on the clock had just passed midnight.

My birthday had only just started.

And yet I felt a strange sense of loneliness.

"......"

I was sure it was because the dream had been overly boisterous. That could be good or bad, depending, but still, I had enjoyed the dream. I wondered, would I go back and finish the rest of it if I went back to sleep?

"......"

By the way—
Setting that aside—
"……"
I got up from my bed.
It was not the time to be lying around in bed, I thought.

"…What's gotten into you all of a sudden, Mistress Elaina? To suddenly start working on my maintenance."

"Nothing, really, nothing special."

Wearing a puzzled look, the girl who looked so much like me sat there while I played with her hair. For some reason, when I turned my broom into a human figure, she looked a lot like me. From behind, although her hair was a different color, she was my exact copy.

"I just thought your split ends were getting pretty bad lately, so I figured I ought to do a little grooming."

"But my split ends won't go away just because you run a comb through them."

"Well, good enough, isn't it?"

"Besides, I don't need you to comb my hair after you go out of your way to turn me into a person. You'll get it done more quickly if you use magic to fix it while I'm still in my broom form."

"Well, good enough, isn't it?"

"……"

"……"

I had gone about straightening out her hair. Her beautiful silky hair flowed like sand, spilling smoothly out between my fingers when I scooped it up.

It was pretty and soft, and I wanted to keep touching it forever.

"Mistress Elaina."

Suddenly, my broom turned around to face me.

"Come to think of it, today is your birthday, isn't it?"

"…Yes it is."

"Happy birthday."

"...Well, thanks."

My broom giggled at my words.

"You must have felt lonely ringing in your birthday all by yourself, Mistress Elaina. That's surprisingly cute of you—ow! That hurts, Mistress Elaina. Be a little more gentle with the comb, plea—"

At any rate—

In this way, I welcomed a peaceful birthday.

While wishing somewhere in my heart that I might have a similar dream again the following year.

[Publication Information] Kakuyomu Post Story
[Author Comments]

This was a bonus story I uploaded on October 17, which is Elaina's birthday.

I myself was always someone who felt uncomfortable about the inhabitants of fantasy worlds having birthdays following the same standards as we do in the real world. (First of all, if it's a fantasy, there's absolutely no reason why their calendar has to be the same as the real-world calendar, right? I'm the kind of irritating person who thinks their calendar isn't even limited to expressing dates in numbers.) But I suppose we ought to be happy that this way we can celebrate her birthday.

CHAPTER 1 STORY 12

The Snowman and the Witch

"Excuse me, miss, are you a mage?"

I was loitering absentmindedly on a street corner in a certain country when someone tugged at my sleeve.

It was a group of little girls, dressed in soft and puffy clothes.

The girls were gazing at me as if I was some kind of curiosity. Depending on how you looked at it, their gazes might have even been envious.

"Indeed, I am a mage," I answered, throwing out my chest somewhat with pride. "Moreover, I'm a witch."

In unison, the little girls said, """"Hmm?"""" and cocked their heads all at once.

"A witch?"

"What's that?"

"Is it something wonderful?"

I see. It seems this country is located in quite a remote region.

"It is something wonderful. Witches are the most exceptional magic users, even among the mages. Which is to say we're strong, the very strongest."

I threw my chest out even more proudly.

The little girls all said, """"Oooh,"""" and their eyes lit up.

"If you're so strong, will you make us a snow sculpture?"

"We want a snow sculpture."

"Make us a snow sculpture!"

Uh-oh, what are you saying all of a sudden?

"Why do I have to make a snow sculpture?"

"There's a snow sculpture over there." One of the girls pointed to the roadside. "We tried our very best to make that one."

As I was being urged to do, I took a look at the side of the road. Sure enough, there was a little snowman sitting there, watching people going down the road with a cheerful smile on its face.

"Oh-hoh…that's quite well-done." From its carrot nose to the bucket it was wearing for a hat, it looked like the kind of snowman one often saw, but it was still unique.

"We want a snow sculpture that's even better than that one."

"We really do. We want a sculpture that surpasses our snowman."

"Well, I don't think she'll ever be able to make a sculpture that's better than ours."

Oh-hoh. Apparently, these girls need to be taught just how superior mages really are.

"Make something that surpasses a cliché little snowman like that one, you say? No problem. Creating a magnificent snow sculpture is a piece of cake."

"All right, then, make one."

"We're waiting!"

"Yeah!"

In order to shut down the group of three little girls with their disrespectful attitude, I took my wand in hand.

"Very well, let me show you! When you talk about magnificent snow sculptures, this is the kind of thing you mean!"

●

In a complete upset, that year's snow sculpture contest was won by a group of three young girls living in the neighborhood. The surprising thing was that this group of three seemingly adorable children had built such an intense snow sculpture. It had overly intricate details and beautiful curves that were almost sublime. This was no longer a simple snow sculpture; it was a work of art that impressed the judges. But there was just one problem.

"...Who on earth could this beautiful woman be?" one of the judges said as they pointed at the snow sculpture.

"Oh, you know, that's the witch who came to our country earlier," said one of the girls. "We begged her to act as our model," she lied smoothly.

"Well, that's... She must really care about her image, huh...?" answered the judge, looking astounded.

"That's what we thought, too." The girls also looked astounded as they gazed up at the best snow sculpture ever.

[Publication Information] Volume 6
Melonbooks Buyer's Bonus
[Author Comments]
　These little girls are going to become big shots in the future, huh...? At least I thought so.

CHAPTER 1 STORY 13
Little Witch

At this point in time, I am a child.

A cute little girl. In this state, it's impossible for me to even do proper magic, but I wouldn't be me if I didn't take advantage of this situation. If you want to know why, it's because I'm a traveler!

All right, let's hurry up and get to the moneymaki—

"And? Why is it that you're dressed like that, again? Whose child could you be?"

I left the inn, and several minutes later, I was nabbed by a guard on his rounds and taken into protective custody.

Apparently, they were wary of witches in this country at the present moment, so it must have looked suspicious for a young girl to be wearing a witch's costume in spite of that, and muttering to herself, "Heh-heh…money…money…"

I apologized through tears. "……Waah! *Sniff*… I'm sorry… I won't do it again…"

Of course, this was an act. I wouldn't be me if I repented just because someone got angry with me.

"Oh no, I don't know why you're crying… Anyway, that outfit is giving people the wrong idea, so stop wearing it, okay?"

"Okaaay…" I nodded, wiping away the tears (eye drops) that spilled from my eyes.

The following day—

Since dressing as a witch was apparently a bad thing, this time I decided to imitate a fortune-teller to make some money. I figured if

I wore my hood low, no one would be able to tell that I was just an ordinary little gir—

"And? Why are you out making money in a place like—? Hey, you again?"

Several minutes after I started telling fortunes, I was nabbed by a soldier on his rounds and taken into protective custody.

Apparently, they had been thoroughly warned in this country against people who planted themselves along the road and conducted shady commerce. It was probably because they already had young girls selling weird tonics in the street. Unforgivable.

"Waah...*sniff*... I'm really sorry... I won't do it again..." Right away, I overdid it with the crying again.

Is there a single adult around who can go up against a little girl's tears? No, of course there isn't.

"...Jeez. Well, fine. Don't cry like that, please. It makes it look like I'm bullying you, see?" The soldier frowned, looking troubled, and crouched down as he said, "Well, I don't think you had any bad intentions, so I'm not going to scold you too badly here. But you mustn't do this sort of thing ever again, you hear?"

"Yeees..."

It seems like he's going to forgive me. Just like I thought, there's nothing as powerful as the tears of a young gir—

"Mm. I'm glad you understand. Now, for the fine."

"Huh? I have to pay?"

"Of course you do."

"...*Sniff.*"

"Crying won't do you any good."

"...Tch."

"Don't you click your tongue!"

Sure enough, doing bad things isn't good. As I pondered that, I slapped the money for the fine into the soldier's hand.

Dressing like a mage was bad. Telling fortunes along the road was bad. Since those things meant I had to pay a fine, in the end, I went back to selling matches.

[**Publication Information**]   Volume 6
Toranoana Buyer's Bonus
[**Author Comments**]
    This is an incident that took place in the spare moments of Priscilla's story. I'm changing the subject here, but I was so happy that little girl Elaina made an appearance in both the comic and the anime. Little Elaina is so cute…

CHAPTER 1 STORY 14
An Academic Anecdote

No one would object to me saying that the school canteen is a war zone.

The only thing found there was wave after wave of bloody conflict. No peaceful exchanges, no friendly conversations admitted. The students headed for the canteen simply held their tongues and marched forward toward their common goal.

That's right, because there at the canteen was: "Bread…limited to ten pieces per day!"

I'd heard a rumor that among the hundreds of pieces of bread the canteen normally had in stock, there was one type they only stocked ten pieces of.

Most students, the second we plunged into the lunchtime break, dashed out into the hallways, the magic-using students even employing their brooms, and charged toward the canteen. Either that or they blasted one another with spells and knocked one another out.

They were probably all after those ten limited pieces of bread.

Of course, I was no exception.

"Ay!" I was riding on my broom, swinging my wand as I went. "Hyah!" As I waved my wand side to side, I knocked down the students who were running toward the canteen one after another.

Those ten limited pieces of bread per day were all for me.

"Now, now, clear the way, please. The bread in the canteen is for me."

I overpowered the students on their brooms one after another.

I soaked the feet of the students who were trying to run away from me in water and froze them. It was easy to leave them all behind.

Then I finally arrived at the canteen.

Luckily, I was the first one there.

The students who showed up after me clicked their tongues and said bitter things like "Tch...she beat us to it, huh...?"

"Well, I'll take some of that limited bread, please." I put my money on the counter and looked expectantly at the woman working the canteen. "The bread that's limited to only ten pieces per day," I continued. "...Don't try to tell me you haven't got any?"

Staring me in the face, the woman blinked. "...Ah, the bread that's limited to ten pieces. Here you go."

Without any particular hesitation, she held out a piece of bread.

"Heh-heh-heh..." Wearing a smile that I couldn't fully suppress, I stepped out of line.

The students who had lined up behind me then, one after another, put in their orders.

"Croissant."

"One croissant."

"Croissant, please!"

What's this? All the students are buying just ordinary...croissants...?

...How strange.

"You're not buying any of the bread that's limited to just ten pieces per day?"

I caught one of the students who had been lined up behind me and tilted my head to the side inquisitively.

Then she said, "Huh? Bread that they only sell ten of each day? Everyone was just hurrying because they wanted lunch, not something like that. The bread here is cheap. Actually, that particular bread is hard to get, but it's not all that tasty."

Really...? How strange.

"Well then, why are they limited to selling ten pieces?"

The student answered me with composure.

"I think it's just because it's super gross and doesn't sell at all, so they only stock ten pieces, maybe?"

[**Publication Information**]   Volume 6
Gamers Buyer's Bonus
[**Author Comments**]

Being rare isn't proof that something is exceptional, is it? This is a concept I dealt with again in Volume 12.

I really like the version of Elaina in her school uniform from this era of stories. I'd like to write more stories in the Royal Magic Academy setting.

With the story of Alte and Linaria in Volume 10, I did write a time-traveling lesbians tale, but I want to write a time travel story that is less in the vein of *Interstellar* (where the future doesn't change even if they time travel), and more like *Back to the Future* (where they change the future through time travel). Though then I would have to treat it less like time travel and more like a parallel storyline.

◀ CHAPTER 1 STORY 15 ▶

Pumpkin Festival

The story so far—

I, the Ashen Witch, Elaina, am a traveler journeying across the world. My purpose in life is to go around looking at country after country, dressed in my black robe and pointed hat, my ash-gray hair fluttering in the wind, and my other purpose in life is to not think of anything in particular except for doing just that.

I arrived in a certain country yesterday.

Once I arrived in this country, which was rumored to be the place where the Pumpkin Festival was held, one of the gate guards called out to me. "Wow, you're really cute! That's terrific! I've never seen such a cute girl before! Wonderful! You know what, because of that, I'm going to give you this candy." And I received a basket brimming with a massive quantity of candy.

Yippee.

Then I went walking around town, but the appearance of the people there was somehow really bizarre.

I saw a big man with bandages wound around him, a vampire, a succubus, a ghost wearing a white sheet, a werewolf, and more.

In other words, the city was overflowing with monsters; everywhere you looked, it was nothing but monsters.

Whoa, how scary.

I felt just like a piece of bait that had been thrown into a pen with fierce beasts.

What on earth is this Pumpkin Festival supposed to be?
Am I in hell?

"Heh-heh-heh, you're awfully cute, missy!"

"What do we have here? A witch came wandering into our town?"

"Why don't you come hang out with me, sweetheart? Fwa-ha-ha-ha-ha…"

"Oh my! This is no place for a kid like you to visit!"

The monsters surrounded me, wearing vulgar smiles.

And then, I fell prey to them right there.

Nothing in this life lasts forever.

Thus, my travels came to an end.

All's well that ends well.

"……"

Well, as you may have suspected, the bit about falling prey to the monsters was a lie. In fact, the story so far has also been a total lie.

The thing about getting the candy? Yep, that was a lie, too.

The truth is it was currency conversion.

Apparently, in this country, on this day, they used candy in place of money.

So I had handed over all the money I had and converted it into candy.

Everything from "Heh-heh-heh, you're awfully cute" onward had happened pretty much the same way I described it.

Carrying my basket of candy, I was then surrounded by the monsters, who said this:

"Trick or treat!"

"…………………"

Apparently, in this country, on this day, terrible acts were allowed—even more awful than I had been told about.

On the day of the local Pumpkin Festival, the government permitted acts of extortion.

"…………Have some candy."

And then I found myself penniless.

Nothing in this life lasts forever.

Oh-hoh-hoh, I don't understand what's going on.

○

I hurriedly walked down the street where the monsters were strutting around.

As I might have expected, walking openly through a town that was filled with monsters seemed like it would be nothing other than a suicidal act.

For example, in my current situation, it would be just terrible if one of them were to say something like "Trick or treat!"

Who could tell what they might do to me, a person with no money (candy)?

"......"

I would have to procure some money (candy) somehow.

But how on earth would I go about doing so? I didn't think that in this town full of magical creatures, there was any place that would employ a totally normal human being like me. Moreover, if I tried to rob someone for the money (candy), I would probably wind up a victim of the monsters (in the sense that they'd eat me up).

......

It was all over for me.

Suddenly all over.

Or rather, somehow I'd fallen into a bind right from the start.

I resented my own foolishness in converting everything I had into this country's currency. I deserved to die ten thousand deaths.

"I'm hungry..."

Head in hands on the side of the road, lamenting my bleak future, I was fed up with my stomach demanding food even in such a sad state of affairs.

"...Are you all right?" A girl was standing before me as I worried over my troubles. "Are you a tourist?"

When I nodded, she clapped her hands together lightly as if she understood. "I see! You can't sit in a place like this, okay? Bad guys might take all your money."

"......"

If I stepped into the back alleys, there would surely be a multitude of awful monsters, and I knew they were out on the main road as well. And I wasn't even allowed to be on the roadside.

There is no safe haven to be found, I suppose. Without a doubt, this place is hell.

I stood up and fixed my eyes on the girl.

She was dressed in a mage-like fashion, with a black robe and a pointed hat. Upon her breast was neither a corsage nor a brooch, indicating to me that she was simply a novice—in other words, the lowest rank among mages.

"I am Lisa. By the way, this outfit is a costume."

Whoops, she isn't even a novice.

"Why are you dressed up as a mage? Is it an interest of yours?"

"Well, it is interesting, but…" Lisa smiled slightly, and she held up the basket that she had in her hands. "It's for this. If you want to make money, you have to wear a costume."

"If you put on a costume, you can make money…?"

I frowned in confusion, and Lisa put on a puzzled expression.

"…Don't tell me you entered this country without knowing anything?"

"Well—that's about right." I held up the basket in my hands and showed it to her. Unlike her basket, which was stuffed full of lots of candy, the inside of my basket was empty.

Lisa let out a little sigh and took me by the hand.

"You dummy. You're guaranteed to have a bad time if you come to this country without any background knowledge—come with me for a minute."

Then she pulled me by the hand and walked off.

Penniless me went along with her, without any resistance.

I thought that, if things went well, she might give me a piece of candy.

After all, I was broke and hungry.

○

"*Trick or treat!* It's a set phrase we use in this country on this day."

As we were observing the gathered monsters from behind a trash can on one side of an open plaza, Lisa said, "Everyone here has gone all out with their outfits, don't you think? This event is held so that we can celebrate the effort everyone put into their looks."

She told me how it worked.

"Trick or treat!"

Whenever someone called out to you with that phrase, if you thought the other person was more impressive than you, you had to give them candy. If you thought you were the more impressive one, you could play a trick on them.

That was the gist of it.

In other words, it was extortion, officially sanctioned by the government.

What are they doing holding an event that's so bad for public order? I don't like it; it's scary.

"So doesn't that mean every time someone talks to you, you're forced to pay them money?"

I mean, who would choose to have a trick played on them?

"No, not at all! Look over there." Lisa pointed into the plaza.

A fistfight had broken out.

Two werewolves were circling wildly around each other, completely oblivious to the crowd that had formed around them, snapping at each other with their fangs and slashing at each other with their claws.

"……"

What's that all about?

"If someone comes up to you and says that set phrase, but you turn them down, that's what happens. They'll compete to determine which one is more impressive."

"……"

Really, what is the deal with this event? It's such a hazard to public safety.

"So in other words, you have two choices, between getting hit or paying out money? Everyone else is a monster, so if anyone speaks to me, it's all over for me during this event."

I let out a sigh, and Lisa tilted her head to the side in confusion.

She looked like she was wondering what I was talking about.

"It's not like there are any real monsters here, right? You really came here without knowing a thing, huh?" She shrugged. "By any chance, did you think the men over there were real monsters? You really are gullible—"

"…What do you mean?"

"They're all just people, wearing costumes. There isn't a single monster among them."

"……Huh?"

"Like I said, I mean, this country isn't teeming with monsters. This is a place where everyone wears costumes, and we all boast to each other about how well-made our outfits are!"

"……"

In other words, I had been extorted into giving money (candy) to normal people who had only been dressed up as monsters.

Oh-hoh.

Huh. I see. How interesting.

I resent that. They deserve to die ten thousand deaths.

"By the way, how have you managed to earn as much as you have?"

"Huh? Oh, they love it when you say 'Trick or treat! ☆' Really, all men are idiots."

"What's the trick?"

"I tie them up and walk away."

"You're a genius."

"It's surprisingly easy. Men are all stupid, after all."

○

From that point on, I was unrivaled.

I showed my true ability. If the others weren't monsters after all, I had nothing to fear.

As I walked around town, I spoke to one person after another, men and women alike.

"Oh, hello, how do you do? I'm a witch."

"Oh. You've got a really cute costu—"

"Candy."

"…Hmm?"

"Candy, please."

"I didn't hear the set phrase, though…?" The man was wearing a giant pumpkin on his head. "But even so, don't you think my costume is even cooler—?"

"Candy."

"…Uhhh?"

"Candy, please."

"No, um…"

I thrust the wand I was holding in my hand at the man's throat.

"Never mind that; give me candy. *Please* give me candy. Give it to me. Quickly, the candy. If you don't, you know what happens, right? By the way, I…am a real witch. Do you understand…what I'm saying?"

I pressed the man, demanding candy as I circled around and around him.

"…Wait, but—"

When, despite all that, the man didn't seem ready to supply me with candy, I cast a spell and conjured a crystal of ice that exploded right beside his head.

"By the way, the tricks I play are on this level. What do you think? Do you want me to play tricks on you?"

Then I clapped a hand down on the man's shoulder.

"Trick or treat, okay? What's your preference? Oh-hoh-hoh!"

After that, I really raked it in.

* * *

Well then, once I had gotten back the amount of money (candy) that I had had in my possession when I first entered the country, I decided to leave.

Apparently, Lisa left the country around the same time I did. I was surprised to encounter her outside the gate.

"Oh, hey, it's been a little while. How'd you do? Were you able to make a lot?"

"No, but I've at least got about as much as I had when I got here."

"Hmm—by the way, want to see my take?"

"…You earned all this?"

There was a huge quantity of gold coins tucked into her coin purse.

What the heck? This is like a normal person's annual income. That's amazing!

"Men are simple creatures. You can generally get what you want if you just expose a little chest."

"……………………………………………Right."

"Ah, sorry."

She lowered her gaze to my chest and drummed on her own head as she giggled, "Tee-hee! ☆"

After suppressing my desire to drop a block of ice on the top of her head, I said, "Anyway, I suppose this just goes to show this is an event that favors people with lots of exposed skin, who use coercive methods, right? Are there any benefits for the people who live here?"

"Of course there are!"

"What are they?"

"They get to talk freely with cute girls. They get to have cute girls play tricks on them."

"……So the men—"

"They're all idiots."

"…………"

Nevertheless—

There was one thing I just couldn't understand about the country I had just visited.

Even if what Lisa had said was true, the workmanship on the costumes the people were wearing when they dressed up as monstrous creatures was amazing, no matter how you looked at it.

So much so that I mistook them for real monsters.

So much so that when I had been surrounded, I'd been frightened out of my wits.

"............"

Perhaps...

Perhaps they weren't really costumes, and it was a country where monsters gathered together to live.

Maybe they held that festival once a year so they could interact with humans or something.

My head was filled with possibilities.

●

After the festival, the residents of the country were talking in the pub.

"This year was amazing yet again!"

"I had some incredible things done to me. I got tied up by a human girl! And abandoned!"

"Fwa-ha-ha, I got swindled out of my candy by a girl dressed like a witch!"

"What? Did that really happen? I also got threatened by a girl dressed up like a witch."

"How was that?"

"...It was the best."

"Human girls really are great..."

"Human boys really are great..."

* * *

"Hey, listen! I got proposed to by a human man!"
"Wow! Then what happened?"
"He sort of turned into a rock."
"…So that rock beside you—"
"Oh, this? Yeah. This is my husband."
"……"

"Tch…kill."
"Hey, who did this? Who picked up the human knight? Go put her back."
"Wait a minute, please, brother orc! That girl is special!"
"Special, my foot! The only thing she's said since she got here is 'Tch…kill.'"
"Well, are you surprised? Look at how she's dressed!"
"She should only be dressed like that at night."
"……"
"Tch…kill."

In the monsters' country, there was a custom of opening up the gates just once a year to hold the Pumpkin Festival.

However, in order to avoid frightening the humans more than necessary, they all pretended they were only dressed up as monsters and let the visiting sightseers enjoy themselves.

Before anyone realized, the festival had become a costume contest for humans and monsters alike. But nobody had a problem with the situation.

If anything, they enjoyed it.

Looking forward to the same time next year, when the gate would be opened again, the monsters in the pub partied wildly until dawn.

[Publication Information]   Kakuyomu Post Story
[Author Comments]

  This is a bonus story that was published in Kakuyomu. When you talk about witches, you think about Halloween, and I think this bonus story was printed to coincide with Halloween. When I started writing it, I meant to write a story that was about four pages long, but it ended up being quite a bit longer than that.

CHAPTER 1 STORY 16

And So Miss Sharon Is At It Again Today

Because Sharon frequently wore a self-satisfied look, and because she dressed herself up like a witch, it seemed that from a stranger's perspective, she often looked like quite a capable person...

"At the last country I visited, see, they asked me, 'Recently, a witch with a rotten disposition has been sitting on street corners pretending to be a fortune-teller and ripping off our citizens, so we'd like you to punish her.' And I'm not a witch, right, so I couldn't forgive someone who would put on an act to fool people, and I readily took the job."

"...Uh-huh..."

A witch pretending to be a fortune-teller and ripping people off?
I've heard that description somewhere before...

"That witch sat on the corner and called out to passersby with stuff like 'You there, young lady. Your fortune today is terrible. It's likely that something very, very bad is going to happen today.' Apparently, she was selling some kind of suspicious jars. A witch, of all people! Isn't that just unbelievable?"

"You're right. She sounds awful, that witch. I think she should face divine punishment."

I nodded in agreement, and Sharon said, "I know, right? Isn't she just the worst? Total trash, huh? No value in her living, right?"

Sharon continued, striking without mercy. I'm not really sure why, but my heart ached terribly.

Maybe you don't have to go that far...?

After that, she eloquently told me of the events that had taken place in that country.

I heard that even when the passersby who had been sold jars and later realized they'd been tricked went back to the witch to complain, she had put her quick wit to use and talked her way out of trouble with nonsense like "You were sold a jar by some strange witch—without a doubt, this is a very, very bad thing, right? In other words, it turns out I wasn't telling lies" and hadn't refunded any of their money.

Sharon, who had been asked to punish this witch, was at her wit's end.

Even though Sharon dressed as a witch, she was an ordinary young woman for her age. If she faced off against a witch, she would be in terrible danger. That meant she needed to stop the witch's wicked deeds while at the same time not meeting the witch. She wondered whether such a feat was really possible.

Sharon was worried. After worrying over things—

"Hey, hello. You there, won't you buy a jar? If you buy this jar, see, you'll become happy like me!"

—she tried her hand at the same kind of rotten trade as the witch. With a face full of confidence.

"Wait, wait, wait," I butted in and interrupted her reminiscence, "…why?"

"I just kind of felt like it."

Somehow or other, she got swept away with the mood of the moment, and Sharon ultimately tried her hand at the same suspicious trade the witch had been plying. But because it was Sharon, things developed in an unexpected direction.

"That's our Lady Sharon! Thanks to you, the witch has completely stopped her shady dealings!"

As a result of Sharon pretending to be a fortune-teller, the witch had abruptly stopped pretending to be a fortune-teller.

"Heh…that's what I thought. Just what you'd expect from me…"

She cut through the crowd, wearing a triumphant expression. But she congratulated herself without knowing the reason why the witch had stopped pretending to be a fortune-teller.

"……"

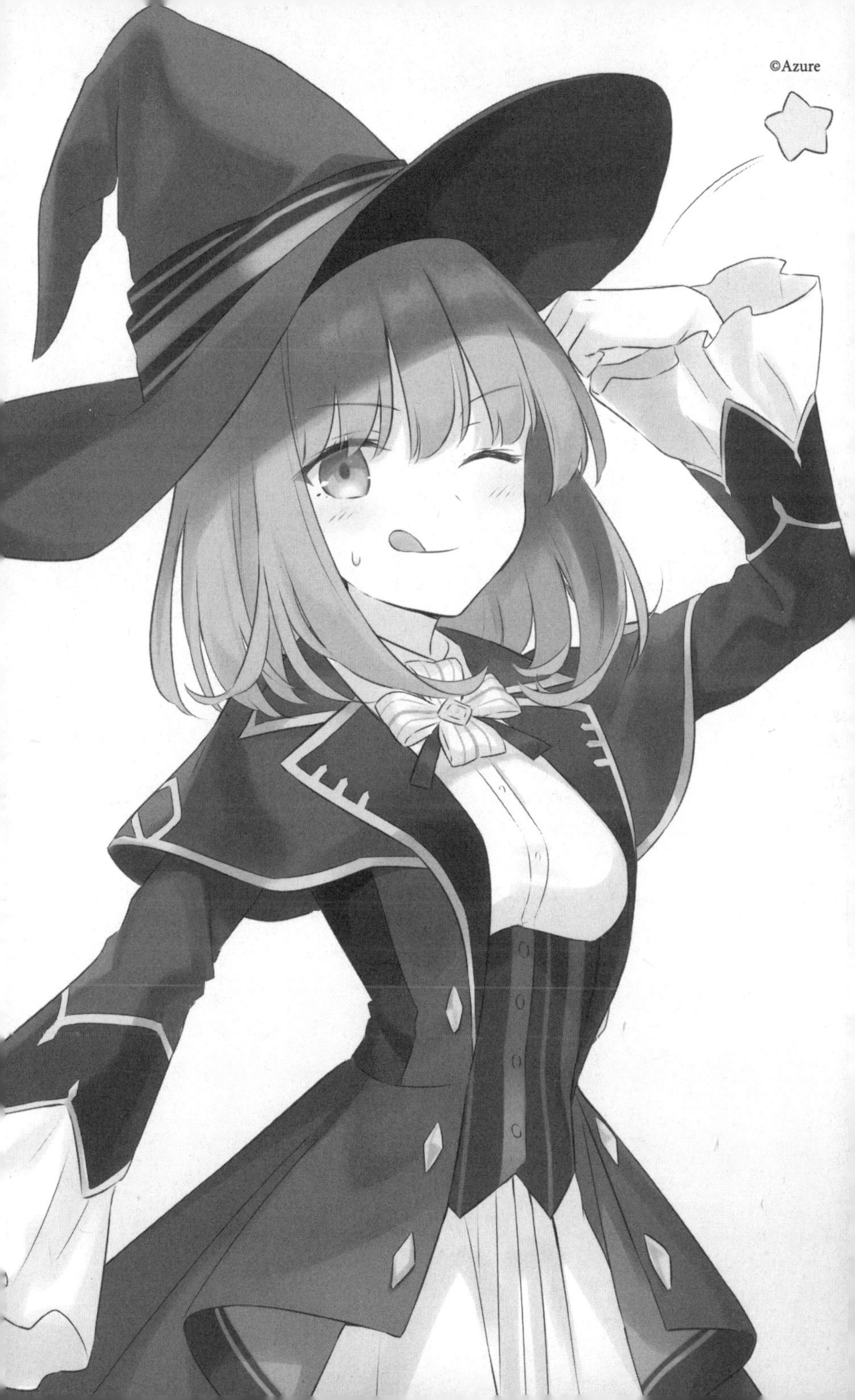
©Azure

Well, given the timing, I stopped because I'd been caught...
But let's not tell her that.

[Publication Information] Volume 7
Melonbooks Buyer's Bonus
[Author Comments]
Both of them are total good-for-nothings, huh...?
Sharon is apparently very, very popular with a certain segment of readers, and my editor is always telling me, "Put her in, put her in!" But I mean, there are lots of characters I'd like to write into the story.

CHAPTER 1 STORY 17

The Selfishness of the Ancient Dragon Luciella

"How strange…!"

Wrinkles appeared on the brow of the famous, the one and only, the ancient dragon Luciella. She groaned as she pondered, "Hmmmm…" At the moment, there was one question that was troubling her.

"Why is it that humans wear clothes? *Must* they wear clothes?"

The desire to not wear clothes was difficult to understand for humans like us.

Or rather, we wondered how she could say that, when we had gone out of our way to buy them and give them to her.

"Ohhh, they're too constricting. I hate this feeling…" Luciella abruptly began to take her clothes off.

"Wait a second, what are you doing? No, really, what are you doing? Stop, please, we're in public here!"

"Graaah, get off me! They're coming off! I'm taking these things off! They feel awful!"

Right in the middle of town.

Luciella put her hands on her clothes while we were in the middle of talking. I forced her to stop. The personality who, until a few moments earlier, had been excited about clothes and even picked some out for herself, had apparently been discarded along with the clothes I had bought for her, and now there was just a girl throwing a terrible temper tantrum.

Because there in the middle of the main avenue, she was shouting and carrying on.

"What's that? What's that?" The people walking down the street started looking at us, wondering if we were fighting.

"Oh, oh no, some kind of quarrel?" As soon as that happened, people began stopping to watch.

"What on earth is all the fuss over here?" Before long, it had gotten to the point that a crowd had formed.

Ignoring the stares of the passing crowd, Luciella kept shaking her head.

"I haaate them! Let me gooo!" She tugged at her clothes vigorously.

"Come on now, listen to what I'm saying! Wait, seriously, cut it out, please!" I pushed her hands back down.

As the spectacle was unfolding, one of the people who had gathered around us went pale and shouted, "The witch is trying to take off that girl's clothes! In public!"

Even though they missed the mark entirely, they shouted these heinous accusations. "It's terrible! Miss Witch! What do you think you're doing?!"

"No, that's not…" But on second glance, our struggles definitely gave precisely that impression. It certainly looked like I was in the middle of perpetrating some inexcusable act against her.

"……"

Ultimately, the struggle ended with me pulling Luciella by the hand and forcing her to flee.

"Ah! The witch plans to take the girl with her to a hidden place and do indecent things to her!" I had a feeling I could hear such things behind me, but I pretended I hadn't heard them and ran through the crowd at top speed.

"I just knew they would be uncomfortable…" After I fought my way through good-natured citizens who were trying to protect what they thought was a girl, Luciella continued to moan and complain.

What on earth can I do to stop her trying to take off her clothes in public like a crazy person?

The answer was in her behavior.

"Ah! Hey, you! I want to eat that ice cream stuff! Buy it for me, won't you?"

In the end, she was so flighty and easily distracted that as soon as she spotted some new thing, that was enough to make even the constriction of clothing into a concern of the past.

"...Yes, of course."

Ultimately, Luciella got her way, much to the detriment of my wallet.

Those days were far too hectic, but contrary to my expectations, also very fun.

[Publication Information] Volume 7
Toranoana Buyer's Bonus
[Author Comments]

I love naive, childlike characters. Even among all the guest characters that show up in each volume, Luciella is the type of girl I particularly like. Well, I call her a girl, but she's really getting up there in years.

CHAPTER 1 STORY 18

Plaster Repair Specialist (Charcoal Witch)

Great Figures Who Built Our History

This is the name of a collection of inspirational newspaper interviews here in our country, intended for people who love our historical heritage more than anything else.

The first guest on our program is this memorable individual:

The Charcoal Witch, Saya.

A witch who is affiliated with the United Magic Association.

Although she is still young, she's blessed with exceptional magical talent. Currently, as she wanders from country to country sightseeing, she also extends a helping hand to those seeking her assistance.

She's particularly unrivaled when it comes to repairing plaster.

People call her—the Plaster Repair Specialist.

—*Thank you so much for joining us today, I know how busy you must be.*

"Actually, this is the first time I've ever been called a Plaster Repair Specialist."

Humility befitting a true specialist. Perhaps this is one of the techniques that made her a master artisan?

"Actually, no one's ever really referred to me as an artisan before either... Well, whatever."

Even though she seemed amazed by the interview, Miss Saya immediately set to work repairing the plaster on the statue. While she was working, she stared at a photograph of a young woman with ash-gray hair, chuckling to herself as she blushed and made a slack expression.

"Eh-heh-heh..."

The person before us no longer seemed like a plaster repair specialist but rather like a lovestruck maiden.

Before she was an artisan, she was just a girl. This was probably one of the reasons why she had become an artisan in the first place.

—*And just who is that person in your photo?*

"This person here? This is the person I love."

That's how she answered as she scratched her cheek bashfully.

—*This person is the spitting image of our statue of the goddess, isn't she? Does she have some connection to the goddess?*

"Huh? What are you talking about? That's completely off the mark."

In a total change from a moment earlier, Miss Saya put on a tense, unsparing expression. She'd gotten angry.

From her serious expression, it was obvious that she had fought her way through many hardships already.

This was what she wanted to say: *"My plaster figures can't be etched onto flimsy pieces of paper like this one. Plaster sculptures should be shown to the wider world."*

It was to our shame that we had thrown out such thoughtless words.

Without a doubt, it was that quality known as the pride of the artisan that we were seeing in that moment.

After that, Miss Saya continued her work in silence for several hours. Occasionally, the word "Elaina…Elaina…" reached my ears, and I reasoned that it was probably a foreign word. It was inspiring to us. She was tremendously stoic.

She continued her work until the sun went down, then—

"All done! It's a statue of Elaina!"

Then finally, our magnificent statue, which had been repaired by a specialist, was com…complete…huh?

We couldn't believe our eyes. Unmistakably, there was a different statue there.

—*This is the famous goddess statue?*

"Huh? What are you talking about? That's completely off the mark."

—*Thank you very much for coming today.*

　　　　　＊　　＊　　＊

※ We'll be terminating the Great Figures Who Built Our History program after the first article.

[**Publication Information**]　Volume 7
Gamers Buyer's Bonus
[**Author Comments**]
　　From about Volume 6 onward, I started using the store-exclusive bonus stories to tell supplementary stories to the events that had transpired in the books. This story is one of those, about when Saya repaired the plaster sculpture.

CHAPTER 1 STORY 19

The World Through His Eyes

That day, a new piece by a famous artist in a certain country to the east debuted in an art gallery.

Now, I'm not someone who is very knowledgeable about art, so as soon as I laid eyes on his painting, which was hanging in an extremely expensive-looking gold frame, the only reaction I could produce was a worthless "Ah, it's a good resemblance!"

However, to the people who lived in that country, that one painting seemed to contain all sorts of meanings. Many voices flew past one another in the crowd of dark-haired viewers that had formed in front of the painting.

"I was excited to hear that he had finally painted something after several years, but this… It's a disappointment."

"It's a beautiful painting, as always. This witch wearing a vain expression is especially wonderful."

"I thought it was great that I would get to see a new piece after so long, but what is this? He's gone astray."

"Well, this route is splendid, too!"

"It's a means of progress. Just what you would expect from someone who has always done innovative stuff."

"Did you say 'progress'? You must have meant regression."

In short, it garnered mixed reviews.

The artist's name was Coulomb. He was a prodigy who was judged to be the best painter in the country despite his youth. His paintings were characterized by a particularly bold use of color…or so I'd heard. That's what was written about him on the placard.

Coulomb's past works were lined up in a row to the side of his new painting. Sure enough, all of them showed a bold use of color, bold enough that even I, in my ignorance about painting, was at least able to come up with a worthless reaction like "Ah, how colorful!"

But what about the new painting?

Hanging on the wall on the other side of the crowd of people was a single painting entitled *The Ashen Witch*. A lone witch wearing a black robe and a pointed hat, as well as a star-shaped brooch, was sitting by a window. She was letting her long gray hair flutter in the wind and wearing a vain-looking expression. She appeared to be simply sitting there, bored.

I could see how the painting didn't seem like the work of the artist Coulomb.

There wasn't the slightest use of any bold colors in the new painting. *The Ashen Witch* had been painted using only white and black and pale gray.

It did look like it was a departure, but I could also see how he seemed to be trying something new—that was probably precisely why the picture was getting mixed reviews.

"……"

Well, leaving all that aside, let's turn our eyes to the painting once more. Even if we skip over everything about it being a departure and whatnot, it is a lovely painting. There's a fair and beautiful witch right there.

By the way, who on earth could have been the model for that painting?

That's right, it was me.

O

This all started when I first came to the country. That was about a week ago.

As I wandered carelessly around town, I grew disheartened, and rightly so.

"...What's going on? This whole place is filthy rich?"

Just from walking down the street a little, it was obvious that the people of this country were fairly well-off and that they put an excessive amount of effort into the arts.

For example, take the bookstore. The exterior looked like an art gallery. A bronze statue of a young boy reading a book while walking was standing in the entryway.

Are you endorsing reading while walking?

For another example, take the butcher shop. Taxidermy animals were lined up around the entryway. In addition to a cow, a pig, and a chicken, there was also a sheep and a boar, a horse, and even a dog.

...A dog?

Add the fact that every store had, as a matter of course, paintings hanging up on the walls.

Even in a furniture store that I somehow wound up visiting (for some reason, the exterior was modeled after an enormous cupboard), they still had paintings on display.

"......"

There was some dark red substance spread thickly over the canvas. The coloring made it look like someone had tried their very best to vent their anger through the painting. The title of it was *Fair Weather Skies*, which was pretty boring.

Was the person who painted this a descendant of the devil or something?

When I averted my gaze downward, trying to escape from the sinister painting, I saw the signature of a man named Coulomb inscribed on it and felt worn out all over again.

It was a name I had seen over and over since coming to the country.

The majority of the shops I visited were decorated with his paintings. They had been painted irresponsibly, one being bright red despite bearing the title *Ocean*, and another being a deep blue color despite bearing the title *Forest*.

Why on earth are these sorts of paintings popular?

"Yoo-hoo! Miss, are you interested in this painting?"

While I was standing there in a daze, I was caught by the shopkeeper. But this was convenient for me.

Let's ask our question straight out, shall we?

"...Tell me, exactly what is good about this painting? I have absolutely no clue what the appeal is."

"Well! Imagine not understanding the appeal of this painting... I take it, miss, that you're not from around here?"

"I'm a traveler."

"I knew it!" The shopkeeper gave an exaggerated nod. "The thing about this painting, you see, is that it's bright red even though it depicts fair skies. The novelty of it is magnificent! Although I don't suppose an amateur who knows little about art could possibly understand."

That's not really much of an explanation...

"This is a furniture store, right? Why do you have paintings here?"

"Well, that's because I'm someone who loves art above anything else, of course!"

"Huh... But this painting—it doesn't match the atmosphere of your shop at all, does it? There are paintings in every shop, but they're just on display. At least, that's how it feels."

This was a question that had been fermenting in my mind since I first arrived in this country, and it had been bubbling there the whole time I was sightseeing.

When I said this, the shopkeeper let his true opinion show for the first time.

"I don't care about the atmosphere or whatever. As long as I have a famous and wonderful painting, that's good enough for me. If you must know why, it's because it's the only thing that can show people my store is doing well! Customers come in to shop at stores that are doing well! And then I can buy another new painting! Wonderful!"

"......"

I left the store, and as I was walking down the street, I thought that this was a very peculiar country.

Initially, I had thought it must be a rich country, but apparently that wasn't the case.

Instead, I got the sense that there were many people there who loved gaudy things.

I couldn't sense any of the placidity characteristic of the wealthy in the people living there. Everywhere, throughout the country, I could see that people were trying to show off by displaying fancy art.

"......"

Well, to put it simply, it's a place with lots of vain people, huh?

Once I changed my way of looking at things, the appearance of the country changed as well. For example, I saw that there were vain people even at the street stalls.

Every conceivable thing was there, at those shops sandwiched in between the flashy buildings.

The street stalls selling vegetables were especially strange and were filled with enormous vegetables the likes of which I had never seen, oddly shaped and defective-looking. However, here in this country, they were apparently quite rare and valuable, and the stalls were doing booming business.

Also, there were many colorful mushrooms on display as well, but I was pretty sure that, regardless of their rarity or their value, they were quite poisonous.

I continued down the street that was lined with stalls for a while, until a fruit shop came into view. But the things being sold there were not normal.

I came to a stop in front of the shop.

There were strangely colored fruits on display. An apple, but it was bright blue. A banana, but it was colored like a peach. A peach, but it was pitch-black.

It really was like—

"These fruits look like they were painted, don't they?"

That's how it seemed.

However, the shop owner shook his head. "Nah, no way, missy. These're rare types of fruits."

"Oh?"

As a test, I picked up a (bright red) orange and scraped at it with my finger.

Scratch, scratch.

"Ah, hey, knock it off! You're gonna damage the merchandise!"

The shop owner snatched the red orange from me in a panic. When I looked at the finger that had done the scratching, it had faint traces of red stuck to it.

......

Shameful…

"—Oh, doesn't that banana look good?!"

A man came to stand beside me as he made this puzzling comment. He was taller than I was and had a slender build. He looked to be about in his mid-twenties. He must have been in the middle of a shopping trip, because he was holding bags in both hands.

The shopkeeper, who had been scowling at me, abruptly changed his attitude with the arrival of a new customer and replied, "Yes, and it's not just the bananas! All of these are rare fruits that I've just recently acquired."

"I see. It's no wonder I thought they were a little oddly colored."

I think it's more than a little.

"How about this peach over here? A pitch-black peach is a rare sight, surely?"

"Hmm… It doesn't look all that tasty to me."

"Don't you worry, sir. The flavor is just like a normal peach."

Well, he did just paint the colors on, after all.

"What are those pale-colored grapes over there?"

"Those are a variety of grape called muscats."

Why are the muscats the only thing you left alone?

The man beside me looked at the shopkeeper and pointed to the red orange. "Interesting… What is that thing you're holding in your hand?"

The shopkeeper threw his shoulders up with a start, then hid the orange behind himself.

"Now, this one's not for sale. That other customer damaged it, you see."

How rude.

"It's not really damaged. It's just lost its value as a product, isn't that right?"

"You hush. Be quiet, little girl! I don't have any fruit to sell you!"

"Oh really?"

I've been refused a sale.

Well, I wasn't planning to buy anything anyway, so it's not much of a problem for me.

"—Hey..."

As I was turning over the shopkeeper's words, I heard a faint voice from beside me.

When I looked over, I saw that a man had been watching the exchange between the fuming-mad shopkeeper and the casually dismissive witch, wearing a dumbfounded expression. It was an expression that was full of surprise, as if he was looking at something he just couldn't believe.

"...You... What's up with your hair?"

"...What?"

"What's with that hair, that color, how is it...?"

The man dropped the bags he had been holding in both hands.

The bags made a rustling sound and collapsed, and from them spilled all sorts of art supplies, paint and brushes of various sizes and colors and whatnot.

Then the man, quite excitedly, said, "Y-you! Please, if you don't mind, won't you come and model for my painting?! I'll pay you handsomely!"

He took my hand.

"...What?"

I answered him with the same question again.

○

"How about five gold pieces?!"

The man who had shouted those words took me to a detached house in the middle of the city.

He was either very much the show-off or a real rich person, because the place he brought me to was obviously a luxurious mansion.

"This is quite a large house you have here."

"Guess so. Despite appearances, I'm a pretty famous artist."

"Could I ask your name?"

The man nodded as he placed his hand on the door to the front entrance.

"Coulomb."

"…Ah. That guy."

"Oh wow. Do you know my work?"

"Yeah. You're the guy with the really unconventional use of color."

"Mm…I'm blushing."

Come to think of it, unconventional *and* weird *are kind of synonyms, huh?*

"Why do you make use of colors in that way?"

"Well, it's because to me, that's how the world looks."

"Huh, does it really?"

"You don't seem very interested…"

"I thought for sure those paintings had been made by someone really strange."

"Strange guys aren't the only people who are able to paint strange paintings, you know."

"I guess you're right. Though it's also true that people who paint strange paintings don't necessarily recognize that they are strange people."

"Ha-ha…that's pretty harsh."

He narrowed his eyes and let out a dry chuckle.

Then the door opened.

I was shown farther inside the house and invited into his atelier.

In the ridiculously spacious room, the fresh scent of flowers hung in the air, mixed with the smell of paint. The curtains by the window flapped in the wind, swaying as they twinkled in the afternoon light.

There was a large workbench sitting right up against the wall, with paints and bottles and things, the use of which I didn't really understand, scattered all over it.

He pulled a canvas out from a corner of the room, set it on an easel, and sat down. As he got ready to paint, he certainly did seem like a popular, famous artist. But the many failed paintings scattered around in the background gave rise to a strange sort of melancholy.

Not everything he paints is a success, the discarded paintings seemed to be saying.

"Well then, where should we begin…? Ah, for now, would you stand over by the window?"

"Sure."

I did as I was told and stood where he indicated. By the way, I stood bolt upright.

"…Um, that's pretty unnatural, so if you could strike some sort of pose, I'd be grateful."

"Huh…"

Even though he was requesting a pose, I couldn't come up with anything very good, so I tried raising both arms in the air.

"No good. It's too unnatural. Please do something more natural looking."

"Like this?" I covered both my ears.

"No. Something different."

"What if I do this?" I covered both my eyes.

"That's even worse. Next."

"What do you think of this?" This time, I covered my mouth.

"Mm, let's move away from covering things, shall we?"

"I see." I was getting tired of this, and I took a seat on the window sill.

"That's great!"

"Oh?"

So you're finally satisfied with this pose? Interesting.

"All right, stay like that. Don't move for a while. I'm starting to sketch now." Then he took out a battered pencil and began staring intensely back and forth between the canvas and me.

"How long do I need to stay still?"

"Until I'm done drawing you."

"So how long will that be?"

"Sorry, but I'm drawing now. I can't concentrate when you're talking, so please be quiet."

"……"

What is this guy's deal…?

After that, I don't remember how much time passed. It could have been one hour, it could have been three; possibly even more time than that went by.

The time I spent just sitting on the windowsill and gazing outside was duller and more punishing than I'd imagined.

"—Okay. Let's take a little break."

Coulomb's words as he sat down his brush and gently stretched sounded to me like a death sentence.

"…Huh? We're coming back to it?"

In response to my question, he nodded, as if the answer was obvious.

"It's only about halfway done yet. You must be tired, too. Have a seat somewhere over there. I'll go get something to drink," he said, and he left the room.

……

I was terribly exhausted, but more importantly, I was curious about how his painting was coming along. I walked over to the spot he had been glued to just a moment earlier and peered at the canvas.

"…Whoa."

On it was a witch lingering by the window, gazing off somewhere in the distance with a sorrowful expression on her face. It wasn't finished, but it was beautiful.

Who on earth could this model be?

This silly joke rose up in my mind, so I stepped away from the canvas and roamed around the atelier.

The failed paintings that were piled up on the floor. The window where I had been sitting. Various items the use of which I did not understand. Those, and the paints scattered across the desktop.

It was all rather charming.

It was as if all the agonizing days of an artist who people called a genius were packed into this one room.

"……?"

As I was looking aimlessly around the room, suddenly, my eyes fell on a glass that was standing alone on top of the desk. Without thinking, I picked it up. The thick, viscous, bloodlike liquid inside it sloshed around, and a single drop spilled over the edge and ran onto my hand.

I sniffed it, thinking it might be a drink, but it had a scent that was obviously not palatable. In fact, it stank like paint.

What on earth could this be?

"Hmm…"

There was no way the answer would come to someone like me who knew so little about painting, no matter how much I puzzled over it.

"Maybe it's a bad batch of paint?" I pondered.

Coulomb came back into the room just as I set the glass down on the desk and started to wipe my hand.

"Okay, sorry for keeping you— Wait, hey. Hey, are you okay?"

He came back carrying two cups, and as soon as he saw me, his eyes went wide.

"…? What do you mean?"

"What do you mean, what do I mean—?" He was starting to panic a little, and without even closing the door, he set the cups down where he was and started trotting around the room. "*You're bleeding, aren't you? Okay, right.* There ought to be something we can use to stop the bleeding over here—"

"……?"

Bleeding?

"Did you happen to touch a blade or something? I'm so sorry. This room is a total mess..." He pulled some strips of cloth out from a corner of the room and handed them to me. "Here, please use these to stop the bleeding. Although it looks like the wound is a shallow one... Doesn't it hurt?"

I took the cloth.

"Um, I'm really not bleeding at all," I said as I wiped away the liquid that was on my hand. Then I said to the stunned Coulomb, "I'm sorry. I was curious about the glass that was on your desk, and I touched it. Looks like some of the liquid that was inside it got on my hand."

"......" For just one short moment, his face twisted. "A-ah. Was that it...? Looks like I jumped to the wrong conclusion."

"Yes—sorry. I shouldn't have touched it."

"No. That's fine. The most important thing is that you're not hurt."

"...Yeah."

When I finished wiping my hand, the liquid soaked into the cloth somewhat. There was no mark left on my hand. It seemed to have wiped away cleanly.

I asked, "By the way, why did you think I had gotten hurt?"

"Uh, um, well...I wonder why... I guess because it looked like blood?"

"That stuff?"

As I pointed at the desk, I asked again.

"You mistook that for blood?"

The stuff I was pointing at—the liquid on the desk that was viscous like blood, the *pitch-black* liquid, was swaying slightly inside the glass.

○

"*...Sigh...*"

After letting out a deep sigh, the man sat in front of the easel that was holding his half-finished painting. He looked vexed.

Perhaps he had realized there was no way to continue to keep his secret hidden.

"Please don't tell a soul what I'm about to say, okay?"
"Sure, I won't."
Though it's not like I have anyone to tell in the first place.
Then he told me—
"I...can't see colors. Ever since I was born, the things people call colors haven't been visible to my eyes. The sky, the sea, the forest—everything I see is black and white and shades of gray. But I thought that was normal. I first began to suspect something when I was a child. My friends were distinguishing things that looked the same to me, calling them 'red' or 'blue.' It made me wonder what on earth they were talking about."
"...Hmm."
"I've never been able to see color myself. I can't see what others see. It came as a serious shock when I realized that fact. Though at this point, that's all in the past."
He lowered his eyes to stare at the floor.
Then, after a long pause, he continued, "Even though I couldn't see colors, I never confessed as much to the people around me. I pretended to be normal. I acted as if I could see things I couldn't see."
"......"
Maybe that's why he's such a show-off.
"Well, even if you can't see colors, you can still live a normal life if you try. The only time I had any trouble was when I was painting—painting pictures has been my hobby since I was small, you see, and even after I knew I couldn't see color, I never wanted to stop. So I kept on painting, purely as a hobby. I didn't have the slightest intention of seeking any recognition..."
"And now you're highly acclaimed, huh?"
"That's right. The funny thing is my paintings were praised anyway. The people of this country who saw my paintings made a big fuss, calling them unique and saying, 'What an unconventional use of color!' and so on."
I wonder whether this is another effect of living in a country full of vain show-offs or whether they really think he's a genius—

"So to make a long story short, you mixed up random colors and painted with them, and before you knew what was happening, you'd become a famous artist. Is that it?"

"Well, I guess that's about how it went, yeah… And so, because of that, I'm struggling now."

"Oh…? Why's that? There's no sweeter deal than making lots of money just by painting things the way you see them, is there?"

"You make it sound so simple, but it's not so easy coming up with these crazy color schemes, you know. The more famous I get, and the more works I produce, the more criticism I face. They say my color balance is off, or that my paintings are starting to look like realistic landscapes, and all sorts of other stuff."

"…Hmm."

"That's why, recently, I've been thinking I should try something new—I'm planning to paint something in only black and white, using that stuff you were holding earlier."

"That stuff…?" I looked toward the desk. "You mean the liquid in that glass?"

"It's charcoal ink. By diluting it with water, I'll be able to paint the world exactly as I see it."

"…Ah."

"I want to try making a new kind of painting using that ink. What do you think?"

Don't ask me…

"What if you paint two and then decide? Two different types, one painting done the same way you have been doing it until now, and one where you use the new charcoal ink or whatever you called it."

"Foolishness. Even if I painted two of the same picture, I wouldn't be able to tell the difference, would I?"

"……"

Oh, right.

"Now, no matter what anybody says, I intend to paint with the ink this time."

"......"
If you had already made up your mind to try painting a picture with the charcoal ink, then why did you ask for my opinion? I don't understand it. Am I just here to be your sounding board?

"I feel like once this painting is complete and put on display, people will see my true abilities for the first time. They'll be able to tell whether I actually have any talent or whether I'm some pitiful guy who simply got lucky and was just elevated by chance—"

In other words, this painting is his way of testing that out.

He must be struggling with the idea of getting real criticism around here. This country is full of nothing but vain show-offs and shams.

That must be all the more reason why he's decided to paint the world exactly as it looks to his eyes.

"Well, that's enough of a break, I think," he said. It sounded like he was indirectly telling me to hurry up and get back to my position.

I did as I was commanded and walked over to the window.

Coulomb stared earnestly at the painting of me on his canvas as he rearranged his brushes.

Then he looked up as if he had remembered something and asked, "Ah—come to think of it, what is your true hair color?"

I answered his question as I took my seat by the window.

"Even you can see that."

[**Publication Information**]   Kakuyomu Post Story
[**Author Comments**]
    I wrote this story for Volume 2, but the content was too gray, in several senses, and it was rejected. Initially, I complained about it and vowed that I would have it published, and because of my persistence, it later wound up being published in Kakuyomu. I really like this kind of story, so I'd like to write these more frequently, but...

CHAPTER 1 STORY 20

Avelia's Secret

"I'm back!"

My older sister and I were still in the middle of our journey.

We spent our days traveling from country to country, earning our daily wages.

"Welcome home."

My sister, who had already gotten home, greeted me by waving her hand in the air. I walked right past her as she enjoyed a cup of tea, and collapsed with a *fwump* on the bed.

I was obviously exhausted, but my sister cocked her head and looked down at me. "How was work?" she asked.

"As you can see..."

"Exhausting, huh...?"

"How did your work go, Big Sister?"

"Just as you can see."

With a bitter look, my sister slapped a bundle of well-worn recruitment magazines and let out a sigh.

My older sister, who was also my traveling companion, had started looking for a job like mine, where she could earn the money we needed. But for some reason, she had encountered a stroke of bad luck and was not presently employed.

"I just can't manage to find a job..." My big sister let out a sigh. "Maybe they don't want help from foreigners here in this country... There are no good jobs at all."

"There are jobs out there if you're not too picky."

"Huh? I wonder..."

"It's true."

"Speaking of which, what was it that you're doing for work, Avelia?"

"That's a secret."

"Why?"

"Because I'm not picky about what jobs I take."

"Somehow, that's got a little bit of a suspicious ring to it…," my sister said as she narrowed her eyes. Then she let out a sigh and mumbled, "I wonder if I'll also find a job right away if I stop being so picky…?"

Honestly, I would have preferred for my sister to stay in our room and not work at all, but given her personality, I knew that could never happen.

The fact that I had started my part-time job before she found anything had probably spurred on my sister's feelings of guilt even more. And so she was frantically searching for work.

I wish we could both quickly find good jobs and escape these worries.

"Ah!" Suddenly, my sister raised her voice. "Hey, how about this cat café right here? I guess it's a store where you can play with cats… Sounds interesting!"

Uh-oh.

"You can't work there."

"Oh? Why not?"

"It doesn't matter why not. If I say you can't, you can't."

Oh no, seriously.

I wish we could both quickly find good jobs and escape these worries.

[**Publication Information**]   Volume 8
Melonbooks Buyer's Bonus
[**Author Comments**]
     There are jobs out there if you're not too picky…! That's this story. I like the conversations between Avelia and Amnesia because they're easy to write.

CHAPTER 1 STORY 21

Amnesia's Anguish

I had been having a hard time finding a business that would hire me, given that I was a mere outsider.

When we'd first arrived in the country, I'd set out looking for work with a lighthearted attitude. "Hmm. For now, I'll find any old place where I can make money, and after making a suitable amount of cash, I can move on."

But I had faced nothing but difficulty in my job search. It was a spectacularly awful disaster, bad enough to make me wish that just once I had chastised the version of myself who had first entered the country, who had been scrutinizing each business so carefully, touting her high ideals.

"Eh? You're a traveler? Which means you'll be leaving before the week is out? Well…we don't really have the leeway to hire someone who's only going to work a few days…"

"We're not recruiting for any short-term jobs… Sorry…"

"If you're just window shopping, get outta here!"

That's all.

That was how my search for a part-time job had gone. Unfortunately, I hadn't found any employment.

Whenever we arrived in a new country, my younger sister, Avelia, and I always searched for jobs so that we could make enough money to live another day, but every single time, I had a terrible time finding work.

"How does Elaina always manage to make money…?" I recalled

my benefactor, the girl who had previously rescued me, and grumbled, "Next time I see her, maybe I'll get her to teach me her moneymaking methods…"

In response to my question, Avelia declared, "I'm not really sure why, but I get the feeling she has a hand in some shady business."

"Why do you think that?" I cocked my head.

"Woman's intuition," Avelia asserted bluntly. Then she said, with some pride, "By the way, I found a job. Since yesterday, I've been working at a café."

"…How did you find a job?"

"That was also thanks to a woman's intuition."

After that, my own sister, who had outmaneuvered me without me knowing a thing, said this: "Big Sister, in order for foreigners to make money, we inevitably have to get our hands into some slightly shady business."

As she told me that, my little sister peered off into the distance. It seemed like somehow, without my knowledge, my sister had embarked into the adult world.

"You've really grown…Avelia…"

"No, I've probably just gotten a little soiled…"

Still, even after we had that exchange, I walked around town looking for a job. But sure enough, it seemed it would be difficult for an outsider to find work through respectable means.

I was tired from walking around being continuously rejected, and I decided to go into a café. It was a café I had found in town, where people were doing dangerous jobs in secret…a dangerous environment.

I casually opened the door.

[Publication Information]   Volume 8
Toranoana Buyer's Bonus
[Author Comments]
　　As a matter of fact, the bonus stories for Volume 8 all wound up being connected to the main storyline. Now, they weren't quite good enough to put into the main book, but still, I wrote them as supplementary stories.

　　This is off-topic, but I love the dialogues between Konomi Kohara (Amnesia) and Miho Okasaki (Avelia) on the drama CDs.

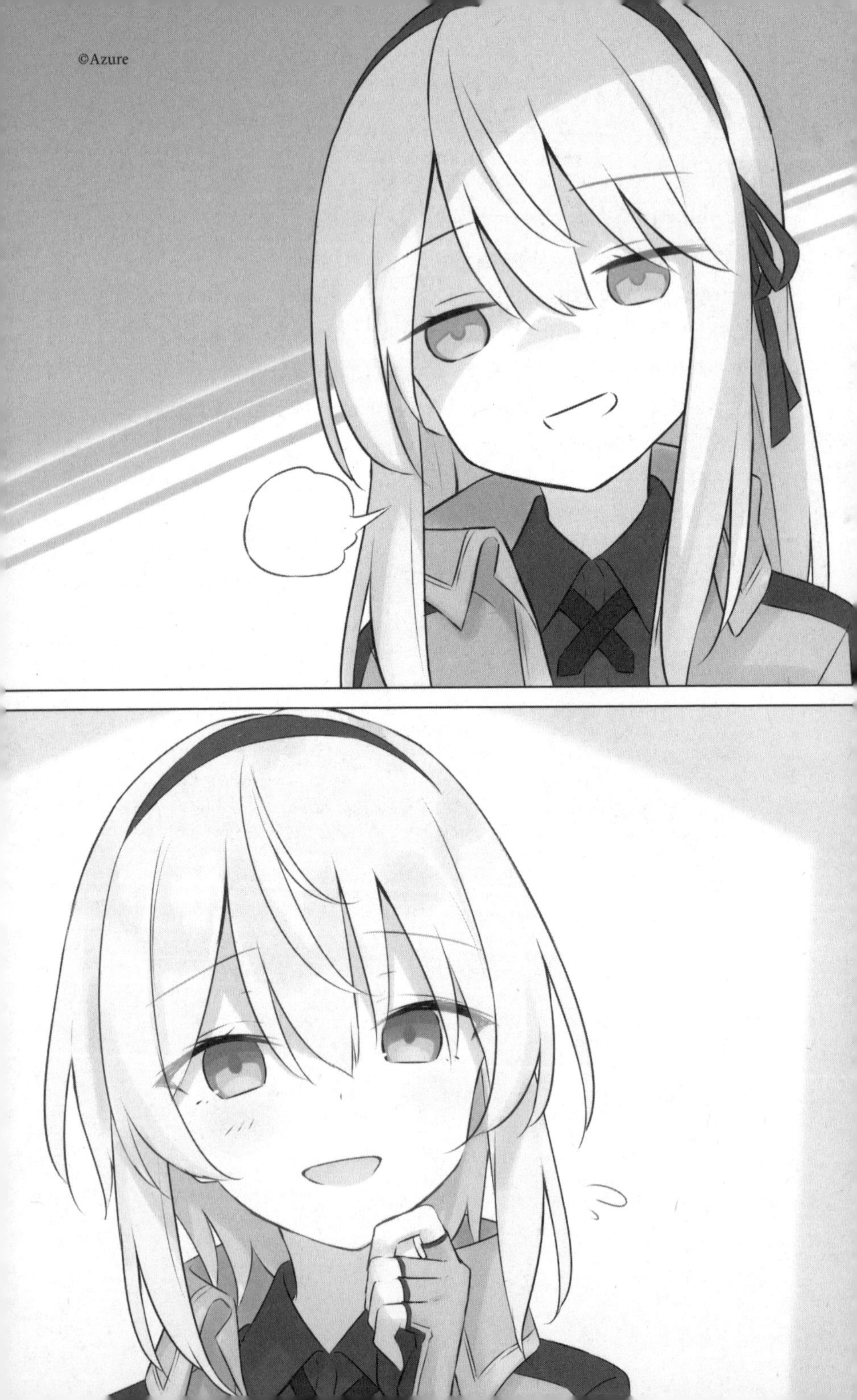
©Azure

CHAPTER 1 STORY 22
Saya's Daily Routine

"Teacher, hey, teacherrr!"

"Huh? What do you want?"

One day I grabbed ahold of the sleeve of my annoying teacher, who was calmly smoking her stupid pipe just to the side of the designated smoking area at a branch office of the United Magic Association.

I knew she would probably say something strikingly amoral, like *"This isn't a cigarette, it's a pipe, so it must be okay if I don't stay in the smoking area, right?"* But her smoking was nothing but a nuisance, and I really wished she would quit. However, on that occasion, I had other reasons for approaching my teacher, besides chiding her for her foolish decisions.

"Teach me some magic, please," I said.

That's right, I want to learn magic.

I had studied magic under my teacher, the Midnight Witch, Sheila, and I was already officially the Charcoal Witch, Saya, but even so, whenever she had free time, I still pestered my teacher to teach me more magic.

Although I was now being treated as an adult, I was still inexperienced, so there were many things I didn't know. I didn't have the time to waste just standing still. I'm always joking around, but as a matter of fact, I think I'm quite a serious girl… Though that's not the sort of thing you say about yourself.

"Ehhh…what a pain…" My teacher was quite an undisciplined witch, so even when I asked for things up front, she generally didn't listen to what I said. "I don't feel like it…"

You see?

But my negligent teacher always dismissed everything I asked her. This was an everyday occurrence. And I already knew what the next words out of her mouth were going to be.

"All right, first things first, go buy me some coffee." That's what you're going to say, right?

"All right, first—"

"Here, have this," I said as I swiftly presented my teacher with a cup of coffee.

"…!" After opening her eyes wide, looking somewhat shocked, my teacher said, "You've got more sense than I thought…" and accepted the coffee.

After this, as a rule, she would continue in a similar fashion.

"All right, next go buy me some bread."

Then it would be tobacco, and then she'd ask for another coffee. I already knew the drill.

"All right then, next some bread—"

"Here you are," I said as I swiftly presented her with a loaf of bread.

"…Okay then, tobacco—"

"Here," I said. I had already purchased it.

"…In that case, another—"

"Coffee, right? Here, please enjoy."

"……"

Then finally, after I had met all her demands, my teacher scratched her head, looking annoyed, and turned to look at me. "…No way out, huh…? Fine. What do you want me to teach you?"

She might have looked like quite a rough-and-tumble witch, but my teacher was by no means a bad person at heart.

And that was more or less how I passed my days together with my undisciplined and negligent teacher.

[Publication Information]   Volume 8
Gamers Buyer's Bonus

[Author Comments]

In Volume 4 of *Wandering Witch*, a clumsy girl named Yuuri, who aspired to be hard-boiled but was in actual fact not hard-boiled at all, made her appearance, but whenever I'm writing Sheila, I think that Sheila is actually the hard-boiled character Yuuri ought to try to be more like.

CHAPTER 1 STORY 23
Elaina's Birthday

"Lady Witch. Today is your birthday, is it not?"

In the middle of my immigration inspection at the border of a certain country, the official working there put on a broad smile and looked straight at me. "Happy birthday. You are a very lucky person to have arrived in our country on your birthday."

My, my.

"Just what do you mean by 'lucky'?"

"In our country, we distribute these special tickets to visitors who arrive here on their birthdays."

As he said that, the official handed me a single slip of paper. The paper, which was just about the right size to use for a bookmark, read: BIRTHDAY TICKET.

"…What is this thing?"

"It's a Birthday Ticket."

I mean, I can tell that by looking at it, but…

"Does it do something? Is it some sort of voucher?"

"Sure. Well, I guess you could call it a voucher."

Then the official very casually disclosed something that was hard for me to believe.

He told me—

"If you present this coupon, you can exchange it to get one and only one of anything in this country."

○

Frankly speaking, everything in town seemed to sparkle. The many tall buildings that lined the streets. The bread and fruit for sale at street stalls. Books that had just recently been released for sale, and clothes worn by proud-looking mannequins. Everything, every last thing seemed to sparkle.

"That, and this… It's all…free?"

By the way, while I was holding my ticket, the officials all seemed to follow me around. Behind me, an official who had been waiting on standby put on the same kind of broad grin I had seen earlier and answered me. "Yes, that's exactly right."

"Are you serious…?"

"Perfectly serious."

The official nodded sharply.

Looking back and forth between my Birthday Ticket and the city around me, I got flustered and started to panic. The Birthday Ticket, which had been handed to me much too readily, apparently meant I could have anything I wanted in the whole city, just by presenting the ticket, and nobody would refuse me.

When it came down to it, did that mean if I were to, for example, act the part of an unthinkable villain and present my ticket to the king while saying something like *"Heh-heh-heh, using this ticket, I take possession of this country!"* he would simply hand over the country like *"Ah, please go right ahead, allow me to transfer the country to you, my lady"*? I wondered.

"…It really sounds too good to be true. I've never heard anything so implausible."

I mean, really…

"Are you telling me all the people living in this country will just say 'Here you go' and hand over anything, just because someone presents them with one of these tickets? Or is there some kind of trick to it…?"

I tried heating the ticket over a flame and doing all sorts of other things to it, but no matter how I looked at it, the ticket was nothing more than a slip of paper, and it didn't seem to have any kind of special magic applied to it.

"Please stop, Lady Witch. No invisible message is going to appear. Besides, if you burn it, that ticket will lose its value." The official rushed to interrupt me. "Everyone in this country is a good person. So as long as you present your ticket, they will comply, without exception. No matter what kind of thing you want, I'm sure they will make the exchange."

"Are you serious…?"

"Perfectly serious."

But this ticket is a little bit too powerful, I think…

"I wonder what I should buy—?"

I was puzzled by this sudden development. For the time being, I wandered indecisively around town. But it didn't matter how far I walked. I was simply a traveler, so I would have no way to use, for example, a house or a whole shop, even if I were to exchange my ticket for them.

But since I got the ticket, I ought to use it.

"How about I exchange this ticket for their most expensive bread—?"

I casually stopped by one of the street stalls, pointed out a piece of bread that looked well baked, and then—

"Excuse me, one piece of this bread, in exchange for this tick—"

—I was about to hand it over.

"……"

But just before I did, I suddenly had a thought.

Supposedly, all the people in this country are good people. No matter what kind of unreasonable request I make, if I hand over this ticket, they'll grant it. I can acquire anything at all by exchanging this ticket.

……

By the way—

—where exactly does the ticket go once I've handed it over?

"Is something the matter, Lady Witch? Would you like to buy our most expensive bread?"

The worker popped her head out from behind the booth. Luckily, I hadn't handed over my Birthday Ticket just yet.

"Could I ask you a question?"

"Anything."

"These tickets—can they only be used by the person whose birthday it is?"

"No, no. That's not how it works."

"So then, in the event that I handed over my ticket here in exchange for some bread—"

"Of course, the right to use the ticket would pass to the owner of this stall."

"……"

"The owner of this stall would get the ticket, the Birthday Ticket, that you can exchange to get one and only one of anything, as well as the right to use it. However, only good people live in our country, so probably, if you exchanged it for something as cheap as bread, he would relinquish the right to use the ticket. You would do that, right, Boss?"

The owner of the bread stall nodded in agreement with his employee.

Additionally, the worker clapped her hands together joyfully.

"I'm so happy, Lady Witch, to learn that you're such a good person. If you were a bad person, then right about now, you would be headed straight for the king, getting ready to try to use the ticket to take possession of the whole country!"

"Well, now! Are there even people who would consider doing something so wicked? What a horrible thought."

There stood a lone witch desperately suppressing the evil deed that had flashed through her mind earlier, as she forcibly willed herself to align with the good-natured worker.

Who could she be?

That's right, it's me.

"So in other words, to make a long story short, this ticket is used to distinguish between bad people and good people?"

And here I thought it was a Birthday Ticket. This is a ridiculously dangerous item, isn't it?

"You're exactly right. By the way, we also have a program where we give tickets to travelers when it's not their birthday and tell them they're our hundredth traveler!"

"Why do you do something so bothersome?"

When I asked her, the worker grinned again and said, "We do it, of course, so that the invisible will become visible."

○

"So that's my story about my birthday the other day."

Later on, I ran into Saya on my journey and recounted the story of these events that had taken place in a strange country. It was another one of my traveling tales.

Saya nodded and agreed that "There sure are some strange countries out there. So then, in the end, what did you get with your ticket, Elaina? Based on what I've heard, I got the sense that as long as it wasn't something overly expensive, they'd exchange it for anything."

Exchanging it for something like the most expensive piece of bread wouldn't have been any problem at all. Certainly, there would have been no issue getting any small thing in exchange for the ticket.

"Well, since it was a rare opportunity, I got one special thing to remember it by."

"What was that?"

"This."

As I spoke, I smoothly pulled a single piece of paper out from the book I had just been reading.

In my hand was a special slip of paper that read: BIRTHDAY TICKET.

[**Publication Information**]   Twitter Post Story
[**Author Comments**]

Once again, we have a story about Elaina's birthday. This one is a story that I put up on Twitter. By the way, I often get asked just how old Elaina is, but I think people would be shocked if I revealed the exact age of the character, so I'm intentionally keeping it a secret. The shock you feel when your own age passes the age of a character you always thought, ever since you were in elementary school, was older than you, is unfathomable, right? I experienced that with *Hell Teacher: Jigoku Sensei Nube*.

CHAPTER 1 STORY 24

A Mysterious Phrase

"Dubya tee eff!"
Immediately after I arrived at the gates of that country, the gate guard turned to me and uttered that mysterious phrase.
"What was that?"
"Dubya tee eff," the guard repeated, this time with some force in his voice. After that, he said, "Oh, sorry, in this country, that phrase means all sorts of things."
"What?" I said again, with discomfort in my voice, as I tilted my head questioningly. "…Huh, well, whatever," I answered indifferently.
I couldn't really see what the landscape rising behind the gate looked like. I had heard elsewhere that it was a lively place with delicious food, where they used unique words. But although I had been interested in visiting for some time, I simply hadn't gotten the chance to set foot in the country yet. I'd been hearing rumors for quite a while about what an interesting country it was, so I was ready for anything, but I'd never expected things to get weird before I even went in.
By the way—
"What does that 'dubya tee eff' phrase mean?"
—I've never heard that phrase before.
"It's a mysterious phrase that will somehow or other get the job done whenever you say it," he replied immediately.
"……"
I don't claim to know much about what goes on in this country, but I still feel like I can say for sure that his explanation was absolutely false…
"All that is to say, Miss Witch, once you go through these gates, please

go ahead and use this phrase whenever someone speaks to you. Is there anything else you would like to know? If you like, I'll be happy to tell you."

"...No, I'm good."

"Dubya tee eff."

"......"

"Dubya tee eff... Ah, that's what we call comedic repetition. It's also a phrase we use when we have the same exchange several times. Do you want to practice?"

"......"

At that point, it occurred to me that I might shake my head and refuse him again, but right before I did, I realized something. This was a trap. If I were to speak the same words again now, that would unmistakably amount to the comedic repetition the guard had mentioned.

I was kind of annoyed at the idea of doing things the way the gate guard had expected, so I shut my mouth before I could open it and took a moment to think.

In this situation, what is the right way to respond?

A moment later, it hit me. Hadn't I just been taught a mysterious phrase that would somehow or other get the job done whenever I said it?

And so I said—

"Dubya tee eff!"

[Publication Information] Volume 8

Animate Osaka Nipponbashi Purchase Perk

[Author Comments]

I was thinking about whether or not it was all right for there to be dialects in a fantasy setting, but I figured it was all right, since Alte is already a rural character who speaks with a dialect. I mean, even in other countries, it's normal for people to have accents depending on what region they're from, right?

CHAPTER 1 STORY 25

Mirror, Oh Mirror

In a certain land, there was an extremely beautiful princess.

She was so beautiful that if you were to look up the word *beautiful* in one of that country's dictionaries, the entry would say something outrageous like: *Did you mean Her Highness?*

Because of her overwhelming beauty, the people, without exception, even prostrated themselves whenever they were in front of her. Hers was a beauty beyond description.

One day, the princess, who wielded such terrible beauty, found herself troubled.

"…Why is it that I haven't been able to marry, when I am so beautiful?"

That's right, she was searching for a marriage partner.

The world's most beautiful princess was aware of her own beauty, but she was so unpopular, it was hard to believe it. The men of her country all just prostrated themselves when they were before her. She hadn't had any luck meeting her soulmate.

And why on earth not?

"Could it be that there is a woman more beautiful than me…?"

The reason why the princess wasn't popular with men was simply that she was of much too high a status, and the common people all thought it was presumptuous to approach her. But the princess had a slightly strange sense of the world.

And so the princess turned to her mirror and mumbled to herself.

As she touched her marvelous, mysterious mirror, which could speak human language, she mumbled—

"Mirror, oh mirror, tell me just who is the most beautiful in the world?"

The mirror, which had been reflecting the beautiful princess, responded to her words. It answered, showing her a new scene.

"That's right, it's me."

There in the mirror was the image of a beautiful young woman with ash-gray hair.

○

"Wow, thanks to you, Miss Witch, our company's performance is through the roof! I can't stop smiling!"

The fairies of the forest were all fawning over me just like that. I'll have to back up several weeks to describe how I came to butt into the small business that several of them were operating.

As I was traveling through a forest, I'd overheard several middle-aged fairy men complaining to one another.

"Look at us… Our architecture skills are top rate, and yet we can't sell a thing…"

Oh my goodness, some kind of trouble?

I approached them to satisfy my curiosity, and when I asked, they answered, "Well, as a matter of fact, we're architects, but we keep building house after house only for those damn wolves to blow them all down, one after the other. Our clients, the pigs, are starting to complain."

Well, that is awful.

Then I realized I could offer them a little bit of wisdom. "How about building a house out of brick?"

As soon as they switched from building wood-frame houses to building brick houses, the fairies started getting words of thanks from their piggy clients. "Oink, oink."

I see, I see.

"I'm sorry, but I haven't got the slightest idea what the pigs are saying," I said.

One of the fairies answered me apologetically. "He said, 'Heh-heh-heh, the girl is cute.'"

"Is it okay if I slap him?"

When I said that, the pig replied once again, "Oink, oink."

"What did he say now?" I asked.

One of the fairies answered me apologetically. "He said, 'Please slap me! I'm begging you!'"

"You filthy pig…"

At any rate, that was how I ended up meddling in the fairies' business. To make a long story short, I confronted their manager and extorted them for money.

I found myself doing the easy work of reviewing the final reports every day at the end of business, while spending a comfortable time relaxing inside one of the houses the fairies had built. Piece of cake. It was a sweet gig.

Sure is great to make money off someone else's mess, huh?

The phrase *smooth sailing* described just such a scenario. All I was doing was earnestly squeezing money out of them.

"Heh-heh-heh…heh-heh-heh-heh…"

It was enough to make a bold laugh spill spontaneously from my lips.

O

"Tch… That's the Ashen Witch, huh…? She's horrible…horrible…! How can she laugh like that?! She's infuriating!"

As she watched the witch quietly reading by herself through the mirror, the princess brought the handkerchief in her hand to her mouth and tugged on it forcefully with her teeth. She was the very picture of stereotypical jealousy, it was easy to see.

The princess, who had been convinced that she must be the most beautiful woman in the world, nevertheless felt herself already surrendering to the charms of the cheerful young witch before her eyes.

Huh...? Wouldn't you know it, when I see her up close, she's pretty cute... Who is that girl...? The princess was angry at herself for thinking that.

By the way, the mirror that could speak human language had stupidly said while still half-asleep, "Elaina is the cutest." So the princess had smashed it to pieces with her fist.

The story got a little off track there, but anyway, that was how much irrational rage the princess was holding toward the Ashen Witch before her eyes.

Her mind was full of resentment.

She loathed that witch.

"......Heh-heh-heh, note this well, little witch. I am the most beautiful in this world... Nowhere in this world does a woman exist who is more beautiful than I am...!"

By the way, do you know what you have to do to become the very best at something?

Put in the effort and wrest the title away. Find a category in which you can take first place. There are all sorts of different methods, but as you might expect, it can be quite difficult to be the best, so it won't be that easy to surpass those above you. That's because there's a great gulf of talent between you and the top spot, and your efforts will be futile.

So then, what is the much easier way to become the very best?

The answer is simple.

All you have to do is get rid of anyone above you.

○

While I was killing time reading my book, I suddenly heard the sound of someone knocking on the door of the forest home.

There were two polite knocks that came slowly, as if the knocker was aware of what I was doing. After that came a voice, resonating clearly. "Pardon me!"

A visitor, perhaps?

"Coming!" Without being on guard at all, I opened the door.

A suspicious-looking woman was standing in the doorway. She wore her hood low over her head, and I couldn't see her face. In her arms, she was holding a small basket, which had a lot of apples in it.

"Good day, Miss Cute Witch. I wonder if I could speak with you for a moment?"

I closed the door.

"Hey! Why do you close the door? Isn't that rude?"

On the other side of the door, the unidentified woman voiced her complaints.

I shook my head. "I'm sorry, but we're not accepting sales calls."

"You've got it wrong! You've got it all wrong! This isn't a sales call!"

"Oh, religious evangelism, is it?"

"It's not evangelism either!"

"Well then, what is it?"

I opened the door a little.

"...Um, I live next door, but, well, I had too many apples, so... um...I thought I would share..."

"Huh... Is that so...? Well, thanks, then."

I opened the door a little bit more. Then the woman wearing her hood low over her head said, "Well then, go ahead. They're very tasty apples. People say that they're so good, you'll ascend into heaven if you eat one."

As she spoke, she pushed the basket of apples into my arms.

"...I see. Very interesting. Are they really that good? Now I'm curious, since you built them up so much." I accepted the apples without issue, then asked the woman, "By the way, I've been wondering this since you showed up: How did you get those wounds on your hand?"

The woman's hand was wrapped up in bandages. She must have been injured.

"Ah, these... I got these when I broke a mirror that was being a little cheeky."

"...What on earth does that mean...?" I didn't really understand her meaning, but I decided not to worry about it. It seemed bothersome.

More importantly—

"It's a good idea to apply ointment when you are injured. Wait just a moment, please. I have some in the hut."

Still holding the apples, I closed the door for a bit.

I soon reopened it.

"Sorry for the wait. Please apply this ointment to your wounds. People say the medicine is so good that your wounds will heal all at once and you'll ascend into heaven."

"Well, how wonderful. Is it really all right for me to take something like that? You really are too kind."

The woman chuckled and removed the bandages that were wound around her hand, then scooped some of my ointment onto a fingertip and began spreading it on her hand.

"Oh my...this medicine—it smells like apples, doesn't it?" The woman looked at me with a puzzled expression.

"It's made from the apples you just gave me. I mashed them up, you see."

"Eh?"

The change came over her body right after she spit out that one idiotic sound.

"*Hyuuu*," she whistled as she fell flat on the floor. Stiff as a board, she lay there in the same position and did not move.

"...So they *did* have poison in them...?"

I didn't know the reason, but apparently she had been after my life.

○

First things first, I used magic to eradicate the poison that was in her body.

Although I was saving her life now, I imagined she would still be upset when she realized I had turned the tables on her and nearly killed her.

So for the time being, I healed her body and then put her to sleep. I decided I would wake her up in a little while.

I began wrapping ropes around and around her body, to keep her from getting violent when she woke up.

I was still working on dealing with the aftermath of our confrontation, when—

—suddenly, a strange man appeared before me.

"Hail, you there!" he cried. "Could I have a moment?"

"And you are?" I replied.

I looked up and saw he was riding on a white horse. And he had a crown sitting on his head. From the way he held himself, I deduced that he was probably a prince.

"I am a prince," he said proudly.

Then he continued with some strange words. "A necrophiliac prince, who just happened to be passing by unexpectedly."

What on earth do you mean, "a necrophiliac prince, who just happened to be passing by unexpectedly"?

I didn't quite understand the whole concept of it, but poking fun at the idea was too much of a pain, so I replied, "Oh really? That's nice."

The prince was delighted. "It sure is. It is nice. But that woman who you're wrapping up in ropes is also…nice. Really nice. Her beautiful face looks like it's sleeping, but as a matter of fact, it also looks dead. It's really, really nice. Nice enough that I want her to be my bride."

"Ha-ha."

Apparently, the prince had some strange predilections. I decided not to delve into it too deeply.

"However, there is another person who I've been madly in love with for some time now, so the thing is, unfortunately I can't fall in love with that woman there."

"Oh, is that so?" From the bottom of my heart, I did not care, but I nodded along anyway.

"That is so. The princess who lives in a nearby country is incredibly beautiful, you see. My goodness, actually, the woman lying over there is the spitting image of— Hmm? Huh? Oh my, oh no! Could it be that the woman you've bound up in ropes is the princess?"

"Huh, is it really?"

How is it that the princess was after my life?

"Oh, there's no doubt. That woman is perfect for me, the very one I've been searching for. She's the princess! What on earth was she doing here in a place like this?"

Trying to kill me.

...But of course there was no way I could have told him that, so I decided to put on a little show.

"Um—actually..."

Once upon a time...

○

Then, several days later...

A lavish wedding was held in a certain country. Right at the heart of the wedding procession was a certain prince whose sexual predilections leaned in a somewhat strange direction. Beside him was the princess, who, although she hadn't yet been able to fully comprehend what was going on, was smiling defiantly at the people, as if she was satisfied for now because she had managed to get married.

After our first encounter, I had approached the prince and whispered to him, "You should know, the princess has decided she wants to understand your sexual predilections, and to that end, I have placed her in a deep sleep. In order to wake her up, all you have to do is give her the kiss of true love."

The prince had fallen head over heels for the beautiful and refined princess who wanted to understand his weird interests, and he had gone right ahead and taken her home to his country, where he kissed her and woke her up.

Although it was less that he woke her up and more that I released my spell on her.

Be that as it may, that is what came to pass, and before they knew what was happening, the two of them wound up getting married.

"Oh my…my goodness… Am I really allowed to be this happy…?"

During a spare moment in the celebration, the princess mumbled that to herself.

"I never could have imagined you would become the cupid to lead me to my love… I see now that you may be the most beautiful person in the world."

She went on and on in that vein.

It was only later that I learned that apparently, she had hunted me down as part of her search for a marriage partner. As long as she wound up married, she probably didn't really care what happened to me.

Still, even so, that unfortunately couldn't erase the fact that she had attacked me.

"Ahh…what a lucky woman I am…!" Her eyes teared up with emotion.

"Yes, that's right. How nice for you." I returned her smile.

Oh-hoh-hoh.

By the way—

"I clearly remember the evil deed that you came to do to me, but—"

Placing my hands on her shoulders, I whispered softly.

"If you don't want everyone else to know… Well, you understand, right?"

"…Huh?"

"You. Under. Stand. Right?"

"……"

And that's how I found my fortune charging ridiculously exorbitant prices selling houses to pigs.

And they all lived happily ever after.

[**Publication Information**] Volume 8
Animate Purchase Bonus: Cast Talk CD Insert
[**Author Comments**]

This is a story I wrote especially for the Cast Talk CD that was a purchase bonus at Animate to go with *Wandering Witch*, Vol. 8, a CD which at this point is quite a rare item. I relistened to the Cast Talk CD for the first time in a while when I was writing Volume 15, and just as I remembered, the reading performance of Kaede Hondo was enthralling.

I feel as if she's been looking after me ever since Volume 1, and I'm certain that if Miss Hondo hadn't taken charge, *Wandering Witch* would never have made it this far.

I wonder if we could resell the CD in conjunction with the reading performance for Volume 1, Chapter 1? I really hope we do.

CHAPTER 1 STORY 26

Alte and Linaria's History Hunt: A Traditional Statue

My history hunt with Linaria was continuing as always.

I said, "with Linaria," but if anything, I had the sense that I was more like Linaria's assistant. I was just kind of along for the ride.

"Hey, look at this statue. So cool!"

My partner, Linaria, was rubbing her cheek against an ordinary-looking statue and chuckling weirdly to herself. "Heh-heh-heh-heh." I had absolutely no clue what was so great about it.

"What's the deal with this statue? I don't really get it."

"I'm glad you asked. Once, there was an incident where a mighty witch said playfully to herself, 'I'm out of money… I know, I'll go pull a few quick scams,' as she went around defrauding the townspeople. In those days, the leader of the city said, 'Let us build a statue so that we will never forget the witch who is doing these ridiculous things,' and that is how this statue came to be built at the city museum. To put it simply, rather than celebrating some great figure, this statue was built for public scorn. Statues like this are a rare sight."

I see, I see.

"I'm sorry, but even after hearing that, I still don't understand."

"You ought to have a little more interest in history."

"And I think you ought to have a little more common sense, Linaria."

"How rude. I've got plenty!" *Rub, rub, rub, rub.* "See, Alte? We almost never get the chance to encounter a statue as rare as this one."

"Well, that is true."

"There's a good chance that we'll never get to see it again after this."

"Yes indeed."

"If I didn't rub my cheek on it now, I'd never get the chance to do it again, don't you think?"

"Sorry, just that last part. I don't really get what you're saying…"

Don't I think? I'm not the one to ask…

"In any case, it's a good experience to rub your cheek on a historical statue, you know. Won't you give it a try?"

"No, I don't really—"

"Don't be shy."

"Uh, I'm not really being shy, but—"

I mean, after all…before we get to that…

"Linaria, you're not allowed to go in there…"

"Oh?"

Linaria cocked her head to one side cutely. The perimeter had been carefully enclosed by a partition, and to make things worse, there was even a notice posted that said: No Entry. Do Not Touch the Statue. And yet Linaria was inside the barrier, rubbing up against the statue.

"—Heeeyyy! You there! What are you doing?!"

Unsurprisingly, Linaria, who was breaking the rules, was arrested right there on the spot by the security guard.

"…Huh? Ah, um…" Linaria's eyes went wide, and she looked to me for help. So after I quietly averted my eyes, I had just one thing to say to her.

"…Well, um, things like this also offer valuable experience, don't you agree…?"

[Publication Information]   Volume 9
Gamers Buyer's Bonus

[Author Comments]

    Initially, the plan for Alte and Linaria's stories was to write them as a new project that had absolutely nothing to do with *Wandering Witch*, but one way or another they ended up getting included in the main narrative. I feel like I wrote out all the details somewhere or other, but anyway, as far as how they fit into the timeline of the story, I think it's nice that they became a way for us to see the world after Elaina has already become an adult. That said, someday I would like to do the stories I originally planned for them (he says, looking over at the publisher).

CHAPTER 1 STORY 27

Hot and Cold Elaina

"So I have a theory. I think you might actually like me, Elaina."

Saya lobbed these nonsensical words at me all of a sudden, so I paused my reading and gave her an incredibly vague reply. "Uh-huh… Is that…so?"

"Apparently, there's this concept called 'hot and cold' in the world, Elaina."

"Hot and cold?"

Well now, what on earth could that be?

According to Saya—

"The idea of hot and cold describes a person who likes someone and can't be honest about their feelings, so they say the exact opposite of what's in their heart."

"Huh…" At that point, I finally raised my head. "So exactly what does that 'hot and cold' thing have to do with me?"

"Because, Elaina, I love you, but you ignore me, right?"

"I do."

"And yet I've never seen you take a liking to anyone else before."

"That's right, you haven't."

"You see? So basically, that makes you hot and cold, right?"

"I think you're totally off base…"

"I thought you might say that, so I prepared a little display for the occasion. Take a look at this, please."

As she spoke, Saya somehow pulled a huge sheet of paper out from somewhere and stuck it up on the wall.

"Here you can see that I've created a visual representation of your usual behavior, Elaina."

"Have you got too much time on your hands?"

"No, I'm very busy researching you."

"I'm sorry, I asked the wrong question. Are you a stalker?"

"Yes."

"I wish you had denied it…"

"Anyway, will you take a look at the results of my research?"

Smoothly warding off my disdainful look, Saya continued, "These are all the responses I've gotten when I confess my love to you, Elaina. You can see that in ninety percent of the cases, I was rejected with 'What are you talking about? I don't get it.'"

"Sure."

"By the way, for the remaining ten percent, you completely ignored me."

"I see."

"So here are the statistics on all the hot and cold girls worldwide. When someone confesses their love to them, they also indicate their rejection, at the same rate of ninety percent, by saying, 'Wh-what a stupid thing for you to say! Well, if you're going to say it anyway…um, I guess I can't…not go out with you, I suppose.'"

"Wait, that's not a rejection, though, is it?"

"When they get to the second half, some convenient noise or something always interferes, and ultimately the other party only hears the 'Wh-what a stupid thing to say?!' part, so in the end the result can be considered the same as a rejection."

"Huh…"

"By the way, in the remaining ten percent of cases, they answer, 'I… like you, too.'"

"That's not 'hot and cold' anymore. That's not anything."

"By the way, this reply always goes unheard by the other party for some reason or other, so it's the same as getting ignored."

"……"

"Anyway, as I've shown here, your behavior corresponds to that of the hot and cold type."

"For the most part, the only thing that corresponds is the percentages, wouldn't you say?"

"No way! Come on, really think about it, Elaina!" Saya pitched forward even more. Then she said, "As a matter of fact, with your typical hot and cold girl, the hot parts of what she says are often not heard by the other party. Because of that, she's thought to be just a cold and prickly girl—those are the results I got from my statistics."

"I waited too long to say this, but you've assembled some extremely stupid statistics, Saya."

"Never mind that!" Now that she'd reached this point, there was no longer any stopping Saya's momentum. She said, "Going by this theory, even if you did say something sweet, Elaina, there's a high probability that I wouldn't hear it!"

"Your theory is already ruined, though…"

"And so, given all that, Elaina, please show me affection."

Sticking to her nonsense, Saya forced the conversation to a close, then put a hand to her ear and waited. "Come on, now…go right ahead," she mumbled.

She seems to be expecting something, but…

I knew what I had to do.

"……"

And so, just like always, or maybe in a demonstration of the remaining ten percent of the statistical breakdown, I went back to my reading.

"Ah…I can just tell that Elaina is answering me with 'I love you, too'…"

Saya, by the way, was thrilled.

[Publication Information] Melonbooks
Fair Buyer's Bonus
[Author Comments]
  Is she my strongest character?

CHAPTER 1 STORY 28

The Tale of the Sweets Shop and the Witch

"Our sweets aren't selling at all…"

On a certain city street corner, a woman who had just established her store was already at her wit's end. Her shop wasn't thriving at all. *Why on earth not,* she wondered. Once again, the cakes and cookies she had put so much effort into making sat desolately arrayed in the storefront all day. Though her shop was the only sweets shop in the area, though she felt her prices were reasonable, though the shopkeeper was such a beauty, still, nothing sold.

And recently, there was more. She was worried about her rough skin, and the sharp rise in prices, and how her mother had started stressing about her future as an only daughter, saying things like "I sure would like to see my grandbaby's face before too long," and "When are you going to bring a boyfriend home?" and "I heard the girl next door is getting married soon. If I remember correctly, she's the same age as you, right?" and "I heard the son of someone your father knows from work is looking for a bride. What do you think of him? Apparently, he earns quite a bit," with the end result that one way or another, she had endless worries to contend with. The shopkeeper was at her wit's end.

"*Sniff*… What on earth am I going to do…?"

As she munched on a piece of cake, tears dripped from the shopkeeper's eyes. But nothing sold.

"Waah…no…I don't want to get married…"

She was feeling so depressed that her personality had even changed.

Then someone extended a helping hand toward the spectacularly sorrowful woman.

"I see. I understand your situation."

Her hair was ash gray, and her eyes were lapis blue. She was a traveler dressed in a pointed hat and a black robe, and she was a witch.

The witch who had rushed over without delay to confront the emergency of unsold sweets ate a piece of the store's cake with relish as she said, "I see. The fact that these aren't selling sure is a problem. A big problem. We have to work out a strategy immediately."

Who on earth could that witch be, who was so quick to offer advice? *That's right, it's me.*

"As long as you turn a profit, that's what counts, right? In which case, how about changing up your prices?"

"Changing…my prices?"

"Yeah. Your current prices are too low, so for the time being, let's set them about four times higher."

"Four times?!" The shopkeeper raised her voice. "There's no way they'll sell for such ridiculous prices!"

"Wait, wait. First of all, the sweets at this shop are super delicious, and after all, your current prices are too cheap. As things stand, even the things that should be selling aren't."

"But I want lots of people to eat my baking…"

"I understand it's a hangup of yours, but the thing you have to realize is that people don't show any interest in stuff that is too cheap. It's precisely when something has a high price that people get their hopes up and expect something delicious. And the sweets at your shop have a flavor that can surpass those hopes. So it's only reasonable to multiply the prices."

"Multiply the prices…? But they'll sell at four times the price?"

"Yeah. Make them cost four times as much, and to make up for it, throw in a freebie."

"A freebie?"

"A handshake ticket."

"Handshake ticket?"

"When they present the handshake ticket that's included with their purchase of any sweet at a later date, you'll give a handshake to the customer. However, you only give handshakes when they come to the register. And then the new sweet they purchase also has a handshake ticket with it. It's a perpetual cycle."

"That's a crooked way of doing business…"

"At first, you do that to increase the number of repeat customers. Then once you've secured a regular customer base, we can think about expanding the shop. If we can get as many cute girls as possible lined up working the counter, we can expect even more new customers."

"I wonder if it will really go that well…"

"Well, how about just trying things out? At the very least, I think the handshake tickets will have about the same value as the prices your shop is selling sweets for now."

"The same value, huh…? By the way, I think that by those calculations, making things three times as expensive would be more appropriate, so why did you say four times?"

"It has to be that way, doesn't it? Since one quarter of those new prices is my take?"

"That's a crooked way of doing business…"

Though she seemed incredibly reluctant, the shopkeeper embarked on a new business undertaking.

So how did it all turn out?

"We're really flourishing."

"Piece of cake, huh?"

A prosperous shop. People say there are two shady women there, who keep making money through shady means.

[Publication Information] Volume 9
Animate Buyer's Bonus

[Author Comments]

I'll delve into my comments on this story as part of the next story, so I'm changing the subject to ask everyone, what kind of sweets do you like? I'm not sure whether I can call it a sweet or not, but recently, whenever I have a free moment, I've been eating the Korean seaweed snacks that Seven-Eleven sells. They're low in calories; I recommend them. Though they don't fill your stomach, so they're an empty snack.

CHAPTER 1 STORY 29

The Tale of the Sweets Shop and the Master and Student

In the middle of my journey with Miss Fran, we just so happened to find our way to a certain country I had visited before.

"Elaina. You've been to this country before, haven't you?" my teacher asked as she walked alongside me. "If you don't mind, would you show me around?"

I didn't know all that much about the place, but it was true that I knew more than she did, so I readily agreed.

"This country is—well, you know, as you can see, it's an ordinary country. It has a main avenue, and pedestrian traffic, and plenty of tasty restaurants. A normal place."

"Ha-ha, you don't say! By the way, I heard the sweets shop here is pretty famous."

"...Where did you hear that?"

"Huh? Oh, a merchant told me about it back when I was traveling alone, but—if I remember correctly, he said that the sweets were reasonably tasty but that the free gift was amazing... He said such strange things... Elaina, have you ever been there?"

"I have not."

"Really? Is that true?"

"I haven't."

That's a lie.

I had. I had been there so much. But since I had gone and done things that I couldn't let my teacher Miss Fran know about, I stuck to feigning complete ignorance.

"......"

But it's a real bother that Miss Fran knows about the existence of this particular sweets shop...

"Miss, right this way."

I walked off, leading Miss Fran behind me. Luckily, I knew the sweets shop was in a spot a little off the main avenue, so even if she had wandered endlessly along the main avenue, she probably would never have happened across the shop in question.

"......"

However—

In the short interval since I had left this country—after I had made easy money and then taken off—apparently the sweets shop in question had achieved more growth than I'd ever imagined.

People crowded together on the main avenue.

At one of the corners stood a shop that had a familiar sign set out in front of it. It was the sweets shop, which had had no presence at all when I'd last visited.

"Uh..."

There was the sweets shop we were looking for, facing the city's main avenue in an enormous building that couldn't even be compared to how it had been before. A long line snaked out the door of the shop.

"My goodness, speak of the devil... So this is where it was."

Miss Fran looked up at the sign, pondering it.

Apparently, the store relocated while I wasn't looking...

"Oh... I was just wondering who was there, and it's Miss Elaina, isn't it?!"

Then, in a continuation of my misfortune, while I was standing there looking up at the shop's sign in a daze, a woman spoke to me from behind.

"......" I turned around and looked at her face. "You're..."

Standing there was a young woman who clearly had too much money, wearing some kind of ridiculous down coat with a perplexingly gargantuan necklace hanging from her neck, and rings fitted onto each and every one of her fingers.

"...Who are you?"

I don't know anybody like you. I tilted my head. When I did, she snickered. "I'm the shopkeeper."
That was what she said.
"......"
...Hasn't your character changed too much?

○

"Oh, Miss Elaina, it's been far too long. I haven't seen you since I got your help that one time, oh-hoh-hoh!"

Wearing a cheerful smile, the shopkeeper ushered us into the VIP room in the back of the store. I was happy that she cared enough to offer me special treatment, but in my current mental state, I didn't really want it. All I wanted to do was hurry up and leave.

But I couldn't leave.

"Well, isn't this wonderful?"

My teacher, Miss Fran, was absurdly excited, so I couldn't leave.

"Look here, Elaina. There's a chandelier on the ceiling! It looks awfully expensive..."

"It sure does."

"Oh! Look here, Elaina. There are strange abstract paintings decorating the room everywhere! I don't really understand what they mean, but they look awfully expensive."

"They sure do."

"By the way, Elaina, what is your connection to this person?"

"...We worked together a little. It was a while ago."

"Huh, you met at work? What kind of work?"

"......"

I was reluctant to answer. The shopkeeper, who couldn't read the room, exclaimed, "Ah!" and clapped her hands together as if she had just realized something.

"As a matter of fact, Elaina came here to my shop before, and she saved my business when sales were sluggish!"

That's what she said.

"Oh, I never realized… But how did you set things up so that business was so successful?"

"With handshake tickets—"

Uh-oh.

"Miss Fran, by the way, aren't you hungry? I'm famished, you know. Oh, that's an idea. Shopkeeper, do you have any cake? Yes, cake. I'd sure like to eat some cake."

"Huh? Ah, cake, is it? Yes. Of course we have cake! *Oh-hoh-hoh!*" The shopkeeper let out a chuckle and, without a pause, clapped her hands twice.

Immediately after she did, the door to the room opened, and men in all-black clothes carried in trays of cake.

"……"

The cakes were covered in gold dust and looked by all accounts like they would be rather difficult to eat.

Nouveau riche…

"Wow!"

But as long as my teacher is happy, these are great.

I would be happy so long as she got absorbed in her cake and forgot once and for all that she had asked me a question.

"By the way, how did you boost sales of these cakes, Elaina?"

"……"

She's persistent…

"That's a trade secret," I replied.

"Oh, is it now?" Miss Fran nodded in understanding as she munched away at her cake. "Miss Shopkeeper, by the way, what is a handshake ticket?"

"They come with your purchase whenever you buy something from our shop. They grant the customer the right to shake hands with any of the cute girls working here."

"Shopkeeper…"

Why are you telling her that?

"Thanks to Miss Elaina coming up with the idea, our business became the most popular shop in the country. I really need to thank you for what you did for me back then..."

"Shopkeeper..."

I don't need your thanks, so could you just keep quiet for a minute?

"You should know, the prices for our cakes are now ridiculously high, but that was also Elaina's idea. Oh, Miss Elaina's ideas are all just wonderful, aren't they? I have to know just what kind of teacher she studied under, to become such a magnificent person..."

"My goodness..."

My magnificent teacher, Miss Fran, just put on a cheerful smile and continued chewing her cake.

"Elaina...you did a really good thing here, didn't you?"

Though she kept wearing her cheerful smile, there was an indescribable air of intimidation in Miss Fran's narrowed eyes.

"...I don't...recall..."

I averted my gaze.

"She's so humble! Elaina's skills really can't be described as anything other than superb!" The shopkeeper was smiling. "It was almost like she had been doing that kind of thing on a regular basis to make money or something."

"Is that so...? Hmm." I felt my teacher's cold eyes on me.

"No...really, I don't remember..."

"Ha-ha-ha! In that case, did you also happen to forget the amount of money we made? No, really, imagine forgetting that you headed home with a disgustingly large sum of money in your pocket...! That's so like you, Miss Elaina!"

"A large sum of money... Hmm." Miss Fran's fingers grabbed ahold of me.

"...Ah, did you say we...made money...?" I had already lost any chance of escape, and the light drained from my eyes.

"Ha-ha-ha! Miss Elaina, you are truly a modest person! But I remember clearly everything you did for me and my business. Now, please. Enjoy your fill of my shop's sweets today, until you are completely satisfied."

Then the shopkeeper once again clapped her hands twice, and again, the black-clothed men brought in every type of sweet the shop offered.

Just the sight of it all was enough to give me indigestion.

"Oh, isn't this wonderful, Elaina? The good work you do comes back to you. Oh-hoh-hoh!"

Miss Fran was still wearing a smile just like always, but there was absolutely no way she was letting me off the hook.

"......"

And then—

—she stealthily brought her face close to mine as I sat there in silence, and she whispered into my ear.

"But the bad you do also comes back to you, and you're going to have to learn that, okay?"

[Publication Information] Animate Previously Published Fair Buyer's Bonus

[Author Comments]

This story is one I originally intended to include in the main narrative, but when I initially wrote the first draft, it was a little on the short side, and it didn't have much of a punchline, so it got rejected. After I got the offer from Animate to write a bonus story, I got all excited and wrote this, thinking, *If the punchline is weak, then I'll just rewrite it. Let's go!* Also, for this bonus story, Animate requested that I write it in two parts, so honestly, it was the perfect opportunity.

CHAPTER 1 STORY 30
Miss Fran's Culinary Awakening

My journey with my teacher was continuing as always.

"Elaina, guess what? To tell you the truth, I've recently learned to cook."

One evening in the midst of our travels, while we were staying at an inn in a certain country, my teacher suddenly came out with this incomprehensible statement.

My teacher had learned to cook.

After digesting those words in my head, I spit out my reply. "…What are you talking about?"

"As you might imagine, I felt embarrassed about the fact that I couldn't prepare even a single dish, even at my age, and I decided I should learn the skills to live a more serious and respectable life. So I took up cooking."

I had thought it was unusual to see her standing in the kitchen, so that must have been it.

"In other words, we're eating your cooking today?"

"Well, that's what it comes down to, yes."

"……………………………………Is that…so…?"

"Why are you making a face like it's the end of the world?"

"It just brought back painful memories of my training days…"

I had a faraway look in my eyes. Once, during my training days, when I was spending every day diligently improving my magic, I had carelessly eaten some of my teacher's cooking and had found myself confined to my bed for several days. Because of that experience, I was very suspicious toward anything she claimed to have cooked, and furthermore, at the time, I had vowed never to let her cook again and had done everything I could so that all she did was wash the dishes. And so the moment words like *cooking* came from my teacher's mouth, the only thing I could imagine was the end of the world.

"Miss, you shouldn't force yourself to work too hard…"

"Elaina, there's no need to worry. I may look young, but I am an adult. Naturally, I have a good understanding of my own cooking abilities. I made sure to try to start with something simple, so there's nothing to worry about."

"Uh, try to start…? What do you mean by that? Are you saying today is your first try?"

"It certainly is, oh-hoh-hoh!" My teacher laughed.

"Please stop this, Miss. People will die."

"Well! What a cruel thing to say," my teacher said with exaggerated surprise, then picked up one of the kitchen knives. "You just watch, Elaina. I'll show you how I've improved."

Then my teacher began to cook.

And several minutes later—

"……" I was looking down at the food my teacher had prepared. "Miss, what is this?"

"Sandwiches."

But they were the same sandwiches the two of us had bought at the shop. The act of cooking my teacher had spoken of was simply cutting the sandwiches.

"That was less cooking and more just cutting with a knife, don't you think?"

"Well, it's not like I'm going to get good at it right away, is it? I've got to start with the simple things so that I can diligently improve my skills day after day."

Then my teacher smiled again. "Just like you during your training."

[Publication Information] Volume 9
Toranoana Buyer's Bonus
[Author Comments]
  I, too, practiced all sorts of skills when I thought for a while that I might become an expert cook. By the way, this is kind of off-topic, but in RPGs and other games, there are often weapons and items that you can't equip because of your level or the cost, aren't there? For me, all the different cooking utensils were basically the same as those items. Even if I bought some equipment that I could afford, my level was too low, and I couldn't make use of it. Darn.

CHAPTER 1 STORY 31
Leveling the Playing Field

"Elaina, let's play a game."

In the midst of our journey, while we were resting at an inn, my teacher suddenly made that suggestion.

With a smile, I answered her. "No thanks."

"The rules are simple. I'll place a piece of paper on the table. On the paper, I've written what you are going to do, according to my predictions. If you act as predicted within the next three minutes, you lose. How about it? Won't you play?"

"I just said no, didn't I?"

"Oh my, not even when it's a game that favors you so heavily? You won't play? If you just take care not to do anything that's written on the paper, that's all you have to do to win, you know?"

"So tell me, if I win, what do I get?"

"My praise and admiration."

"And if I lose?"

"I'm afraid you'll have to treat me to dinner."

"…I thought the game was supposed to work out overwhelmingly in my favor?"

"Since it works so overwhelmingly in your favor, isn't it only natural that the penalty for losing would be steep?"

"……"

But still…

"Just being praised doesn't get me very motivated."

"My, how selfish."

What are you talking about?

With a sigh, I replied, "I just mean that those conditions don't get me interested. If I can get some better terms, well, I guess I'd be willing to cooperate with your game to kill some time."

"Better terms like what?"

"Isn't it obvious?" I made a slightly wicked face. "You have to treat me to a luxurious dinner, Miss."

"My, my, how selfish."

What are you talking about?

"Don't you think the stakes of the competition ought to be equal?"

"……"

After falling silent for a little while, my teacher suddenly broke into a smile and said, "Well…you're right, the stakes ought to be equal. That's fine. If I lose, I'll treat you."

Now we're talking.

At that point, I finally got on board, and I extended a hand toward the paper that had been placed on the table.

Then I opened it up.

Only one thing was written there.

You played the game.

……

"Miss Fran. Isn't this a little dishonest?"

I glared at her, and my teacher smiled.

"How ridiculous. It's not dishonest! We leveled the playing field, didn't we?"

[Publication Information] Volume 10
Toranoana Buyer's Bonus
[Author Comments]
Somehow, it seems like Miss Fran is a little more excitable than usual, but in Volume 10, she was often more energetic. It's by design.

Leaving that aside, the acting for Miss Fran in the *Wandering Witch* anime was incredible, wasn't it? Since I was used to listening to the version of Miss Fran who had comedic exchanges with Elaina every time they reunited at some destination on the drama CDs, it was really a fresh experience to see Miss Fran adopt a more mysterious presence. Kana Hanazawa sure is amazing…

CHAPTER 1 STORY 32

A Tale of Teachers and Students

"What do you think makes someone a 'witchy' witch?"

Saya suddenly asked me this question as I was teaching her magic in the Country of Mages. In other words, when I was gripping my wand, right in the middle of expounding on how to do this and that to a girl who was at her wit's end because she just wasn't making any progress, she interrupted me with that sort of question.

And so I also wound up tilting my head and asking her, "What's this all of a sudden?"

Up on the roof of a house, surrounded by the kind of scenery that abounded in that country, she suddenly started talking about some strange thing. It was extremely puzzling.

This is what she said next:

"I'm working on being an apprentice now, and someday I'd also like to become a witch, but—even among witches, there's a lot of variety, isn't there? There are witches who give their lives for their countries and witches who live their lives devoted to their own desires, and then there are people like you, Elaina, who are free-spirited and spend their time traveling."

"…That is true." Certainly, even when talking about witches, it wasn't that simple to lump them all together. There were all sorts of different witches living different lives.

"It just sort of occurred to me while you were in the middle of teaching me a spell, but I've got a very vague reason for wanting to become a witch, I think."

"There's not really anything wrong with that."

"Why did you decide to become a witch, Elaina?"

"...Hmm..." At that juncture, I remembered that we hadn't taken a break in our magical training for some time. I took a seat near Saya. "Let's take a little breather, shall we?" I patted the roof tiles to tell her to sit down beside me.

Saya did as I urged, and as soon as the somewhat nervous-seeming girl had sat down beside me, I began reminiscing as I looked up at the blue sky.

"There's a book called *The Adventures of Niche* that everyone's read, right? It's just a collection of short stories about a lone witch wandering through the world, but back when I was little, I was very, very enamored with the world that unfolded in the book. How happy I would be, if I could travel the world like her—if I could see such a world with my own eyes, reach out and touch it, how much fun would that be, I thought, admiring her as I got absorbed in the story."

"...Mm-hmm." Saya had picked up on the signs that this was going to be a long anecdote, and she started nodding along, with an attentive look on her face.

"So since I wanted to travel after reading that book, I made that my goal. I was told that if I wanted to become a traveler, I had to become a witch, so I became a witch."

"...Mm-hmm."

"The end."

"...Huh? Story's over?"

"It's over."

"Wha...?"

She seemed like she might be irritated by how quickly I finished my reminiscent story after going out of my way to make her sit down, because she asked quizzically, with some reservation, "There wasn't, like...some kind of episode where a witch saved your life or something...?"

"There wasn't."

"You didn't, like, aspire to become a witch so you could wrap men around your finger, or make tons of money, or something...?

"I didn't."

Though I can't deny the second part.

"……" A few moments later, Saya cocked her head and asked, "So the reason why you became a witch was, in short, because you read a book? Is that all?"

"That's all."

"Isn't that a shallow reason…?"

"How rude," I replied.

First of all—

"You don't need a special reason to become a witch," I said. "It's not as if every girl who becomes a witch has some splendid sense of purpose, or that only really sincere people can become witches. Some witches are total jerks, and although they have the skills, their terrible personalities make you wonder why they even became witches in the first place. And there are some people who just simply felt like it, so they became witches."

"……"

"So to sum up, not everyone who is wearing a witch's brooch is some sincere person who has amazing, magnificent goals in life. There are a few absolute jerks in the mix, too. We're not all wonderful people. But that's the world we live in."

There was no need to go all out in order to become a witch. It was all right to take it easy.

I said, "In short, even if your spellcasting doesn't improve, that's not really because you lack a strong sense of purpose, or any reason like that, is what I'm saying."

Beside me, I could tell that Saya had opened her eyes wide.

I kept talking.

"Maybe you thought it wouldn't be appropriate for you to become a witch, since you don't have any clear purpose of your own—but that's not really something to concern yourself over. Even if you don't especially have any amazing, magnificent goals, you can still become a witch."

"……" After a few moments of silence, Saya cast her eyes down and answered, "…I wonder if I can."

I nodded.

"Probably, if you keep working hard at your training. But before you become a witch, Saya, you have to become an apprentice witch."

"…I wonder if I can."

"……"

"Huh, wait a second, why didn't you say anything?"

"Well, to be completely frank, becoming an apprentice is much more difficult than becoming a witch."

In order to become an apprentice, she would need to pass an exam, but after that, to become a witch, she'd have to find a teacher, then go through training, and only when her teacher approved her could she finally become a witch.

In short, achieving the title of "witch," for better or for worse, depended a great deal on the discretion of one's teacher.

"Becoming a witch is easy?"

"It's so easy that if you put your mind to it, it would be possible to become a witch in just one day."

"Seriously?!" Saya nodded hopefully.

"If you capture a nearby witch and give her drugs or something to brainwash her, you could acquire the title of 'witch' in a single day."

"Isn't that a crime?"

"Not everyone who is wearing a witch's brooch is some sincere person who has amazing, magnificent goals in life, I told you…"

"But hearing that remark now only makes me feel anxious…"

"That's the world we live in."

"…By the way, what kind of person was your teacher, Elaina?"

Saya narrowed her eyes sharply. She was suspicious of me. She was wondering whether I might have become a witch through criminal means.

No, no, unfortunately, I apprenticed under a teacher to earn my title in the proper way.

"She was kind of hard to pin down."

"Oh?"

"She couldn't handle mornings, and she always left the cooking up to me, and she always ran off chasing butterflies when I thought she was coming to train me, and she spent night after night absorbed in her own research, and I spent a whole year with her, but she only spent the tiniest amount of time actually teaching me magic."

"Elaina, that's not someone who's hard to pin down, that's just a total jerk."

"But she did teach me something. Not magic, but something even more important."

"...What?"

"She taught me that when humans are corrupt, they can fall to incredible depths..."

"I knew it. She was a total jerk, wasn't she...?"

"But she was a good person. I felt disgusted with her while I was in training, but looking back on it, I can now see how all of that was actually for my benefit."

"......"

After keeping silent for a brief while, Saya frowned and tilted her head. "But why did that witch end up giving you your brooch, Elaina?"

I answered her.

"One way or another, a year passed, and she gave it to me."

"Sounds sloppy."

"That's the kind of teacher she was."

Well, regarding the particular details, we can talk about that another time.

●

I had been studying with my teacher for about a month when I remembered what had happened to me while I was in the Country of Mages.

Miss Sheila, my teacher, was another person who was extremely hard to pin down, and just like Elaina's teacher, she spent her days lazing around and seemed like a useless person with too much time on her hands.

For example, even if I said, "Teacher! Take a look at my spell!" and triumphantly shot off a magic spell, she would just barely acknowledge me.

"Huh? ...Seems fine to me?"

For example, even if I threw a girly tantrum and whined, "Teacherrr! Hey, teacher! Teach me some magic nooow!" my teacher would just blow a cloud of tobacco smoke in my face.

"Ah, sorry, I'm kinda busy right now, so..."

It stinks! Damn you!

Since I almost always received this kind of awful treatment from my awful teacher, I suppose it was inevitable that my heart became blackened, just like a lung polluted by tobacco smoke.

At the same time, my teacher showed her dislike of me by blowing comments like "Huh? No way. Can't do it" at me like puffs of smoke.

I was getting worried.

"This is bad... If this keeps up, I'll be an apprentice witch forever..."

I felt hopeless. At any rate, as things were, my teacher wasn't paying proper attention to me. I wondered what was wrong with me.

Oh, if only Elaina was here at times like these...

Even if she made an unpleasant face, surely Elaina would have some sort of advice for me, I thought.

Help me, Elaina!

Actually, I have a feeling Elaina said something like "Becoming a witch is easier than becoming an apprentice," but that's not true at all, now, is it?

I was at my wit's end.

And then—

"No, no, you've got it all wrong. Becoming a witch is easy."

—I heard a voice echo through my mind.

"That voice...! Elaina!" I raised my head at once and looked around. But she wasn't there. In fact, the only person around was my teacher, who was wearing a puzzled expression. "...What's up?"

"Saya... Saya... I'm talking to you inside your mind right now..."

Ah, Elaina's voice is inside my head...

Holding myself in check before my excitement boiled over, I whispered, "Elaina...! Are you watching me from somewhere...?"

I exercised my self-control because I didn't want my teacher to think I was a weird girl.

But even my hushed voice seemed to reach Elaina.

"Saya, unfortunately, the real me is in the middle of a journey right now. I'm probably nowhere near you..."

"You're probably not here...?"

"Not even I know where the real Elaina is or what she's doing right now," the voice echoing in my head was quick to say. "That's because I'm the version of Elaina that you made up in your own mind."

"...What's going on here?"

"Basically, I'm a fantasy you made up. I'm me, but I'm not me."

That's kind of a philosophical way of putting things. So in other words, that means—

"...You're saying that the person talking to me inside my head is a fantasy I made up? An imaginary Elaina...?"

"To put it clearly and directly, that is what I'm saying."

"Are you serious?"

"Yes."

"Isn't it totally crazy that I can do this?"

"I think so, too."

Ah. That dry delivery was very Elaina-like...

"So then, Imaginary Elaina, what do you want with me...?"

"Saya, let me help you solve what's troubling you—you recall it often, the conversation you had with me in the Country of Mages—you call to mind the conversation we had while we took a break... There's a hint hidden there..."

My exchange with Elaina...?

I put my head in my hands and groaned. "Ummm..."

The conversation back then, I think it went—

* * *

"Saya...I, my feelings for you... Um, I know this is a weird thing to say, since we're both girls, but...I...love you."

"I'm so happy...! I've always had feelings for you, too, Elaina—"

"I would appreciate it if you would avoid fabricating false memories..."

"Oh, but I do feel like we had a conversation like that at least once."

"Do you have trouble distinguishing between fantasy and reality...?"

Well, if I was good at distinguishing between them, then Imaginary Elaina wouldn't have suddenly appeared with no warning, would she?

After letting out a disgusted sigh, the Elaina in my head said, *"What I'm trying to talk to you about wasn't that stuff. When we were up on the roof, you asked me about my teacher, remember? Please, think back on that."*

Think back on that...

I put my head in my hands again.

That time...I think...it went—

"Saya, becoming a witch once you're already an apprentice is a total walk in the park! All you have to do is make some kind of love potion for your teacher and make her fall in love with you... If you do that, everything will turn out fine. Oh-hoh-hoh...!"

I see! So that's what I need to do!

"Thank you so much, Elaina! I'm gonna go make a love potion!"

"Huh? No, that's not what I said..."

Ignoring the exasperated Elaina in my head, I dashed out of the room in order to go make a potion that could brainwash someone.

Then, several days later—

"Miss Sheila! Thank you for all you do! This is from my heart... Won't you please accept it...?"

With big puppy dog eyes, I openly flattered my teacher as I handed her my homemade cookies (with ultra-powerful love potion in them).

Once she eats these, my teacher will become my slave and do whatever I say...!

"...Hmm?"

My teacher took the cookies from me and said bluntly, "Sorry, but I don't like cookies. You can have them." She crammed a cookie into my mouth.

"Mmph...!"

Unfortunately, I'm a person who is usually pretty unguarded, and so the cookie my teacher shoved in my mouth went straight down my throat and right into my belly.

I ate my own ultra-powerful love potion cookie.

My teacher had probably seen right through what I had been trying to do. She had probably figured me out.

"Uuuuugh...ugh, I already have someone, named Elaina..." I writhed in agony there on the spot.

Looking down at me in my suffering with frigid eyes, my teacher said, "So it was a love potion, huh...?" and blew out a puff of smoke. She looked disgusted with me. "If you want to make me do what you want, you'll have to improve your magic skills a little more."

Then, with a sneering grin, my teacher sat me up and said, "For now, though, rub my shoulders." For as long as time permitted, for as long as the potion was in effect, she ordered me around like her slave.

"After that, make some dinner."

"Go buy me tobacco."

"Go buy some bread."

"Gimme a light, a light."

And so on, like that.

The sad thing is, the love potion I had made seemed to work perfectly, so even in the face of that kind of treatment, I answered my teacher in a sickly sweet voice, "Eh-heh-heh...of course I will. I love my teacher!" as I followed her every command.

What's more, even as she kept on pushing me around like her little

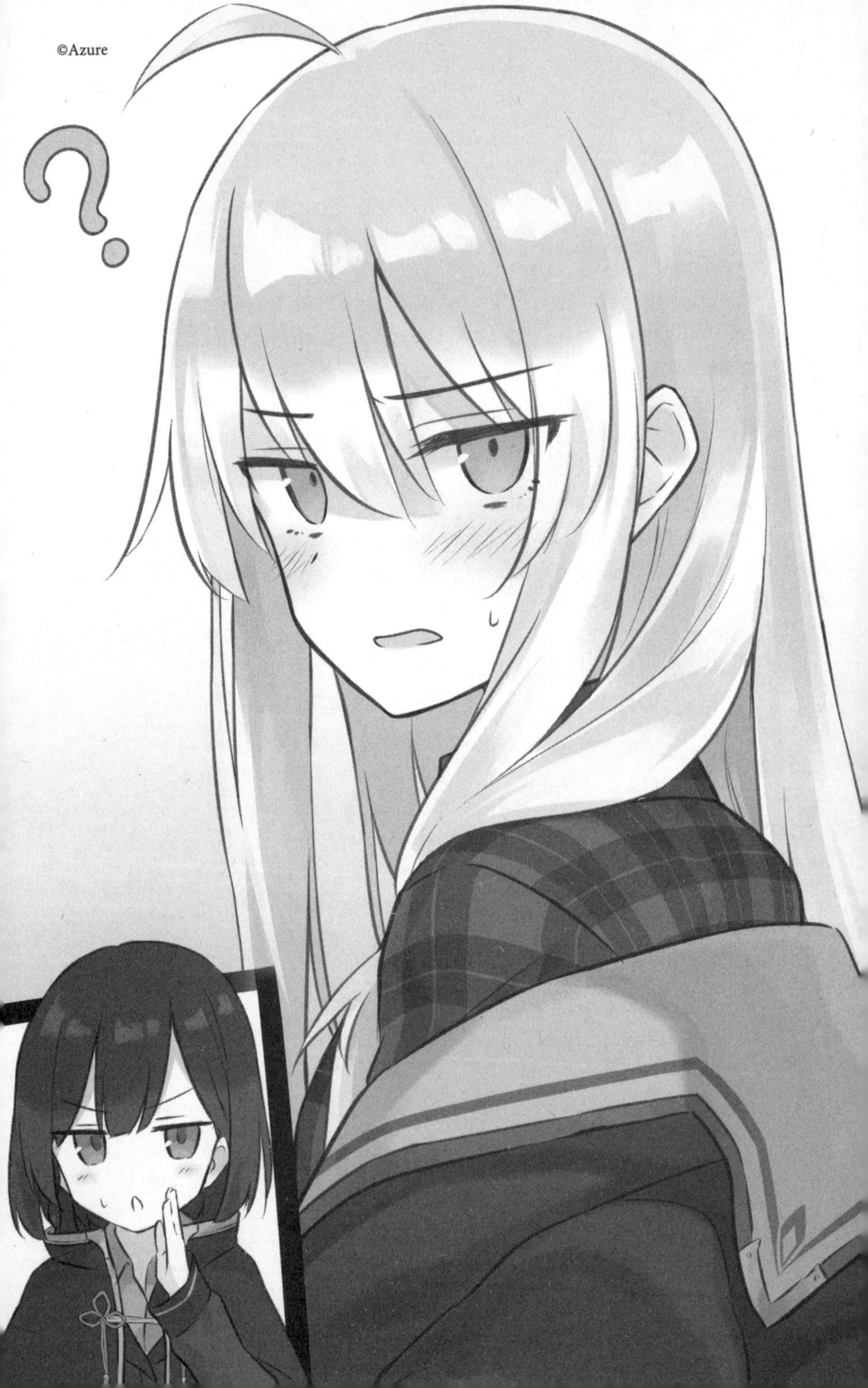

servant, I proclaimed, "Eh-heh-heh... How are you such a good person, Miss...?"

Just then, I suddenly remembered something. Elaina had told me that her own teacher was a good person, but could that possibly have meant...?

After that, I had an opportunity to meet up with Elaina, so I stealthily whispered something into her ear.

I said—

"Elaina, did your teacher force-feed you a love potion? Are you all right? Are you still feeling the effects?"

"Huh? Sorry, what are you talking about?"

[**Publication Information**]   Animate Previously Published Fair Buyer's Bonus

[**Author Comments**]

I always had a feeling I would be collecting these stories into a bonus story volume someday, but many of the bonus stories are quite long, huh? I made a big fuss, begging them to put out a bonus story volume, and as a result I got the opportunity to publish this one, but if you never ask, you never get your way! There was no way I could bring myself to leave this many bonus stories as only limited-time offers and then scrap them.

If I ever get the chance, I also want them to put out a drama CD volume, too!!!!!!!!!!!!

CHAPTER 1 STORY 33
Another Scary Story

Saya, whom I encountered for the first time in a while during my travels, had said something strange.

"Ohhh...Elaina's scary... I'm scared of Elaina..."

This "Elaina" whose name spilled from Saya's mouth from time to time, who on earth could she be?

There's no need to tell you, is there?

That's right, it's me.

However, for what possible reason was she frightened of me? I didn't have any memory at all of doing anything to threaten her.

Well then, why is that?

"What's the matter, Saya?"

"Kyah! Stop, please, Elaina! Don't touch me!"

She raised her voice. Saya backed away from me while shaking her head no, but rather than looking scared, instead, she looked delighted. As she glanced over at me, her quivering face had a look of expectation, as if she wanted to say, *"Come on, now, startle me more!"*

I sighed.

"...Um, did something happen?"

"Stop it, please! Don't get any closer to me! I'm scared!"

"Wait, even if you say that all of a sudden..."

...I still don't know how to deal with you.

At any rate, the only possible way to describe Saya's behavior that day was "strange." I was certainly confused.

Fortunately, I just so happened to have plans to meet up with Saya's teacher, Sheila, later that day, so in the course of our conversation, I talked to her about Saya's sudden transformation, but—

"Ah, right."

Sheila nodded as if she understood something about it, and moreover, she said, "Must be because she likes you," and made a somewhat unpleasant face.

"She called me scary because she likes me? I don't really understand what you mean…"

"Her birthplace is in the East, see, and apparently they have some kind of legend about publicly proclaiming that they are afraid of their favorite foods so that other people who want to cause mischief give them that food or something."

"…Huh?"

So in other words, if I grumbled about being afraid of bread in an Eastern country, I would receive lots of bread? Good to know…

"In short, I think maybe she was trying to act out that story with you."

"So she thought that by continuing to say she was afraid of me, I would go to her…? But wouldn't that be pointless, unless I already knew about that Eastern legend…?"

"Well, she's always doing weird stuff. In fact, I tried to give her a little warning about it." Sheila said that, and then, still holding her pipe in her mouth, she left.

The following day—

"Sheila's scary… I'm afraid of Miss Sheila…afraid of my teacher…"

Saya was there, teeth chattering and trembling with fear. She was sitting in a corner, shaking so badly that I didn't even feel like asking her what on earth Sheila might have done to her.

I looked at her like that, and for some reason or other, I felt a desire to cause mischief smoldering away deep in my heart.

And so I spoke up and presented her with a single question.

I asked—

"Which meaning of *scary* would that be?"

[Publication Information]   GA Novels Published Fair Buyer's Bonus
[Author Comments]
 I truly was not aware of this in the least, but this turned out to be like a sequel to the bonus story I wrote for Volume 1. Elaina finally found out the meaning of "scary *manjuu*" in Volume 10. Life is interesting sometimes. I surprised myself.

CHAPTER 1 STORY 34

A Story About a Psychological Test

I was in a café, eating a meal with Saya.

Saya looked at me, wearing a somewhat proud expression, and then asked, "Elaina, do you know about this kind of psychological test?"

"Never heard of it," I immediately replied.

"But I haven't even told you anything about it yet."

"Generally, I don't have any use for that sort of frivolous speculation."

"I think that's biased, though..." Saya frowned. She seemed a little surprised by my dismissive attitude. "Anyway, in the psychological test, they ask you something like this: 'You have some bread sitting before you. Now, how many pieces are there?'"

"That's an incredibly vague psychological test..."

Psychological tests usually didn't have a correct answer set up from the start; they were like a game where you surmised things about the other person based on their answers to the questions.

Well, roughly speaking, to put it simply, that means I can just answer without having to think too hard about it.

How many pieces of bread are in front of me, huh?

"There are two pieces," I said as I looked at the bread that was sitting on the table.

There were exactly two. In short, all I had to do was answer according to what I saw.

"Oh...is that what you think?"

"*Heh-heh-heh.*" Saya put on a bold smile. It looked a little triumphant. "By the way, Elaina, did you know? Supposedly, the number of pieces of bread in this question tells you the number of people you're interested in at the moment."

"I see." I nodded as I chewed away, eating both pieces of bread at once.

I saw what was going on.

In short, Saya had come up with a scheme to kill time by teasing me.

"Elaina, who are you interested in right now?"

That's what's going on, right? Right, I knew it.

"By the way, Saya, have you ever heard *this* fact before?"

"Nope," she answered immediately.

"Didn't think so."

Generally, I don't have any use for that sort of frivolous speculation.

But then, given how Saya was acting at the moment, it was probably precisely because she didn't know that she had challenged me to the psychological test.

I said—

Wearing a somewhat triumphant smile, I said—

"Psychological tests are something you only give to people you're interested in."

[Publication Information] Volume 12
Toranoana Buyer's Bonus
[Author Comments]

This was a story about Elaina teasing Saya by asking "Is it possible that you like me?" before Saya could tease her by asking "Who do you like right now?"

Elaina said this in the punchline, too, but psychological tests aren't something you give to someone unless you're already interested, right?

I think "get them before they get you" is a very Elaina-like stance to take.

CHAPTER 1 STORY 35

Am I Pretty?

"Saya. When I say 'summer,' do you know what that means?"

"Well, that can only mean one thing, Elaina. Summer means the ocean—"

"That's right, ghost stories."

"Uh, no, the ocean—"

"Ghost stories, that's right. Yes indeed."

Elaina rapidly set up some candles on the table, then turned to me and said enthusiastically, "And so let's tell some ghost stories today."

Normally, I would gladly leap at the chance to do just about anything as long as Elaina invited me to, but in this particular instance, I screwed up my face in a grimace beside the enthusiastic Elaina.

"I'm not really one of those witches who is very good at telling ghost stories, you know."

"Now, this is something that really happened to a friend of a friend of mine—"

"Ah, hang on… Elaina, are you ignoring me?"

"Of course, when it's summertime, you always want to tell stories that will send a shiver down your spine, isn't that right?"

"I can't really handle spine-tingling stories."

"Saya, do you know the story of the scary *manjuu*?"

"That's the story where someone tries to harass a man who says he's afraid of *manjuu* by giving him *manjuu* to scare him, right? I think the punchline was that the man was actually lying because he wanted to eat *manjuu*, though."

"That's right."

"So what about it?"

"I bet when you say you can't handle spine-tingling stories, you're basically doing it for the same reason as that man did."

"Wrong."

"Well, setting that aside, this is something that really happened to a friend of a friend of mine—"

"So I take it that you intend to force me to listen to your story anyway, Elaina?"

Sitting in front of the gently flickering candles, Elaina wore a bewitching smile as she presented the following ghost story to me.

One evening, a woman walking down a back alley in a certain country felt a strange presence behind her.

Someone somewhere is watching me—that's what she felt. Every time she took a step forward through the darkness, she heard the *clonk, clonk* of heavy footsteps echo through the night.

The only footsteps she was hearing were her own. Even when she got up her nerve and turned around to look, the only thing behind her was a dark alleyway. There wasn't anyone there.

Still, she had the feeling that somewhere, someone was watching her. But the feeling was all she had. Once she had that worry on her mind, she could no longer pay attention to anything else.

The woman started feeling like everything was some suspicious creature waiting to attack her in the dark, from her own shadow as she walked along, to the clouds roiling ominously in the sky, to even her own reflection in the windows she passed.

But she kept walking, pretending to be calm.

"……"

Then, before too long, she saw another woman wearing a coat walking toward her from the direction she was headed. *Clonk, clonk*—her heels struck the cobblestones. The woman was brimming with a mysterious aura. She was hanging her head low and had a scarf wound around her mouth so that nothing was visible below her eyes. The little bit of her skin that was visible was shockingly white, and her figure, illuminated by the moonlight, looked almost translucent.

The first woman was afraid.

It was the height of summer, you see.

So wearing a coat was extremely out of season—

Before long, the two women passed by each other.

So as not to make eye contact with the eerie woman, the first woman lowered her head in the same manner and tried to slip past her.

But—

"Hey, you."

The stranger tightly gripped the woman's shoulder. Startled, she looked up, and the eerie woman's face was right next to hers.

The woman was terrified.

It was at that point that she remembered something. She recalled an extremely famous ghost story. Someone was walking alone at night when a lone woman came from the opposite direction. That woman was grotesque, a creepy, uncanny creature whose mouth had been cut open all the way up to her ears.

Night after night, she appeared before people walking alone and asked them one question.

"Am I pretty...?"

And so just like the story—

—the woman unwound the scarf that had been covering her mouth.

The scarf gently fell onto the ground.

"Uh, ah..."

The first woman began to tremble.

She looked at the other woman before her eyes. The grotesque creature that had removed its scarf was, to her surprise, a very beautiful young lady with ash-gray hair. Her mouth wasn't slashed at all. The weirdest thing about her was that she was supercute. Who on earth could she have been?

That's right, it's—

"Wait just a minute, please."

"Sure. What's the matter?"

Elaina was in the middle of her story, but I called for a time-out.

Wait, wait, wait, wait.

"What was that story just now?"

I thought it was going to be a scary story, but then Elaina showed up.

"The punchline is that I'm the supposedly grotesque creature. To put it even more simply, it's a story about how I'm pretty."

"......"

"So what did you think?"

"It turned into a story that had me shaking for a different reason..."

It was just like in the story about scary *manjuu* that Elaina herself had brought up earlier.

"Well, in the end, my beauty was the most frightening thing, huh? You got me, you got me."

It wasn't a scary story or really much of a story at all.

......

I thought I was ready, but she still got me.

"I was sure you were going to tell me an incredibly scary story, one that would leave me trembling..."

I breathed a sigh of relief. I can't handle scary stories.

Actually—

"What about that story was supposed to be scary, Elaina...?"

I was relieved, but at the same time, I was a little disappointed.

Elaina looked at me in my disappointment and let out a little chuckle.

"Let me see..."

She blew out the candles and said—

"My beauty, I suppose..."

○

Not long after that, Elaina left my room. She had suddenly shown up that afternoon and then left after only telling just one scary story, so

I really didn't understand what was going on with her that day! If I'd gotten the chance, I would have liked to ask her about having lunch together or something, but...

Such thoughts were circling around my mind when—

"Saya. Hello."

—Elaina appeared again. Acting as if it was the first time we had seen each other that day, she tilted her head and asked, "Saya, have you had lunch already? If you haven't, how about eating with me now?"

And so—

"Gladly, so long as you don't tell any more weird stories like earlier," I agreed.

To which Elaina asked quizzically, "Earlier...? Weird stories...? What are you talking about?"

Then, looking at me very, very curiously, she said, "But I was in my room reading a book until just a minute ago..."

[Publication Information] GA Novels Published Fair Buyer's Bonus

[Author Comments]

I think this is a little different from a supernatural encounter, but I myself have also had some strange experiences. For example, one day, back when I was a student, I was gazing vacantly out the window when I heard footsteps approaching me from behind, and when I turned around to see who it could be, no one was there. Well, although it's not like that experience became the basis for me writing this story or anything.

CHAPTER 1 STORY 36
Amnesia and Avelia

"Apparently, if two people have a really good relationship, they can enjoy a conversation even if it doesn't really go anywhere."

"What's this all of a sudden, Avelia?"

In response to my overly abrupt statement, my older sister questioned me, tilting her head to the side adorably. Her expression was so puzzled, I could almost see the question mark hovering above her head.

I regurgitated the contents of the book I had read earlier.

"Apparently, being able to have a pleasant and entertaining conversation with someone even when the topic is trivial is proof that you have a deep connection with that person. Isn't that wonderful?"

"Huh… Well, I guess so."

"Which means, Big Sister…"

"Yeah?"

"Let's talk about something trivial."

"I thought you were going to say that."

My sister screwed up her face unpleasantly.

However, I persisted.

"Please?"

"Fine."

"What I'm asking for is a conversation about something trivial, which furthermore has no real climax or conclusion, and that concerns a topic even I can understand."

"That's asking a lot."

"I think I'll get depressed if it turns into a boring conversation, so…"

"It's hard to come up with an interesting conversation on demand, though…"

I'd raised the bar for our conversation too high, and as a result, my big sister let out a sigh. Despite how suddenly I had made the request, my sister still folded her arms.

"An interesting conversation, huh…?" She hummed in thought—"Hmm…"—and pondered the question for a little while.

Then she said, "I've got nothing."

She quickly, abruptly gave up and ended the conversation.

"Do *you* have anything interesting to talk about, Avelia?"

"Something interesting to talk about?"

Just like my big sister, I folded my arms, hummed, and pondered—actually, I didn't do any of that. I immediately answered, "Nothing here."

"Right." My sister nodded slightly to me after I answered. Then she asked, "By the way, Avelia, were you bored just now, conversing with me?"

Again, I immediately answered, "I wasn't bored."

To which my sister nodded. "Right." And then she smiled softly. "Me neither."

Our conversation didn't really have any other conclusion.

[**Publication Information**]   Volume 12
Melonbooks Buyer's Bonus
[**Author Comments**]

On the fourth drama CD, there's a scene where Amnesia talks about Elaina being a bad person, but after we were done recording the CD, I learned that there are some very similar famous lines in a certain anime that Konomi Kohara appears in. *Oh no, without meaning to, I wrote a parody!* I thought, but, well, it turns out the anime didn't use those lines in the main storyline either!

CHAPTER 1 STORY 37

The Cursed Box

"Apparently, there's a demon inside this box."

In a certain country I was visiting, a man appeared before me wearing a troubled expression.

According to him, he was "in possession of a cursed box." When I asked to hear more, he said that box was bringing all sorts of disasters down upon him.

"Oh-hoh. Just what sorts of troubles have you had?"

When I asked, he said very sorrowfully, "For example, yesterday, a flower vase fell on me. It really hurt! And the day before yesterday, the floor in my house suddenly gave out, and I fell through it."

Apparently, the man had been struck by frequent misfortune. It wasn't just the flower vase and the floor; he had been struck with every conceivable type of mundane disaster.

For example, bird poop fell on him whenever he was walking down the street, and he never won anything when he drew lots. On top of that, if he sat down on a bench, it was always the one that had just been painted, and he lost his wallet a lot. He was apparently the victim of all sorts of bad luck.

So I said, "Oh, tough break," and felt a modest sort of pity for him.

"I just know it's because of this box. There's no question."

The man said that he had only started to meet with these strange-seeming situations after he had acquired the box. The small wooden box was locked and couldn't be opened. Apparently, he had purchased it at a curio shop.

The owner of the curio shop had evidently had some words for the man when he bought the box.

"I wouldn't buy that if I were you. That's a cursed object."

But the man didn't believe him. Ultimately, he had ignored the owner's objections and purchased the box. Since he'd been suffering through strange experiences ever since, he was convinced he had been struck with bad luck because of the box.

"If that box is the cause, couldn't you just throw it away?" I foolishly suggested.

"If it was possible, I would. But I don't think I can." The man shook his head. "After all, I'm suffering through all this just because I have the box, right? If I dump it, I'm sure something even worse will happen."

"Mm-hmm…"

"Which leads me to ask, Miss Witch, if you might be able to do anything?"

"……"

He probably thought I could solve his problem with my magic. He asked me the question with a frown on his face.

I thought it over briefly. It was hard to suddenly believe in a box that gave people bad luck, but it did seem to be true that this man had been plagued with misfortune.

I wonder if there is anything I can do?

"……" One idea occurred to me. "Lend me the box for three days. Let me remove the curse that hangs over that box for you."

Less than a week later…

"Wow, Miss Witch, you're really amazing! Ever since you took the box, I haven't had a single accident!"

The man appeared before me, overjoyed. During the three days when I had borrowed the box from him, I had lifted the curse—or so I'd told him when I'd given it back.

As for how the result turned out, the curse was gone.

"Every day has truly been a blessing since then! I got a girlfriend, and I stopped having bad luck, and I just can't help but enjoy every passing day," he told me, his eyes sparkling.

"My, my. That's wonderful! *Oh-hoh-hoh-hoh.*" I laughed as I extended my hand toward him. "Well then, could I get my fee?" We'd established earlier that if he saw real results, I would get paid.

"Ah, of course!" The man pulled out his wallet, then cocked his head. "How much was it? I'm sure that lifting a curse was hard work, so I'll pay you your proper reward."

Now then, by the way—

To be perfectly clear, I had indeed taken charge of the box for three days, but after that, I hadn't really done much of anything.

I hadn't done a thing to it, really.

Initially, I had opened up the box, but there hadn't been anything inside. No curses or anything. The box was just an ordinary antique-style box. It must have been the man's imagination that had him convinced it was definitely cursed. It was one of those things where anything can turn out good or bad, depending on your frame of mind. All I had to do was convince him that it was not cursed, nothing more.

And so I answered him—

"I'll take whatever amount you feel is right."

[Publication Information] Volume 10
Melonbooks Buyer's Bonus
[Author Comments]

If, for example, a fortune-teller told you in the morning that you would have an unlucky day and then some disaster would befall you, you would probably attribute anything bad that happened to you to the fact that the fortune-teller had said that it was an unlucky day. Even if it really had nothing to do with that, if you put your mind to it, you can connect just about anything, I figure.

CHAPTER 1 STORY 38
A Scam Story

No matter where you are, if you walk down the street, there will always be someone doing something baffling. That held true for the country I visited that day as well, where someone was doing something very strange.

"…Oh-hoh-hoh. Oh-hoh-hoh-hoh!"

The person was a mage, sitting tucked away in a recess just off the street, laughing weakly. She was stroking her pointed hat, then putting it back on, stroking it and putting it back on, repeating these bizarre actions.

At first glance, it was obvious that she was a suspicious person.

By the way, who on earth was this mage repeating these incomprehensible actions?

……

Well, it was me, you know.

"Miss, exactly what are you doing over there?"

Apparently, my incomprehensible actions looked incredibly strange to the people who lived there. A man who had been wandering down the main avenue turned to stare at me, as if he was seeing something incredibly strange.

"Oh-hoh-hoh!" I laughed as I answered, "I'm making money."

"Huh…? You can make money doing stuff like that? What on earth do you mean?"

What possible purpose could there be to repeatedly stroking and putting on my hat? The man seemed to find it extremely strange, but even so, at the same time, he seemed curious.

"Would you be so kind as to teach me the details?" he asked.

My, my…

"Of course, there's no way I can teach you an incredible way of making money like this for free."

"Oh… Well then, how much do I have to pay to get you to teach me?"

"Let me see—how about two copper coins?"

That's exactly what it costs for a night at a cheap inn nearby.

"Is that really enough? Sounds good to me." The man nodded and dropped two copper coins into my hand with a *clink*.

"Pleasure doing business with you. Oh-hoh-hoh!" I smiled boldly again and then told him, "Making money this way is extremely simple."

"Is it? To me, it just looks like you're doing some pointless nonsense…"

Really now, how can you say such a thing?

"Well, if you sit here and do something confusing, sooner or later someone will come up and talk to you, right? I tell the people who come up to talk to me that I'm making money. And when I do, they ask me again how I'm able to make money doing these incomprehensible things, right?"

Just like what's happening now.

"And so I answer that I'll teach them how, if they give me a couple of copper coins."

"…And then what?"

Oh my, you're not too quick, are you?

"I turn a profit."

[**Publication Information**]   Volume 11
Melonbooks Buyer's Bonus
[**Author Comments**]
Usually, Elaina sits by the roadside conducting her strange business and ends up being forced by a soldier to pay a penalty or something, but I bet her schemes usually go something like this, so that's what the story's about. Making something out of nothing. She's a real moneymaker, isn't she...?

CHAPTER 1 STORY 39

A Story of Staple Foods

I visited a certain country, and as always, I bought some bread in town and walked around on the street munching away. To a discerning observer, I must have looked quite rude. People pointing at the unfamiliar traveler and saying, "Wow, what bad manners!" wasn't an unusual occurrence no matter where I was.

And so I did as I always did and walked around town chowing down on some bread. But—

"Hey, hey…look over there…!"

"Whoa… She's walking around eating bread… She definitely must be ill…"

"Poor thing, and she's so young, too… No question about it, she's definitely going to die an early death."

The people I passed in town whispered to each other as they looked at me.

"……"

My goodness.

Apparently, the country I had arrived at that day was, as I mentioned above, kind of a strange place.

"Allow me to explain!"

When I made it to an inn in town, the innkeeper told me what was going on as she hung up an enormous sign. Apparently, most of the travelers who arrived in this country had questions like I did, so she was ready for mine, because she had already answered questions from others.

"In our country, the health risks that come from eating bread are considered a real problem. Eating bread on a daily basis causes a considerable decline in intellect, you see."

"You're saying that it makes you stupid?"

"Exactly! Bread is quite harmful to the body! The majority of people who eat bread regularly end up losing their lives to some sort of illness!"

"Huh…"

I think it's very common when anybody dies for them to be suffering from some sort of disease, though.

"And that's not all. Would you believe that among people who ate bread daily, in about half of all cases, they died sooner than the average life span in this country?! It's just dreadful!"

"Uh-huh…"

"Lots of other data has also been gathered about the dangers of bread. First of all, people who eat nothing but bread every day are at risk for nutritional imbalances, and if you give bread to very young children, they seem to enter a rebellious phase around age fifteen! Bread is avoided here in our country as the devil's food."

Then the innkeeper went on an eloquent diatribe about the dangers of bread.

And in conclusion—

"I understand that there aren't very many people who eat bread in this country," I said. "But in that case, what is the staple food here?"

"Rice, of course!" the innkeeper answered immediately.

Oh-hoh. Is that so? I see.

"Did you know?" I said. "Apparently, among people who eat rice on a daily basis, about half of them pass away before they reach the average life span—"

[**Publication Information**]   Volume 11
Toranoana Buyer's Bonus

[**Author Comments**]

    I wrote about this after the "The Cursed Box" story. This is also a story about how, when you're determined to stretch the truth, everything can get stretched and strained beyond belief.

By the way, everyone, did you know this? Apparently, there's an amazing book out there that will greatly enrich your life if you carry it with you always and enthusiastically recommend it to every single person you encounter. It's called *Wandering Witch*.

CHAPTER 1 STORY 40

The Ghost in the Teapot

"*I am the ghost in the teapot.*"

In a certain country, there is a story about a spirit that comes out when you rub a teapot and grants you wishes. One time, when a man was organizing his family's storehouse, he rubbed the teapot, and a billow of smoke rose out of the spout. The figure of a pure-white ghost appeared and declared itself.

The man was extremely surprised.

The ghost in the teapot folded its arms and said, looking down on the man from above, "*I will grant you just one single wish.*" Apparently, the story was true.

"Seriously?" The man was even more surprised. It's worth mentioning that he was in terrible debt after losing a lot of money gambling, so he decided he would try to get some money. The man was kind of a loser.

"All right, how about some mone—?"

The man spoke up right away.

That's when it happened.

"I have heard your request."

A witch suddenly appeared beside him.

Who was she?

That's right, it was me.

"Are you sure you really want to do that?" I asked. "You're all right asking for money from a dead person?"

The man was making an incredibly perplexed face at this unknown witch who had suddenly appeared to stoke his anxiety.

"Who are you?"

"In these circumstances, it doesn't really matter who I am, does it?"

"I mean, this is my home, so—"

"Are you listening? The ghost in the teapot is, as it were, a dead person. Whenever you accept items or money from a dead person, you incur an inheritance tax. That means unless you pay money, you won't be able to get any money. That's a little different from what you were hoping, isn't it?"

"Hmm, that certainly would be a problem…"

The man sighed.

But he didn't need to worry. I had already thought up a plan.

"What will you do? You may make one wish."

"Uh, actually, I don't really have a wish right now, so could I ask you to go back inside?"

"Is that what you want for your wish?"

"Of course not; don't be ridiculous. I'll call for you again later, so hurry up and go back inside, please."

"Very well."

In a roiling cloud, the ghost went back inside the teapot.

Holding the teapot, I said to the man, "Even if you can't get money directly from the ghost in the teapot, there are all sorts of other ways to make money from it."

Then I took the man along with me, and we set off to sell the teapot that contained a ghost that would grant any wish. And it goes without saying that we sold it for a high price.

And everyone lived happily ever after.

[Publication Information] Volume 13
Melonbooks Buyer's Bonus

[Author Comments]
    If it sounds too good to be true, it probably is. I thought to myself that if a genie came out of a lamp and offered to grant me any wish I wanted, I might go sell the lamp itself, and that's where the idea for this story came from. Generally, things don't work out all that well when people try to take advantage of power they've been granted out of the blue.

CHAPTER 1 STORY 41
A Strange Presence

One time, when I was sightseeing around a certain country, I arrived at an open plaza, where I caught sight of a lone man worrying over something. The man stood before a green lawn, racking his brain.

"This is awful... What am I supposed to do here...?"

It was easy to see he was troubled, so I tried to speak to him, and he said, "The fact is that there's no end to the people walking on this grass..."

He showed me the tragic scene that spread out before us. The lawn in the plaza was apparently just there to beautify the scenery, and a sign stating KEEP OFF THE GRASS had been erected.

However, the citizens of the city ignored the sign and went right in. They sat down and started enjoying their picnics. No matter how many times the man warned them off, and despite the fact that he had set up a fence, it seemed like everybody ignored the rules, he said.

"What to do...?"

The man let out a sigh.

I see, I see.

"Well, if that's the problem—"

A witch suddenly appeared beside him. Who was she?

That's right, it was me.

"Why don't you leave this up to me?"

"Firstly, who are you?"

"I can definitely solve your grass problem for you."

"Sure. By the way, who are you?"

And just like that, I undertook the task of getting rid of every last one of the rude people who were trespassing on the lawn. Well, actually, my method for dealing with a problem like this one was as simple as could be.

The following day—

A young man and woman appeared. They walked right onto the lawn and started to enjoy a picnic. Disregarding the KEEP OFF THE GRASS sign, they laughed and flirted the whole time.

Oh dear, no morals at all, huh?

And so I quickly approached the couple and spoke to them.

"Good afternoon! Could I speak to the two of you for a moment?"

Both of them looked at me blankly, and I said, "As a matter of fact, recently, I've been handing out presents like this to people like you. Oh-hoh-hoh-hoh-hoh-hoh-hoh!"

As I spoke, I offered them a bright red apple.

"I'll be sure to offer you presents whenever you picnic on the grass from now on. Oh-hoh-hoh!"

"Uh-huh…" Although the two of them had a questionable reaction to my extremely suspicious behavior, they still continued their picnic.

Meanwhile, I continued walking around handing out apples to all the people who stepped on the grass.

Eventually, a credible rumor began to circulate that there was a strange, suspicious witch walking around handing out apples on the forbidden lawn, and one by one, people stopped approaching the grass.

"I see. Rather than warning them off, you endorsed them going on the lawn and then made it uncomfortable, and everyone stopped going?" The man slapped his knee as he handed me my reward.

I nodded in the affirmative.

"Because they want to keep their distance from the strange lady, you see."

[Publication Information] Volume 13
Toranoana Buyer's Bonus
[Author Comments]
　　Rather than "No, don't do it!" it produces a stronger reaction against something to be told "Yes, please go ahead, do it, please, heh-heh-heh-heh-heh..." It's the same psychological phenomenon that instructs us to not push, never push.

CHAPTER 1 STORY 42

A Certain Country's Specialty

In a country where they sold certain famous products, a man and a woman were arguing in the street.

When I listened in on my way past, I could hear that they were apparently fighting over a very trivial topic.

"What did you just say was the most delicious food in this country? I can tell you it's the bread, of course!"

"Oh, no, it's the hamburg steaks! Though I don't suppose you'd understand that, with your soft, spongy face like well-proofed bread dough!"

"Why, you, what did you say?!"

Two popular shops sat side by side along the main avenue.

One was a butcher shop famous for its hamburg steaks, and the other was a bakery famous for its fluffy bread, and both of them were fighting over whose dishes were more delicious.

"If that's how you're going to be, then why don't we get that witch to decide for us what is better: my bread or your hamburg steaks?!"

"That's a good idea! Although I know, of course, that my hamburg steaks are tastier!"

Their argument, as heated as a simmering hamburg steak, then dragged me, a neutral traveler, into the mix.

And I, the traveler who had been watching their exchange from a distance, tilted my head in confusion at this sudden development.

"Huuuh…?" But the two shopkeepers didn't care about the traveler's wishes.

"Say, you there, traveler! My bread is delicious! Come try some," the man said, holding out some bread.

"Say, you there, traveler! Everyone knows that hamburg steaks are delicious! Give mine a try!" The woman thrust some hamburger at me.

The traveler was very perplexed by the two of them.

Couldn't they just skip all that and work together instead?

So the traveler took the bread and the hamburg steak that she had been handed and combined them to make a hamburger sandwich. She showed them they ought to consider not which one was the best but the fact that they could make something even better if they put them together.

The two of them were startled.

"Put the bread and the hamburger together…you say…?"

"I never thought of that…!"

The two of them looked at each other. Then they shook hands and made peace.

"Should we also work together, like the bread and the hamburg steak?"

"What a coincidence… I was just thinking the same thing…"

In this way, the two rivals who had been competing against each other got married, and the two of them merged their shops, and the country's most famous food, the hamburger sandwich, was born.

"How do you like them, Miss Witch?! Our country's famous hamburgers?"

I looked around the town as I was eating a hamburger sandwich that was as piping hot as the anecdote about the two shopkeepers in love. Now there were hamburger shops lining the streets everywhere.

"They give me indigestion."

[Publication Information] Volume 14
Toranoana Buyer's Bonus
[Author Comments]
  I had the idea of writing a story that had something to do with hamburg steaks down in the comments section, but I couldn't come up with anything good off the cuff. Sure enough, it takes time to prepare for something like that. Yes, just like making hamburg steaks.
  Hamburgeeeeeeeeeeer!

CHAPTER 1 STORY 43

A Story of the Country of Stories

"A-alert! Aleeert!"

A man's loud shouting echoed out of a certain house in the Peaceful Country of Robetta.

The birds that had been settled in a nearby tree flew off in surprise, and a housewife who happened to be passing by giggled and said, "Oh my goodness, not again?"

Inside the house, the man's wife let out a sigh. "Looks like it's happening again."

The reason for the man's panic was always the same.

"Alert! Alert! We got a delivery from Elaina!"

Every time any kind of package arrived from his beloved daughter, who was off traveling the world, the man kicked up a big fuss, as if a natural disaster had occurred.

His wife always smiled in amusement at him and said, "You've never been able to let go, no matter how much time passes, have you?"

But recently, his behavior had become a source of worry for her. "That's enough. Aren't you used to this by now? After all, it's normal to get mail when someone's out traveling, dear. You're making too much fuss."

"The fact that mail has shown up is proof that Elaina is getting along well. Isn't that wonderful…?!"

The man had been awfully worried, practically beside himself, really, especially since there hadn't been any letters recently.

His wife let out a sigh. "She's getting along well, even if you don't worry over her. The fact that there was a break in the letters just proves she's been enjoying her travels. That girl will be just fine, whether she's sending us tidings or not."

As she said that, the woman looked at the package that had arrived from her daughter—the package the man was holding so preciously. The package, large enough that he was holding it in both arms, was obviously quite heavy.

"You're always so calm."

With a smile, the man set the package down on the table.

It was misleading to say the woman was always calm.

"I just have confidence in the girl. I also get flustered, when it's warranted."

For example, when she saw strange black creatures in the kitchen. For example, when she saw a ghost. For example, when books full of embarrassing anecdotes that she had written long ago appeared unexpectedly.

She was often told she was always calm, but she was a totally normal woman, who got flustered in situations like those.

That said, it had been a long time since she had seen any black creatures in the kitchen, and she hadn't run into any ghosts lately. Nothing had been happening to get her flustered, so her husband certainly might think that she was always calm.

"Well then, okay, I wonder what Elaina sent us this time?"

The man hummed to himself as he opened the package.

Inside were several booklets, about ten of them.

"Hmm…? What do we have here? Books…?" The man picked up one of the volumes that was inside and ran his fingers over the cover.

From the side, the woman peeked at the cover.

Written on it was—

The Story of the Country of Stories

"Ah!"

They were books full of embarrassing content the woman had written on her travels long ago.

And the woman was, understandably, flustered.

[**Publication Information**] Volume 14
Melonbooks Buyer's Bonus

[**Author Comments**]

I had originally planned to include this bonus story in Volume 14 of *Wandering Witch*, but it wasn't that great of a fit, and it was kind of off-topic for the volume, and there was nowhere to put it, so it ended up in the bonus stories volume. At that point, we had already decided that Volume 15 was going to be a bonus stories volume, so you could also say I made a bold decision to relocate it.

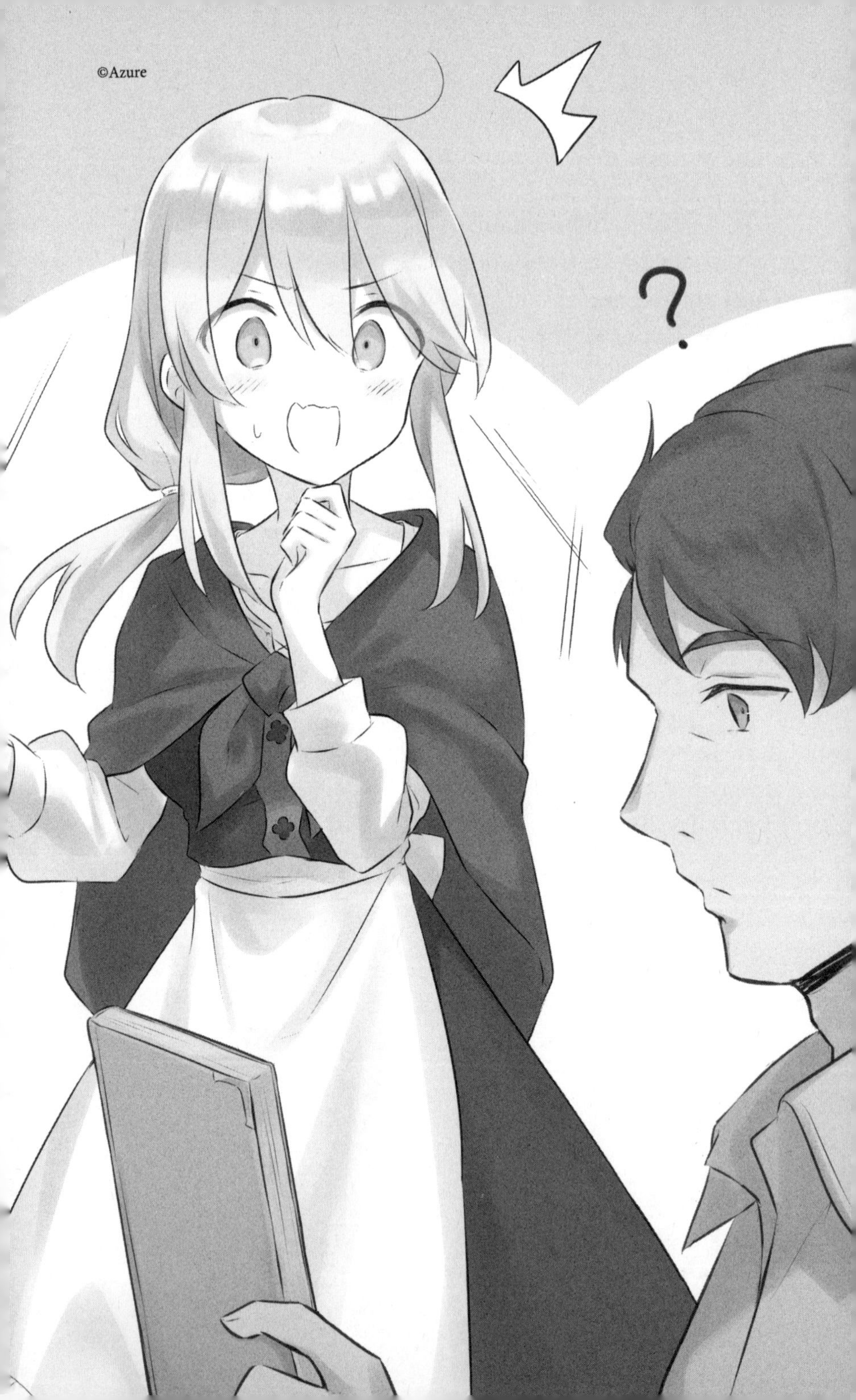
©Azure

CHAPTER 2

The Cursed Doll That Always Comes Back No Matter How Many Times You Get Rid of It

A young girl living in a certain country picked up a doll she found on the side of the road.

Its golden hair was glossy. The pink dress it was wearing was very beautiful. Its blue eyes sparkled like gemstones. With a single glance, in that moment, the girl was captivated by the incredibly beautiful doll. She didn't know whom it belonged to, but she liked the doll so much that she took it right home with her.

However, the girl's mother took one look at the doll she'd brought home and frowned, and she scolded the young girl lightly.

"Oh no, you shouldn't pick things like this up. Take it right back to where you found it immediately."

To all appearances, the incredibly beautiful doll did not look like something that would have been thrown away. It had likely been lost. The owner might have been looking for it at that very moment. Her daughter needed to return it to where she'd originally found it before anyone got the idea that she'd stolen the doll, the mother thought.

"Awww...," the daughter whined. She was disappointed because she'd felt so very lucky to find the doll.

But her mother reasoned with her—"If you want a doll, I'll buy one for you"—and suggested that they go together to get rid of the old doll and then go right to the doll shop, where her daughter could pick out a pretty new doll that her mother would buy her as a present.

"...You will?" the girl asked. All the new dolls that lined the shelves of the doll shop were rather fancy and rather expensive.

"It's okay. Your mother's been making a pretty penny at her side job."

"What's your side job?"

"Resale."

This is a digression, but the lady had been earning a decent amount doing small jobs from home.

"Yay! Thank you!"

The girl forgot all about the doll she had found and went home with her mother, hugging her new doll instead.

Then, the following day—

While the mother was making breakfast in the kitchen, she suddenly felt a chill run up her spine. She sensed an uncomfortable set of eyes on her, as if she was being watched by somebody.

So she turned around.

"……?"

Then she tilted her head to the side in confusion.

There was nobody behind her.

However, there was a doll sitting in one of the dining room chairs where the family usually had their breakfast.

The doll, with its glossy golden hair, dressed in a very pretty pink dress, with blue eyes that sparkled like gemstones, was the very same doll that she was certain she had helped her daughter get rid of the day before.

"My husband must have happened to pick it up." The mother didn't give it too much more thought and went to discard it on the roadside just as she had the day before.

But it was the strangest thing.

During breakfast, when she asked her husband about the doll, he just looked puzzled and said, "I never picked up any doll?"

And of course their daughter hadn't picked it up again.

So then, exactly who had placed it in the dining room?

"It's almost like the doll walked in by itself." The husband laughed jokingly as he nibbled at his bread.

"…Don't say weird things like that." The wife smiled, caught up in her husband's easygoing mood. Even as she smiled, she felt those uncomfortable eyes on her again from somewhere.

Ultimately, no matter how much thought she gave it, she couldn't figure out what could have caused the doll to come back on its own. But this time, she had gotten rid of it for certain, so she was sure everything was all right.

However, that evening—

When she came home from work, the mother froze as soon as she opened the door to the house.

"...How?"

There in the entryway. Right in front of the door.

The doll was sitting there, waiting for the mother's return. It was sitting flat on the floor, looking up at her with its manufactured smile.

The woman got goose bumps. She was afraid. At that point, she finally understood that something supernatural was taking place.

Then, from that day forward, the doll started to follow her whole family around.

No matter how many times they got rid of it, the doll always came back.

Whether they returned it to the road where they had picked it up, or threw it away in a garbage can, or guiltily gave it to someone else, or tried to sell it to a store, no matter what they did, no matter what happened, the doll seemed to have taken a great liking to them and always managed to come back to them.

No matter how many days passed, no matter how many times they discarded it.

The doll always followed the family around.

Then one day, when she returned home to find the doll, which was waiting for her in the entryway as always with a creepy smile on its face, the mother finally reached the limits of her patience.

"Oh, give it a rest already! Quit following our family around! What on earth are you after?!"

Overwhelmed by the weirdness of it all, the mother sank to the floor and started crying.

"I have heard of your predicament."

By the way, it just so happened that there was a wandering witch there, leaning back against the door that was standing ajar, wearing an unruffled expression on her face.

Who could she be?

The lady of the house raised her head and inquired, "A-and you are…?"

When she asked, the witch tossed her hair dramatically and replied, "I am the Ashen Witch, Elaina. A powerful and clever witch. Today, I got wind of someone in trouble, and I came here."

"A powerful and clever witch…?" The woman cocked her head, obviously wondering what this stranger was talking about. I'd meant it as a joke to break the tension, but she seemed to have taken it rather more seriously.

"Well, more importantly, you, madam, seem to be suffering abuse at the hands of a supernatural stalker."

I, the powerful and clever witch, glossed over my own overenthusiastic gaffe and moved the conversation forward.

"Th-that's right…! Th-the doll is…! No matter how many times we get rid of it, it always comes back…!"

The woman grabbed on to my skirt and clung to it as she sobbed furiously like a child.

What are you doing?

"This doll is likely what's known as a cursed doll," I said. "It probably set its eye on you when your daughter first picked it up."

"Huh…? How did you know my daughter picked the doll up…?"

"Because I was there."

"…Are you a stalker, too?"

"Not at all."

I just happened to be there.

"…Can you lift the curse on this doll?"

"Ah, sorry. I forgot to say so, but curses are not one of my areas of expertise." I shook my head. "So it's not possible."

"Y-you're kidding…" The woman slumped her shoulders.

"Stay strong, madam. This sort of cursed doll lies in wait for the moment of its owner's mental weakness. You mustn't show any vulnerability."

This was something I had learned by reading it in a book. Apparently, many cursed dolls wore away at their victims' sanity over time, before eventually taking their lives.

"But, but… If I stay strong, like you said, then how on earth—?"

"Money."

"Huh?"

"Let's make some money, madam."

The woman was bewildered.

"What in the world are you talking about…?"

With a very, very serious face, I told her, "Can't you just smell the business opportunity coming off of this doll?"

"Hold on, I genuinely do not understand what you are saying."

In that case, it seems like you need me to explain the particulars.

I crouched and whispered into the woman's ear, even though there was no one else around.

"No matter where you leave it, this doll comes back to you, is that right?"

"Yes…"

"And, madam, I cannot help but notice, it looks like you send a lot of packages."

Looking into the house from the entryway, I could see several wrapped parcels. She appeared to be making a little money on the side buying and selling household goods.

"What would you think about enclosing the cursed doll in one of those packages?" I suggested.

"Even if I do something like that, the doll will somehow come back to me…"

"That's right. But don't you think it will be good publicity if you attach advertising notices to the doll?"

I'd heard that some people involved in that kind of sales business would include little treats or notes in their packages to show their gratitude to their customers. The woman could package up the doll in much the same way and get her customers to leave the doll on their doorsteps after they had accepted their packages.

As long as they did that, the doll would come back to the woman's house on its own, and along the way, it could do advertising duty.

In short, while she was working her side gig, she would also be able to pull in ad revenue.

"…!"

With the advent of a new business opportunity, the woman's eyes got their light back. She said, "I never thought of that!" clapped her hands together, and picked up the doll.

No longer was the doll in her arms simply a cursed doll. It was her business partner.

"Thank you, Lady Witch! I'm going to give it a try!"

In this way, the woman rose to sudden fame as someone who had invented an entirely new business using a cursed doll. All sorts of different businesses took notice and approached her wanting to embroider their business names onto the clothes of her famous cursed doll, and there was no shortage of people who wanted to get a look at the intriguing doll and placed regular orders, hoping it would show up.

By that point, the sight of the doll parading through town covered in logos from various businesses had become one of the country's better-known attractions.

"Oh, that's just wonderful."

I was a little excited by the extra income I was making, so I was in a fairly expensive café having a leisurely breakfast when I saw that there was a special interest article on the woman who had started the doll business adorning the front of the newspaper.

According to the article—

"It's all thanks to my keen sense of smell that allows me to sniff out good business opportunities at any moment."

That was the gist of it.

The article continued to note that much of the credit for the woman's incredible success was owed to a certain witch who had put the idea in her head.

And who on earth could that be?

That's right, it's me.

CHAPTER 3

A Story of Saya and Sheila's Tobacco

"Teacher, tell me, why do you smoke tobacco?"

This happened while I was working odd jobs at the United Magic Association.

I suddenly became curious about my teacher, the Midnight Witch, Sheila, who, despite the fact that smoking was prohibited indoors, always had her pipe in her mouth, blowing out little puffs of smoke and shortening her own life span.

When I threw out my question, my teacher looked at me and asked, "Huh? You want a puff?"

"I have trouble understanding how you would come up with that idea…"

"Well, you're looking at my pipe like you want it."

"Like I want it…?" *I was just staring at it, but…* "Pipes and cigarettes—all they do is damage your body when you smoke them, right? Plus they make your clothes stink. What's so good about smoking them?"

"Oh-hoh, so you are interested?" For some reason, my teacher nodded meaningfully. "Let me think…" Then she thought for a short while as she gazed up at the cloud of smoke hanging in the air.

"For example, say there's someone you like." For some reason, she launched into a strange hypothetical. "People act strangely when they're in love, and all they can think about is that other person, right? Whether they're working or playing, thoughts of that person rise at unexpected times from a corner of their mind. They can't seem to forget about them, no matter how they try, and in fact, the more they try to forget, the more insistent their thoughts of that person become."

"Um… That kind of makes sense, I think…"

"In other words, to me, that's what tobacco is."

"Uh-huh. So to put it simply, you're in love with tobacco?"

"Well, I guess you could say that."

"…That's unexpected. I didn't think you'd ever experienced love, Miss."

"Hey, hey, who do you think you're talking to here? I'm still your teacher, you know?" Then, after tapping the ash out of her pipe, my teacher said, "I never have experienced love, I don't think."

"……"

"Everything I just said was only from my imagination." She snorted proudly. "Now, I know what you're going to say. You're probably going to tell me I should quit smoking, right?"

"Bingo. It's bad for your body, you know?"

I nodded, but my teacher said, "Sorry for using the love metaphor again, but do you know what you should do when you're feeling impatient because the person you love is moving too slowly?"

"Um…just hang in there and endure the waiting or something?"

"No, wrong." My teacher shook her head, then held out her hand to me. "Mm."

She had been holding a gold coin.

"…What's this for?"

My teacher said simply, "I'm out of tobacco leaves, so go buy some."

I see, so she's trying to tell me that the only way to suppress your desire to smoke tobacco is to go ahead and smoke it.

…She's not interested in quitting at all, huh?

"Which is to say, every day, I'm annoyed at my teacher… Because of her, my chest hurts every day."

"Huh."

I had reunited with Elaina in Qunorts, the Free City.

I was casually complaining to Elaina about my recent troubles with my teacher being a heavy smoker and the harm I was suffering because of it.

Elaina's teacher, Fran, had known my teacher for a long time, and so my ulterior motive was to get my complaints to pass to Fran through Elaina, and then for Fran to speak to my teacher and get her to quit smoking.

When calling an adult's attention to something, the best approach is to follow the proper procedure and get another adult to pass your opinion along. It was obvious that whenever I talked to Sheila directly, she always ended up getting annoyed with me. Even though I was the one who was annoyed!

To that end, I had explained the situation to Elaina, from start to finish. But—

Munch, munch, munch, munch.

Elaina was eating her bread.

The way she was eating, carefully taking little bites, holding her bread close to her in both hands with her fingers wrapped around it, she looked just like a little animal. She was embodying the very concept of cuteness. I was enchanted.

Finally, Elaina looked in my direction and tilted her head quizzically.

"Ah, sorry. What was it you were talking about?"

She's so cute. Wait, but—

"Weren't you listening to me?"

"Huh? Sure, I was listening…" Elaina's eyes shifted around.

Adorable.

"Well then, what was I talking about? Do you remember?"

"Saya. That's my question." She snapped into a smug expression.

Adorable.

"I was talking about how my chest hurts every day because of my teacher."

"Ah, that's right. That was it. In other words, you've got a little crush on your teacher, huh?"

"Incorrect."

"Now, now, you don't have to be embarrassed, Saya. You are at that age. Lots of people have similar problems, you know."

"You've got it wrong. It's not love." Then I put on a smug expression of my own and said, "You're the only one I have feelings for, Elaina…"

"Sure, sure." Elaina waved her hand dismissively.

Adorable.

"Oh my, what's this? Elaina…by any chance, are you feeling embarrassed?"

"I'm not embarrassed."

"I see, so you're saying that when two people are as close as we are, a little thing like a love confession is nothing to get embarrassed about, is that it…?"

"Where does that boundless optimism of yours even come from…?" Elaina asked with a sigh.

I'm not sure how to answer that question; this is just what I'm like. I guess if you must ask, well, there's nothing to say except that I'm just out here laying myself bare, as always.

"Setting that aside, Elaina, please give me some advice."

This is somewhat off-topic, but the piece of bread Elaina is eating right now is one I bought.

I hadn't known what to do with the bread I had bought for my own lunch, which turned out to be tough and unpleasant enough that I had no desire to eat it. "Oh? Looks like you've got something good there, haven't you?" Elaina had pestered me like some kind of delinquent, after which I'd handed it over to her. Since she was eating even that poor excuse for bread as if it was delicious, I think it would be fair to call Elaina a peerless lover of bread. And because I gave her bread, surely I was entitled to request one piece of advice.

"Let me see…" Elaina, who had listened carefully to my story, no matter what she wanted me to believe, put her finger to her mouth for a moment and pondered the question adorably. "Hmm…"

Eventually, she said, "I wonder if it might be best to tell her honestly that she's giving you chest pains."

……

Talk to her honestly.
That's not much in the way of advice…

"That's an incredibly basic suggestion…"

"That was incredibly basic bread…"

Thinking that next time I would have to present her with more respectable bread, I then had a lively chat with Elaina.

○

Who on earth could that perceptive girl be?

That's right, it's me.

I had been listening to Saya talk about her problems while I was eating my bread, but of course, I had been aware of her true motives. Going out of her way to speak to me about her troubles with Sheila's smoking must have been part of a bigger plan.

Given her position, it would obviously be quite a difficult thing for Saya, the pupil, to directly admonish her teacher, Sheila.

And knowing that, this perceptive girl immediately went to see a certain person.

I had to at least put in the work equal to the bread I had received, after all.

"Good afternoon, Miss."

Wham! I opened the door at the inn.

"Oh, Elaina. Good afternoon."

Miss Fran, who had been relaxing in her room, greeted me with a smile upon my sudden visit. "Please remember to knock," she reprimanded me, still smiling.

Setting that aside—

"Please hear me out, Miss. The fact is that recently, one of my friends has been at her wit's end dealing with a certain problem."

"Oh my, is that so? What kind of problem?"

I said, "Apparently, she's suffering because whenever she's near her teacher, she gets chest pains."

Since this was my teacher, Miss Fran, whom I was talking to, I figured she would probably demonstrate her quick wit and grasp everything I was trying to say just from this little bit of information.

"I see…"

However, contrary to what I had imagined, Miss Fran reacted strangely. "…By the way, would that friend of yours happen to be you yourself, Elaina?"

"Huh?"

What are you talking about?

"Substituting a friend for yourself and watching the reaction of the person you ask for advice. It's an old trick when you want advice on a topic that's difficult to ask others about."

"Is it, now? That's not what's going on here, though."

"Oh, but your chest hurts whenever we're together…? In other words, you hate being with me, Elaina, is that what you're saying…? How heartbreaking for your teacher…"

"Incorrect."

"Oh, I'm wrong? Well then, that means your chest is hurting for a different reason…?"

"No, um, Miss, the person who needs advice isn't me at all…" Perceptively, I picked up on her extreme lack of understanding and the fact that a strange atmosphere was starting to fill the room. Shaking my head, I let out a sigh. "Saya is having trouble with her teacher, Sheila."

"My goodness."

I'm sure now that I've explained this much, I can expect her to understand what I'm trying to say.

That's what I thought, but a moment later, my teacher defied my expectations.

"That must mean... What are you trying to say, Elaina?"

You don't get it, huh?

I guess I shouldn't behave like I'm so clever and dance around the issue.

"I want you to tell Sheila what we just talked about."

"I see... Passing along your own opinions through a third party. An old trick for when you need to convey something that's hard to talk about."

"Righto." I nodded roughly.

Please just help me.

"I don't mind talking to her, but...but are you sure it's all right? It won't cause problems if I tell Sheila about this conversation?"

Saya's already in enough of a bind to come ask me for advice, so I don't think it will cause any more trouble.

Besides—

"That's what she wants."

When Sheila smokes around her, the smell sticks to her clothes, and it has an effect on her health. There's nothing good about it. It really does a lot of harm with no benefit.

"I see... If that's the situation, then I understand. I'll try to help."

My teacher nodded gravely, taking the responsibility very seriously for some reason.

●

"Sheila... So you are guilty, I see."

"Huh?"

I was in my room smoking my pipe after lunch.

After knocking hesitantly on the door and opening it slowly, Fran came in wearing a serious face and said to me, "It's about your pupil, Saya. Don't you think she's been acting strangely lately?"

"...?"

Since she asked, I tried to think back on my recent conversations with Saya. But she was always acting strangely anyway, so to put it another way, I could say her behavior had never not been unusual. In other words, normal.

"Nah, she's been the same as ever."

"Huh… Are you sure that's true?"

As if she wasn't satisfied with my answer, Fran sighed dramatically and looked up at the ceiling.

"What is it?"

"Sheila, will you keep calm and listen, please?"

"Sure."

"Apparently, recently, when Saya is with you, her chest hurts."

"Her chest hurts…?"

What are you trying to say?

I cocked my head, and at that point Fran repeated herself.

"So you are guilty, Sheila…"

That's what she said.

"…Huh?"

When she said her chest hurt, that's what it meant? Not that she was physically in pain but that she was hurting because of psychological causes? Seriously?

"Well, I wasn't expecting that…" Thinking back on things, she had never acted that way toward me, and she was always talking about Elaina and nothing else, so I'd been sure she had those feelings for Elaina, and I had never given it any more thought.

I was bewildered by this sudden discussion, and Fran nodded with a know-it-all look on her face.

"People are quick to fall in love, after all."

"What are you talking about?"

"You often hear of people who consult with a close friend on matters of love, then inadvertently fall for the friend who they were consulting with…"

"Wait, I'm not her friend, I'm her teacher…"

○

"Kyaaahhh! It hurts! My chest hurts!"

The next day, I tried to implement the advice Elaina had given me and have an honest talk with my teacher, Sheila.

I went to the room in the inn where my teacher was staying, checked that she was there blowing smoke out the window as usual, then dived onto the bed.

As soon as I did, I started yelling about the pain in my chest.

I tried to strike honestly and directly and make my objection to her smoking impossible to miss.

So then, how do you think my teacher reacted?

"Ah, o-oh…does it…? Your chest…hurts…?"

……

Hmm?

What's with this weird reaction?

"What's the matter, Miss? I feel like you're acting a little strange."

"I'm acting…strange…? Am I? Is that how it looks…?" my teacher said, putting on a serious air as she puffed on her pipe. "Ah, I really thought I was treating you the same as always, but, uh… I'm sorry, I don't have much experience in that realm, so I'm not exactly comfortable…"

"Huh?"

I don't really understand what's going on here, but she seems troubled by something.

"Are you all right, Miss?" I asked. "If you want, I could lend you an ear."

"Uh…no, that's all right… It's not something I can talk to you about."

"Come on, now, don't hold back." I shoved my way over and closed the distance between us. "But maybe, in exchange for me listening to your troubles, Miss, you would take some advice from me?"

"Now I want to talk to you even less."

"Well, if you prefer, you could just take my advice?"

"That's awfully selfish."

"Right, so then, I will just talk, okay? My chest hurts, Miss."

"This really is one-sided."

And so I spoke to her honestly, just as I had been advised to do.

The whole time I was telling her this and that, I stared at her intensely, certain that Elaina had carefully considered my intentions and managed to indirectly ask my teacher to temper the use of her pipe.

The fact that Miss Sheila seemed to have been having trouble breathing ever since we met up that day was surely proof that I was right.

I'm sure she's already gotten a warning from Miss Fran. Elaina sure is a dependable friend!

Expecting the best, I puffed out my chest as I honestly complained to my teacher about her tobacco use.

To which my teacher responded:

"…Sorry, Saya. Right now, I've got my hands full with work, you see, and I don't have the time to be dating."

"?????"

"So listen…I can't return your feelings."

"????????????"

The inside of my mind started whirling at a terrifying velocity, around and around and around like a spinning top. What on earth had possibly happened to make it seem like I had just delivered a love confession to my teacher, I wondered. I turned the question over in my mind, stuck in the perplexing and somewhat awkward situation of having been somehow rejected by someone I hadn't even been confessing my love to.

Let's think this through in chronological order. First, there can be no doubt that this all started when I went to Elaina for advice yesterday.

Elaina is very perceptive, so I'm certain she communicated my concerns to Miss Fran, for sure. By the way, when you're passing a message from person to person, the more people it goes through, the more the substance changes bit by bit, isn't that right? So then what happened was a transmission error? That has to be it! How totally embarrassing!

Having arrived at this conclusion, I pointed out the mistake to my teacher, clearly and directly.

"Miss, what I'm saying is that my chest hurts because of your smoking."

Immediately after I did, the light returned to my teacher's grave expression.

"Huh? Uh, what? You mean this?" My teacher tapped her pipe out to get rid of the ash, and she let out a white puff of relief. "That damned Fran… She almost gave me a heart attack, telling me that way!"

Just as I thought, it sounds like it was a communication failure.

My teacher had her hand on her chest.

By the way—

"Tobacco is also bad for your heart, you know."

"Yeah, yeah."

My teacher waved her hand dismissively.

Back to her usual self, my teacher then packed fresh leaves into her pipe and asked me, "By the way, do you know what you're supposed to do when you're confronted with a situation that makes your heart stop?"

After some hesitation, I answered—

"Um…pause and take a deep breath or something?"

"No, wrong." My teacher shook her head, then held out her hand to me. "Mm."

She was holding a gold coin.

"…Somehow, I feel like we had this same exchange yesterday."

I stared intently at her.

Then my teacher said simply—

"I'm out of tobacco leaves, so go buy some."

In short, she seems to be trying to tell me that when you're confronted with a heart-stopping situation, the first thing to do is to smoke some tobacco to settle your heart down.

I see, I see.

…I knew it. She's not interested in quitting at all.

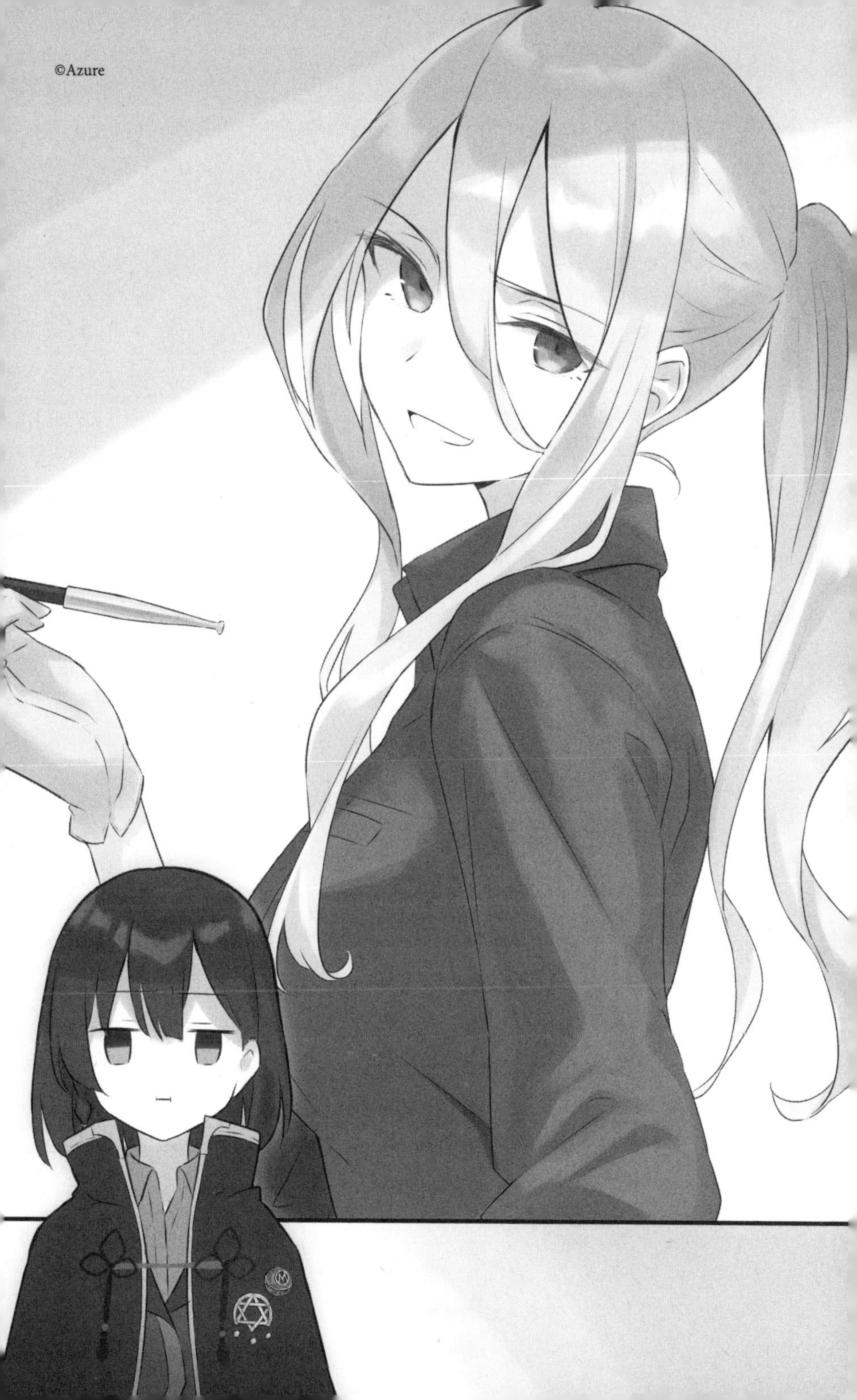

CHAPTER 4

The Tale of a Certain Traveler

I never knew the names of my birth parents.

Tracing my oldest memories back through my mind, I arrived at some ruins standing by the seaside, where the smell of salt air assailed my nose. Broken timbers, beds covered in sand, pieces of clothing plastered to the ground, dolls buried in the sand, and only the skeleton of the house remaining. Everything I could see was wrecked and covered in sand. In the middle of this incoherent landscape, where everything was broken into little pieces and scattered around like a puzzle, I lay collapsed on the ground.

When I asked about it, I was told this was the scene after everything humans had built was washed away by water and the place had fallen into ruin.

And it was my birthplace, which no longer existed. I was the sole survivor, somehow discovered among all that wreckage. That was what my caretaker at the orphanage told me, casting her eyes down sadly. When I asked why she made such a sad face, my caretaker looked even sadder as she embraced me. I knew then that I had asked something I wasn't supposed to ask, and I never raised the same question again.

My days at the orphanage seemed like endless tedium.

We got up at a set time, ate breakfast, and played until the afternoon. Then we ate again, and then took a little afternoon nap before playing some more. If we were lucky, we did some reading and writing or studied the world outside, then in the evening we ate dinner, had a bath, and everyone went peacefully to sleep.

Day after day, we repeated the same activities.

I don't recall how many years and months passed at the orphanage. Before I knew it, I was eight years old.

While I lived out my boring days confined in this little terrarium, the teachers at the orphanage stood at their lecterns and told us every day about what a broad and beautiful place the world was.

"—Certain people, known as mages, are capable of commanding a mysterious power called magic. They can use magic to make amusing things like this happen, right in their hands."

Our teacher waved her wand, and the next thing she showed us was a dazzlingly beautiful burst of glittering stars. As the sparkling beads of light flickered around us, the teacher told us that this was an example of the sort of magical power that mages could wield.

At the sight of this beautiful spectacle that filled the room, all the children erupted into delighted applause.

I realized that applause was the appropriate reaction and, a moment later than the others, clapped my hands together quietly.

Before long, the teacher explained that there might be a mage among us and handed out wands to each and every child. Those who directed their energy into the wand and got bluish-white light to come out were mages, the teacher told us.

I was the only one to produce any light. I was showered with a sparse round of applause, half surprise and half confusion.

The teachers at the orphanage taught me the bare minimum of how to use my magic, telling me that it might help me in the future. How to channel magical energy. How to fly on a broom.

"When will this help me?" I asked them.

One teacher answered me with a broad smile. "I'm sure it will come in handy once you leave here."

Once I leave here.

I didn't know when that might be, but at the time, I couldn't help but feel like my teacher was talking about some impossibly distant future.

From time to time, an unfamiliar adult would visit the orphanage.

Whenever someone came, I would be instructed by a teacher to go greet them, so every time someone visited, I gave them a polite bow.

When the adults saw me do that, they were pleased. "What excellent manners you have," they would say. Apparently, I could expect praise for proper greetings. Without fail, every time one of the adults visited, one of the children was no longer there.

It wasn't like I was especially close to any of the other children there, so I never felt a sense of loss when they left, but it did make me curious whenever someone suddenly disappeared.

One time I asked, "Where did those other kids go?"

When I did, the caretaker averted her eyes from me as if she felt guilty about something and answered, "We got those grown-ups to take them with them into the outside world."

"The outside world?"

"Yes." The caretaker frowned and patted me on the head. "Don't worry. I'm sure you'll be taken away someday, too. You're such a good girl."

"If you're a good girl, you get to go to the outside world?"

I fixed my eyes on the door of the orphanage.

The big door the adults always opened and came through. The dazzling sunlight of the outdoors streamed through the round cut-out window.

It doesn't seem like anyone's coming today either.

"Yes... If you keep being good and wait long enough, someone will find you."

The caretaker patted my head.

I don't know the names of the people who gave birth to me.
I don't know where my own hometown is.
I don't know the world outside that door, not a thing about it.
I don't know anything.
I don't even know what it means to be a good girl.
I have nothing.
The only thing I do have is this heavy feeling.

I was certain there was no way I was a normal child, since I was having these kinds of thoughts.

Locked away in this limited world, I had lived my life knowing nothing. The only thing I had was the heavy, stifling feeling of being swept away and submerged by flowing water.

The more time passed, the more distant the light beyond the door seemed to grow.

"…Boring."

The boredom I suffered through every day gnawed at my mind.

"Boring, boring, boring…"

If I was a good girl and waited long enough, someday a grown-up would come and take me away. Those words my caretaker had spoken to me kept me confined to the orphanage.

"Every day, I'm always bored—"

I was convinced that I must actually be a bad girl.

"I've had enough—"

When I was around ten years old—

—I snuck away from the orphanage, alone.

I didn't run away from the orphanage because there was anything bad about the place. In fact, I didn't want for anything in life, and I could have lived out the rest of my days there without giving it any thought.

But I just wasn't satisfied.

I had been told often and from a young age that I mustn't take it upon myself to go outside the orphanage alone, but as I walked through the outside world on my own, it felt free, and wide, and pleasant.

"Leaving the country?"

As soon as I left the orphanage, I headed for the border.

I had a feeling that if I stayed in the country, my teachers would come and take me back to the orphanage.

"Leaving the country."

I nodded, and the guard who was standing in front of the gate put his hand on his chin and made a sour face.

It was exactly the same expression the adults, who often came to the orphanage to talk to the teachers, made whenever they looked at me from afar.

I never knew what kind of conversations those adults were having about me, but even at that time, I could tell such expressions were not the product of good feelings.

And, so as not to let me know what they were feeling, the moment they made eye contact with me, the adults always put on fake smiles.

The gate guard crouched down and asked me, "Young lady, is your papa or your mama nearby?"

When I shook my head, he made an even more exaggerated sour face than before.

"Hmm, I see… Then I'm sorry about this, Little Lady. At your age, without consent from your papa or mama, you can't go out of this gate. Go on home for now, and come back again after you talk to them."

"……"

I answered him with silence.

"Did you understand me?"

"……"

I took out my broom, set it gently floating in the air, and sat down firmly on top of it. After my position was stable and I took a deep breath, I kicked off the ground lightly. My body floated up off the ground.

"…Hmm? What are you doing, Little Lady? Were you listening to what I said?"

"……"

I directed magical energy into my broom.

"…Little lady?"

"Leaving the country."

Immediately after I said that, I flew off on my broom, leaving no room for argument.

"H-hey! Wait a second! Come on! You can't do that! Heeeeeeyyy!"

The guard's voice echoed behind my back.

When I turned around, I could see the guard running after me.

His voice rang out in the distance, but I kept on flying on my broom until I couldn't hear him any longer.

I sucked in deep, deep breaths and kept on flying on my broom.

Flying through a world full of freedom.

○

My journey began because of my selfish curiosity, which would not allow me to stay in that narrow world.

The first place I visited was a tiny little village.

"Oh my, what a cute traveler you are."

The people of the village, living a humble life in the forest, greeted me, a rare visitor, warmly. It wasn't normal to see a child of only ten traveling alone. It was obvious there was something going on.

But they said nothing and accepted me in.

There were no lodging establishments in the settlement, so one of the old women in the village let me stay with her. It was obvious to see that I had no proper luggage or clothing with me, and the old woman gave me a bag with several changes of clothes in it, saying, "These may be a little old-fashioned for a young girl today, but…"

"…Are you sure I can have these?"

I didn't have a single thing I could give her in return.

"Yes, it's fine. Anyway, they're not doing old folks like us any good."

Along with the clothes, she also gave me a very mage-like robe to be part of my outfit. It was a gorgeous white robe. When I put my arms through the sleeves, it smelled of wood. It seemed like it had been lying unused in a wardrobe for a very long time. It wasn't the right size, so it was baggy on me, but the old woman adjusted it for me so that it fit perfectly.

Gazing at me nostalgically after I got changed, the old woman told me the story of the people who lived in that settlement.

Those people living in their village in the woods all had various reasons for leaving their hometowns. All of them had found regular life stifling.

People who were wandering the outside world for similar reasons naturally gathered together, and in finding one another, they had formed a village.

"That's why even though you arrived here alone, no one will ask you anything."

The old woman prepared dinner for me.

She said that the local cuisine out there in the forest was based on mushrooms. We ate mushroom pasta and mushroom soup. It was a simple meal, but to these self-sufficient people, it was a feast.

After dinner, the old woman told me that if I wanted to, I was welcome to live in the village.

And that the other villagers were hoping I would stay.

They were such kind people.

"Thank you very much. But I can't stay here."

The following day, I left the village at sunrise.

As a parting gift, they gave me plenty of food and money.

They were the kindest people in the world.

But I knew I was not normal.

There was no way I could continue to rely on the goodwill of those kind people, who had never once pointed out that I was not normal. And so, after bowing deeply to the villagers, I once again flew off on my broom.

I definitely didn't leave because I couldn't stomach the mushrooms.

○

I flew for about two days after leaving the village, before I happened across a caravan crossing a plain.

Beside the wagons, three children and a young man and woman were having a friendly chat. I was gazing admiringly at the tranquil scene when their eyes eventually landed on me.

"Heeey! Traveling witch! Where are you headed?"

Where am I headed?

I myself didn't have the answer to that question. My broom naturally came to a stop in front of them. As a matter of fact, I didn't even know whether there were even any countries in the direction that I was flying.

So I opened my mouth and immediately asked, "Are there any countries around here?"

"Any countries around here…? No, none right nearby, but—," the man who seemed to be the leader of the caravan party answered me. He seemed perplexed. "Do you mean to say that you've been flying along on your broom without even knowing where you're headed…?"

"Yes."

"You're quite the strange one, huh…?"

I understand that already.

"Miss, are you lost?" a young child asked from behind the man who seemed to be the leader. It was a boy, about five years old.

I didn't even know whether or not I was lost.

To begin with, what does being lost mean?

I didn't even know the definition.

"…If you don't mind, would you tell us about yourself?"

The man who seemed to be the leader of the caravan party smiled kindly at me when I was stumped for an answer.

They were kind people as well.

When I asked, they told me they were a family-operated caravan. Apparently, they went around trading their wares as they traveled the wide world as a family.

The man who was the leader was the head of the family and the head of the enterprise. Second-in-command was his wife. It sounded like the three children mostly assisted them.

"We wanted the kids to know how big the world is from the time they were small, you see—that's why I decided we would do this job as a family."

After hearing a bit about my circumstances and sympathizing with me a little, the leader launched into an energetic explanation about everything that led him to want to start this caravan.

Sitting beside him, his wife said, "The kids are happy with it," and stroked the children's heads.

The oldest was seven, the middle child was five, and the youngest was three. Two boys and a girl, with the girl being the middle child.

"Having this unique experience at a young age will definitely be an asset to them in the future."

The man talked about the details of forming his caravan business. He looked just like an innocent child who was lost in a dream. Looking at his bright eyes reminded me of some of the children who had been with me while I was at the orphanage.

The man estimated that even if I kept flying on my broom, it would probably take me three days to reach the closest country.

That kind man told me I could travel with the caravan for a little while.

I took him up on that offer.

I traveled with their family for about a week.

They were peaceful days. I spent almost every day playing with the children. Occasionally, we studied together. Apparently, the second-in-command could use a little bit of magic, and she taught me some of the principles of spellcasting, since I couldn't properly handle even the barest basics.

All I did during those days was take advantage of those people's generosity.

"Is there nothing I can do for you?" I asked the leader.

With a smile, he said, "You've been a big help to us already, just by playing with the children. The experience of playing with a girl a little older than them for a week will also be an asset to them, I'm sure."

He told me, "I want them to try all sorts of things, come in contact with all sorts of stuff, and meet, talk to, and get along with all sorts of different people. If they experience a lot of different things, that will lay the foundation for the rest of their lives."

After a week had gone by, we arrived at a certain country.

I separated from them there.

"We are planning to go do business in a country a little farther down the road, you see, so—we came here along the way."

He said that, and then the head of the family business verified my identity to the gate guard and shouldered the expense of my entry.

As a parting gift, he handed me some amount of money.

I protested that I hadn't done anything to deserve the money he was offering—I shook my head, and the man laughed and stroked his children's hair.

My journey had been nothing if not blessed by kind people.

The caravan left the country, and I stood there waving as their wagons grew ever smaller.

And vowing that I would experience a lot of different things in this new country.

○

Then, a week after that happened—

"…Why?"

—I was penniless.

I stood in the street as my stomach growled and grumbled. Too much had happened, and I felt like I might lose my mind. I looked from the back alley I was standing in over to the main road and saw soldiers and shady men going every which way, looking for me. They were going around asking everyone they passed if they had seen a child with ash-gray hair.

"How did this happen…?"

For a little while, everything had been going well for me in that country.

I knew the money I had been given would only be enough to survive on for about a week. I needed a place to live, food to eat, clothes to wear. I would need a lot of money to keep on living.

First things first, I would have to find work.

Cafés, restaurants, inns, clothing shops, bookstores…there were lots of different businesses lining the streets. I wondered what kind of place I could work to get some good experience. I wondered who would employ a ten-year-old mage.

Carefully scrutinizing each shop, I walked down the street.

"You! Hey, you! You over there!"

That was when someone called out to me. When I looked in the direction of the voice, I saw a man beckoning to me from a small alleyway right beside a roadside stall.

"You, by any chance are you looking for a job? I've got a good job for you!"

Well! Can he read my mind?

I was very surprised when it happened, and I walked over giddily, as if being drawn into the narrow, gloomy alley where the man was standing.

"What's this good job?"

I suddenly got excited, thinking I would be able to quickly gain some valuable experience.

"I want you to walk around handing these out to the people of the city."

The man handed me a small basket. The inside was packed with lots of candies.

According to him, he had built a candy shop on a corner of one of the streets in town. His shop was going to open in a week. He said he wanted me to go around handing out the candies as advertising.

I had been walking around looking for a job, and the man had been looking for a publicist. Our interests were aligned. I readily agreed and walked off holding the basket full of candy.

For the next few days, I walked around handing out candy to people on the street.

"A new candy store is opening! Please come check it out!"

Every day, I did my job, shouting enthusiastically.

The man kindly prepared meals for me every day. I was incredibly grateful not to have to worry about food expenses, when I was using up what little money I had every day just to stay at an inn.

As the shop's opening day approached, the man talked to me about his dreams. He told me how difficult it had been to get to the point where he could open a shop of his own and how happy he was to be able to open his candy shop.

However, a week later—

The very first people to open the door of the candy shop, the shop the man had always dreamed of opening, were some rude, shady-looking men.

"'Ey, you! You didn't forget about the money you borrowed from us, didja? Before you relax an' open up a shop like this, first you oughtta pay us back, don'cha think?"

The suspicious men pressed the shopkeeper.

Apparently, the shopkeeper had borrowed money from these shady characters.

"S-sorry…! I'm sorry! I don't have the money right now—but once the shop takes off, I'll definitely pay you back! I just need a little more—"

"What makes you think we're gonna wait? Pay us now!"

One of the vulgar-looking men grabbed the shopkeeper by the collar. He was angry, and he threatened that if the man didn't pay up, they would get their money by selling his organs.

At that moment, I remembered the man's tale of hardships.

I was sure the reason the man didn't have any money on hand was because he had been paying me a daily wage and preparing meals for me. My chest ached. Once I realized that, I stood up in front of these criminals.

"W-wait, please! If it's money you want—if it's money, I'll pay it!"

Then I handed the shady man all the money I had.

I was penniless again.

But it was all right. Because I had been penniless before I entered the country and penniless right when I started my journey. I was sure this, too, would be an important life experience—

"Hey, hey, don'chu treat me like a fool, missy. Your pocket change isn't gonna cut it!"

……

Huh? It's not enough?

After frantically shoving all the money I had into his pocket, the vulgar fellow looked at me like he was appraising me.

"Missy, now that I get a good look atcha, you've got a real pretty little face. I could get a good price if I sold ya!"

……

I had a bad feeling.

"In exchange fer you not payin' us back, we could just take her. That'd work fine."

A really bad feeling.

In the threatening atmosphere, I gave the shopkeeper a look asking for help.

"……"

He immediately averted his eyes from me.

He said only—

"I'm sorry. All right then, please sell the child."

That's when I became convinced he was scum.

After that, everything happened so fast. I promptly pulled out my broom and escaped the shop. Just like when I had left my hometown, I fled with all my might.

"Ah, wait a second! Hey, you guys! Chase her, chase her! Don't you dare let 'er get away!"

I knew I would attract a lot of attention, flying down the main avenue on my broom. So as soon as I managed to slip into the crowd, I put my broom away and started walking.

I had been walking away for a little while when I saw some of the country's soldiers speaking to passersby.

That's it, I'll ask the soldiers for help.

"Mister soldier! Help me, please! Some scary people are chasing me!"

I clung to one of the soldiers.

"Hmm? Oh really...?" The soldier raised his eyebrows, looking a little surprised at me after I suddenly appeared in the middle of his conversation. Then he placed his hands on my shoulders. "Is that a true story, I wonder?" he asked. "Where might those scary people be now?"

"Um..."

I turned back to look around.

My frantic escape must have been effective, because the criminals were nowhere to be seen.

I wondered how on earth I was supposed to explain my current situation. I thought about it, with my young brain.

"But this is actually perfect. I was just out searching for you, too. You must be the little girl who's been walking around handing out candies for the past week, right?"

"Uh, ah, yes...I am, but..."

"Do you know what was in those candies you were handing out?"

"...Huh?"

"When we examined them, it turns out that the candies you were giving out had an addictive substance in them, bordering on illegal, and we have no idea where it came from. Where did you get those candies, I wonder? I'd like to ask you a few—"

I see. This isn't going to work.

I ran off.

"Ah, hey! Waaaaaait!"

And so, on top of being penniless, I found myself being chased by both the soldiers and the criminals.

I wasn't sure whether my luck was bad or whether I'd simply had exceptionally good luck before then. But I had lost everything in the blink of an eye. I was reduced to sneaking through back alleys, trying to escape.

I was afraid I would have to live my life huddling up next to garbage forever, or at least until they forgot all about me.

But my pursuers easily outwitted a ten-year-old girl, even if she could use magic.

Almost as if the criminals and the soldiers had conspired to work together, they organized a search of all the back alleys. In no time at all, I was caught.

The one small mercy was the fact that the soldiers and the criminals had not in fact been working together to chase me down.

"Hey, what're you soldiers doin' here? This little girl is our valuable property! Don't you touch her!"

Apparently, I had already become property in the criminals' eyes.

"We should be the ones asking you. We have a number of questions we want to ask the girl. We've received multiple complaints about the dodgy candies she made. We have to bring her to justice!"

Apparently, I had already become a villain who made poison candy in the soldiers' eyes.

Ahh, this is bad.

"Um, um, I-I'm not—"

How on earth am I going to explain this?

All I could do was stand there, utterly terrified, surrounded by the adults. Though I was a mage, I was only ten years old. When it came down to it, the only thing I could do was to break into tears right there on the spot.

But it was only natural that a large group of adults surrounding a young girl and shouting at each other in the street would attract attention from the public.

It was also only natural that someone should appear to protest against them.

"What on earth is going on here?"

Wedging her way in between the soldiers and the criminals who were fighting over me was a woman with hair so white, it was nearly see-through.

She was wearing a robe that was the same bright white as her hair, and upon her breast was a star-shaped brooch.

She looked like she was about in her late thirties.

"Do good people have fights over little girls in broad daylight?"

Her tone of voice was calm, but there was a forceful drive behind the mage's words. The soldiers took one step back and straightened up, and the criminals dejectedly backed down.

One of the soldiers opened his mouth to speak to the mage who had suddenly appeared. He was probably going to try to explain the situation.

However, before the soldier's voice could come out, the mage shook her head and said, "Regardless of the circumstances, your approach was all wrong, wasn't it? The child is frightened, can't you see?"

Then the mage ordered the soldiers to withdraw and drove the criminals off. "Away with you all," she said. "I shall take charge of this child."

And then, after she had cleared away all the dangerous people who had been around me, the mage looked down at me.

"I don't know what happened here, but it looks like it is a complicated situation. Come with me," she said, and she took my hand.

The woman who whisked me away from that place said her name was the White Witch.

○

The White Witch told me she was a witch who lived in that country.

It was my first time seeing a being known as a witch. Apparently, that's what people were called once they developed their magical abilities and they received a star-shaped brooch from their teacher.

She invited me to stay at her estate.

"May I see you use your magic?" she asked as she handed me a wand.

There was hardly anything in the parlor of her mansion—just the barest furnishings of a table, a sofa, and a bookshelf—but even someone as ignorant as me could see that the furnishings were of good quality, and it was obvious that she lived an affluent life.

And so I carefully channeled some magical energy through the wand, making sure not to accidentally hit anything.

Light came from the tip of the wand.

"I see."

She shook her head and told me that was enough, and then asked me, "Now then, would you tell me your story?"

My story.

"…Where should I start?"

I figured she probably wanted to know the sequence of events that led to me being chased by the soldiers and the criminals. I was stumped as to where exactly to start my explanation.

She smiled gently at me as I hesitated.

"Anywhere you like," the White Witch said. "As much as time will permit, as much as you feel like telling, talk to me about whatever you like." And then, because it seemed like it was going to be a long story, she brought over several plates of cookies and macarons, as well as some tea.

I talked.

I told her everything that had happened before I got there.

I told her my oldest memory of being buried in the ruins by the seaside. I told her about how, the next thing I knew, I was living in the orphanage. I told her how life in the orphanage was stifling, and boring, and heartbreaking, and how I had been certain that I wasn't normal, and how I had fled. I told her about arriving at that kind village when I first set out on my journey. I told her about how after that, after flying across the plains for several days, I had encountered the caravan party and made my way there.

"A lot of people helped me before I got to this place." During my journey, the old woman and the others in the village, as well as the people in the caravan, had all treated me with kindness. "I thought that being friendly to people in trouble was normal."

While I was traveling, I had thought normal people lived their lives doing good things. Like all the people who had shown me kindness, I had also wanted to be kind to other people.

The White Witch asked me, "Are you traveling because you want to become normal?"

"……" I couldn't answer her. "I still don't really understand what normal is."

The world was brimming with things I didn't understand.

I had thought that if I could live kindly and treat people well, like those others had done for me, that that would be a normal way of living, but…

As a result of that thinking, in the week since I had entered this country, a group of men had taken advantage of me, and I had quickly lost everything.

"Is it not normal to extend a helping hand, to be nice when someone you know is struggling before your eyes?" I asked the White Witch.

She shook her head.

"I don't know whether it's normal or not, but as far as I can tell from hearing your story, I have no doubt that in this instance, your way of handling things was foolish." The woman admonished me in a gentle tone of voice. "You mustn't offer help solely out of a desire to be kind, without looking at the sequence of events that led the other person to wind up in trouble in the first place. You've got to think about what will happen after you help them."

Kindness had to be something you did in consideration of others; it couldn't be something you did for your own satisfaction.

That's what she told me.

I wondered whether that was what it meant to be normal.

I thought about it while I was listening to her speak so earnestly. The White Witch must have been able to tell exactly what I was thinking.

She opened her mouth to speak again.

"This *normal* that you keep talking about—to put it another way, we can call it common sense. And common sense doesn't have a definite form to it. It takes a different form for each person. By way of example, take these plates," she said as she picked up a cookie.

"There are several different plates on the table, and they may look the same, but the pattern is a little bit different on each one. Common sense is much the same. It may seem identical, but it's a little bit different in each person," she said.

"For example, don't the cookies and macarons served up on a beautiful plate look delicious? But if this plate was dirty and misshapen, would they look just as delicious, I wonder?"

I imagined it. Then I shook my head.

"...They wouldn't."

"Exactly," the White Witch agreed.

People's knowledge and experiences were built on top of their common sense, and if their version of common sense was peculiar, then the way they viewed their knowledge and experience would be different, too, she told me as she waved her wand and lifted all the cookies up off all the plates.

"And unfortunately, there's no correct answer as to which plates are clean and beautiful and which plates are dirty and misshapen."

"......"

I lowered my gaze.

To me at least, the plates that were left behind on the table looked like the kind of thing that anybody would say was beautiful.

"The people I met before coming to this country were good people."

The old woman and the others who had been living in the small settlement and the members of the family caravan had all treated me, a complete stranger, with kindness. I felt certain that if I could be more like those kinds of people, I could become a normal person.

"Were they really? It doesn't seem that way to me." The White Witch simply shook her head. "For example, the lady who gave you that robe you're wearing right now—do you really know who she was?"

"...?"

"Once, there was a mage in a country nearby here who killed her own husband. The mage was arrested and spent ten years in prison, after which she completed her rehabilitation into society. But the fact that she'd murdered her husband kept her at a distance, robbed her of her place in the community, and she fled from the country. The robe you're wearing is the very same robe the mage wore at the time of the incident."

"......Eh?"

"It sounds like you also encountered a family-owned caravan on your journey. From your perspective, how did they seem?"

"How did they seem...?" I was confused and at a loss for words, but I still managed to squeeze out a few words in reply. "They seemed... happy."

"Did they? By the way, they came to this country once before, but they faced harsh criticism from the citizens here, because they were abusing their children. The people felt bad for the kids, who were forced to work from a young age and never given the opportunity to get a proper education."

And so, unable to stand the criticism they faced, the family left, fleeing the country, she said.

"...But..." At least, those people had treated me, a complete stranger, with kindness. They didn't seem like bad people at all. Not to me anyway.

I hung my head, and she nodded.

"People who seem good from your perspective may seem very bad from another angle. That's what I'm saying."

In other words, she was telling me there was no such thing as one correct version of "common sense" or one true version of "normal," no matter whose perspective you looked at it from.

"As far as I can tell from what I've heard, your common sense hasn't completely developed yet. You simply copy the behavior of the people around you who seem normal and naturally treat them as if they are decent people."

Then the White Witch put her wand away.

The cookies that had been floating lightly in the air all fell down to the table and broke.

"...Well then, what am I supposed to do?" I asked. I wondered what I could do in order to acquire this common sense she was talking about. "What can I do to achieve normalcy?"

I didn't know. I didn't know anything. I only knew that I was ignorant. Other than that, I knew nothing.

I pleaded with her, desperate for any help I could get, and she simply shook her head and answered, "I wonder? That's something I don't really know either."

Then, smiling gently and kindly, she continued, "So why don't you join me in my studies?"

○

The White Witch was certainly a strange character.

She had used the metaphor of the plates to explain to me that each person's definition of a beautiful plate was different. But if I were to follow that example, I think her plate would probably have been quite odd looking to most people.

After all, she took me, a complete stranger with absolutely no blood relation to her, as her pupil to study magic. She said it was wasteful for her to live alone in her overly large mansion and provided me with a room. Then she taught me everything about magic, starting with the fundamentals.

"I'm sure you're eager to get back to your travels as soon as possible, but you can't. There are too many bad people out there, and a young girl like you traveling on her own is a tempting target, easy to trick. It's plainly obvious that if I let you go as you are now, you'll be tricked in the same way again."

"Well then, what should I do?"

I tilted my head questioningly, and she told me, as if it was the simplest thing in the world, "Become a witch. Show me proof that you are a mage in possession of advanced knowledge and skills and that you are powerful enough to use them. After all, I'm not going to permit you to return to your travels until you become a witch," she said.

She was a strict but kind witch.

Day by day, she taught me not only how to handle my magic but also guidelines for traveling and other things that would generally be considered common sense.

Apparently, she was a witch of some standing in that country.

Every day, all kinds of people knocked on the gates to her estate with various requests. Whether she gave them the help they were seeking depended on the money they offered. She wouldn't take a job for too little money, and she wouldn't take one for too much money either.

When I asked her why, she answered, "Respectable people know better than to try to hire a witch for a pittance. And people who offer too much money almost always have hidden circumstances that they don't disclose at the time they make their request."

So she only accepted commissions from just the right type of people who offered her just the right amount of money, she said.

"Is that your definition of normal, Miss?"

"I suppose it is." The White Witch nodded.

About five years after that, on my fifteenth birthday, I fastened a corsage of bellflowers to my chest. My training had begun to bear fruit, and so I became a witch's apprentice.

My intense training in genuine magic began the day my apprenticeship started.

If I wanted to spend my life traveling, then I had to learn every possible kind of spell that would allow me to defeat any looming dangers—that's what the White Witch told me as she instructed me in various spells.

After turning fifteen and becoming an apprentice, I also started lending a hand with the witch's jobs.

We did everything from concocting potions, to exterminating pests, to locating things and people, to making and destroying objects.

She used her magic for the sake of the world and for the sake of other people.

But people didn't always express gratitude toward the witch or her assistant. That was because when magic was used to help one person, it sometimes ended up hindering another.

Together with my teacher, I was sometimes appreciated and sometimes despised as I learned magic in that country.

"Why are you being so kind as to teach me magic?"

On the day I turned eighteen and became an adult, the White Witch said, "I think it's about the right time for you to become a witch."

And so, on the day of my birthday, I was recognized as a witch. "Congratulations. You've finally completed all the preparations to head out on your journey."

The White Witch smiled gently, as she had when we'd first met.

I wore the black robe I had purchased for my travels while I was working as her apprentice. She fixed the star-shaped brooch to the breast of the robe.

Its modest weight pressed against my chest.

"I'm glad that I met you."

These words, which I normally never would have said, came naturally spilling out of my mouth.

I must have been in high spirits at the prospect of setting off again.

"That's my line." She must have been in the same state as I was. "You could say that I was also saved by having you in my life."

I shook my head.

"I'm not powerful enough to save you," I replied.

But she shook her head, too, as if following my lead.

"No, no. I was saved as soon as we met...because I learned for a fact that I was not the only strange human out there."

"......"

"And so these past few years have been fulfilling for me in their own way."

At that point, I remembered something.

She never accepted jobs from the people who came to her for help unless they offered proper compensation.

If the compensation they presented to her was too high, she didn't trust them, and if it was too low, she didn't even show any interest. She had only ever accepted commissions from people whose sense of values aligned with hers, even just a little bit.

Whenever there was a gap between what she was being offered and what she was being asked, she entirely refused to hear the request.

The days I spent with her after we met had been happy ones for me. I thought they had probably been happy for her, too.

"What kind of name do you want for your witch name?" she asked me.

I cocked my head.

"What kind of name would be good?"

For one thing, she was the only witch I really knew. I had never met another witch. I wondered what kind of names were appropriate to signify a witch.

At this point, I found myself asking her once again what was *normal*. She answered me plainly.

"In this country, it's considered normal to take a name that is connected to your hair color."

"I see."

I looked at her. She had beautiful white hair. And that's why she was the White Witch. I felt like it was a little too simplistic, but—

"Well then, I'll do the same. Please use the color of my hair."

I bowed once.

She nodded. "All right, let's do that."

And then I received my witch name from her.

A simple name, connected to my hair color.

"The Ashen Witch."

O

After that, I went on a long, long journey as the Ashen Witch.

I flew around the world on my broom, often veering off the beaten path. Sometimes good things happened to me, and sometimes bad things happened instead.

The world was overflowing with every conceivable definition of normal.

Every day was perfect.

After a number of years had passed since I began my journey, I took on two students of my own. From then on, I continued traveling while raising the two of them as apprentice witches.

Then those two both became witches, and each of them went down her own path, and I found myself alone again.

"Welcome to our country! Are you here for some sightseeing?"

I arrived at a certain remote country, far from any other civilization. It was a peaceful place, a small, unremarkable country without any notable sights.

Perhaps because they very rarely got any sightseers, the guard at the gate greeted me with a stiff salute.

I shook my head.

"Homecoming."

"Oh? Homecoming, you say?" The guard's eyes went wide, and he dropped his salute. "Excuse me, but what is your name?"

"I am called the Ashen Witch."

"Wait just a moment, please! I'll check the departure logs!"

If I was coming home, that meant I must have left once. Apparently, the guard needed to examine the records to confirm I had left the country some time before.

This was my first experience ever coming home, so I was confused.

"We don't have a record of your departure, but—"

When I first left the country, I wasn't yet the Ashen Witch, so understandably, I wasn't going to be in the records.

It was even less likely, since I hadn't exactly departed under the best circumstances.

"Try looking under the name Victorica."

I told him to look back over a decade prior in his records.

It was already quite a long time ago. I gave him the name of the naive young mage who had taken it upon herself to sneak out of the orphanage, fearing that she was not normal, and then forced her way out of the front gates.

Once I designated the specific year for him, he easily found the record of my departure.

As soon as he found it, the guard furrowed his brow.

"...It says here that it was an unlawful exit."

"And that's why I came back to pay the fine." Nodding to him, I asked, "Any chance you're going to let me in?"

"Well, if you don't come in, then you can't pay the fine, so..."

The gate guard stepped aside and ushered me in. Familiar, peaceful scenery spread out before me on the other side of the gate.

"Welcome home, Lady Witch."

Then I bowed back to the saluting guard and walked through the gates.

The Peaceful Country of Robetta.

The final country I visited on my journey was my hometown, the very place I'd started.

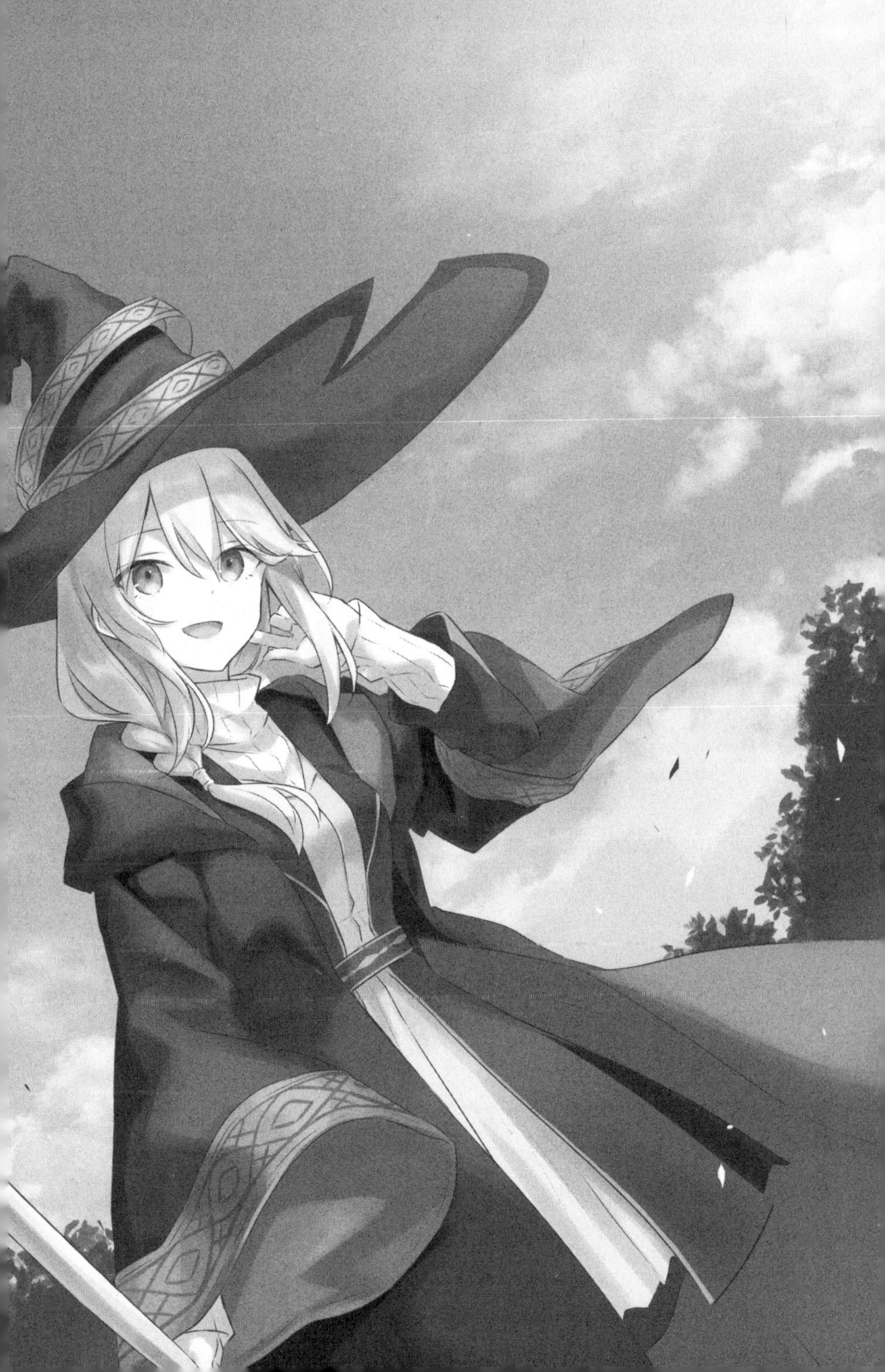

Afterword

Good afternoon, good evening, good morning. It's been two months! I'm Jougi Shiraishi.

I'm going to launch right into it with my impressions of the anime. It was incredible, huh? Led by Director Kubooka, the setting the anime staff drew for *Journey of Elaina* was a far more beautiful and vibrant world than I had even imagined. Completely enchanted by their setting, which was just brimming over with charm, I watched every week, thinking to myself, *I'd sure like to travel through this world!* It really was ridiculously pretty. Also, I loved the way Elaina conducted the music with her wand in the opening theme. The ending theme by ChouCho was also amazingly great, right? And the various other songs that added flair to the series, too. My heart leaped for joy when they played during Elaina's travels.

The Elaina that Azure drew in the original books was cute, and Itsuki Nanao's Elaina in the comicalizations was cute, too. Elaina is basically always cute, and she was cute in the anime, too, wasn't she? Personally, my favorite was Elaina in Episode 7, the grape-stomping story, when she was talking to the village head. Because she flipped through a lot of different expressions, and that was funny. I liked that, and in the anime, I always enjoyed listening to the performances of the voice cast, starting with Kaede Hondo of course. Personally, there were way too many things about it that made me happy, and I can't possibly write them all down, but I'll just say that even during my busiest, most hectic days, I clearly remember that I always looked forward to work that was related to the anime, if nothing else. It was a great year… Though it was over before I knew it, seriously.

I'm changing the subject here, but due to various circumstances at my main job, from January 2021 onward, I'm going to be living in the Tokyo metropolitan area. Up to now, I've had the privilege of visiting my local bookstore in Aichi every time a new volume of *Journey of Elaina* came out, but from now on I guess it's going to be a little too far to go. While I'm still here, I think I'd like to visit the bookstore just like I always have. I want to sign a lot of books there. Inside, there's a part of me that feels like 2020 was a real turning point in my life, so I do feel anxious that taking advantage of this opportunity might change everything, but I also feel excited, like I'm going on a journey to a new place. Well, but it's not like I'm getting married or starting a relationship or anything. I'm only changing locations for work, so the only things that will change are my address and lifestyle, and I'll be getting rid of my car. The first thing I'm doing right now is hunting for an apartment that allows pets. Since I'm going through all the effort of moving, I'd like to keep a cat or a dog. I want to get a hedgehog. Hedgehogs are so, so cute…

Now we're at the end of the year, and the anime work has settled down a little. I've gone on at length about everything here, but basically that's how this year went. Everything was hectic, but there was plenty to be happy about, too.

If next year could bring me days of nothing but that kind of happiness, that would be great.

Well then, from this point on, I'm going to start my commentary on each chapter.

There are probably going to be spoilers as well, so anyone who's like, "I haven't read the book yet!" please turn around here!

- Chapter One

I'm so happy to have finally achieved my greatest wish and been able to put out a volume of bonus stories! Hooray! Because of that, we had the strange situation of the publication of Volume 15 suddenly moving up to December, but including the new sections I wrote for it, the page count was just about perfect, so that was a relief. Taking another look at the collected list of bonus stories I've put out so far, I was surprised to see that the page count was actually huge. I couldn't believe I'd written that much...

- Chapter Two

This was an original short story I wrote in the same spirit that I always write my bonus stories. The idea of a doll or some other toy that always comes back to you no matter how many times you throw it away is a standard among ghost stories, right? In fact, it's too conventional, to where I almost feel like it's become a stereotype that gets written into comedy pieces.

- Chapter Three

For this chapter, I made a medium-length story out of a bonus story I put out to go with Volume 9. I wrote it thinking that since I was finally getting my long-awaited bonus story volume, it might be interesting to try and write a kind of continuation of one of those bonus stories.

- Chapter Four

This was a story about you-know-who. I wonder if that witch, who set off on her journey yearning to be normal but not knowing what normal was, found her own version of normal after returning to her hometown?

I wrote out the witch's real name without any hesitation, but I should tell you that there is a goddess who fulfills the same role in both Roman and Greek legends, and it's a tweaked version of her name from Roman mythology that was the original source for the witch's true name. The name that comes from Greek mythology was the source for her pen name. Really, I would have been just fine putting her name out there at any point, but I didn't have a good opportunity, and after I saw that she would make an appearance in the anime, I decided to reveal it in this volume. Volume 15 was almost all bonus stories anyway, so somehow or other I thought it would be nice to have one story that was connected to the main narrative.

And so that was Volume 15 of *Wandering Witch: The Journey of Elaina*!

I made *The Adventures of Niche* five volumes long out of superstition, wishing that *Journey of Elaina* would make it to five volumes, too, but before I knew it, I had put out three times that many books. Ever since the anime started, we are constantly doing reprints, and I've had the pleasure of hearing all sorts of people tell me that they watched the anime, which made me really happy. I got into the spirit of things and contributed anonymously to *Wandering Witch WEB Radio (Broadcasting Witch)*, which resulted in a strange accident where I was totally doxed by Miss Hondo, but even including that incident, I've been having a lot of fun.

Somehow, this turned into an afterword that feels like I might be announcing the end of the series itself, but I think the main *Journey of Elaina* book series is going to continue on, so I would love it if I could depend on your support as always.

I expect that the series will continue on next year, and personally, writing that plus full comedy stories like the ones on the drama CDs means lots of fun for me, so I'll be happy if the drama CD releases continue to be frequent.

Well then, I'm going to use up all my pages before too long, so I think it's about time I wrapped things up. I'll write all my acknowledgments together, as far as the space allows. Regardless of whether you worked on the anime, the original books, or the manga, to everyone who has had a hand in making *Journey of Elaina*, truly, thank you so much. I would be very glad if we could continue working together in the future.

And to all of you who have come in contact with the world of *Journey of Elaina*, thank you!

Elaina's travels are going to keep on going, so I'm counting on you to cheer her on!

Well then, see you in Volume 16!

HAVE YOU BEEN TURNED ON TO LIGHT NOVELS YET?

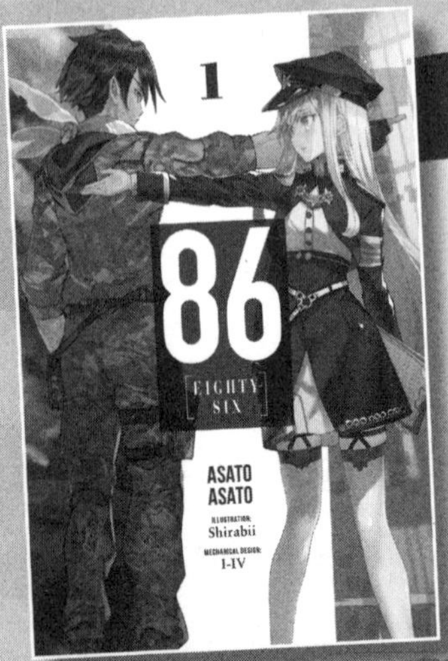
1
86
EIGHTY SIX
ASATO ASATO
ILLUSTRATION: Shirabii
MECHANICAL DESIGN: I-IV

86—EIGHTY-SIX, VOL. 1–13

In truth, there is no such thing as a bloodless war. Beyond the fortified walls protecting the eighty-five Republic Sectors lies the "nonexistent" Eighty-Sixth Sector. The young men and women of this forsaken land are branded the Eighty-Six and, stripped of their humanity, pilot "unmanned" weapons into battle...

Manga adaptation available now!

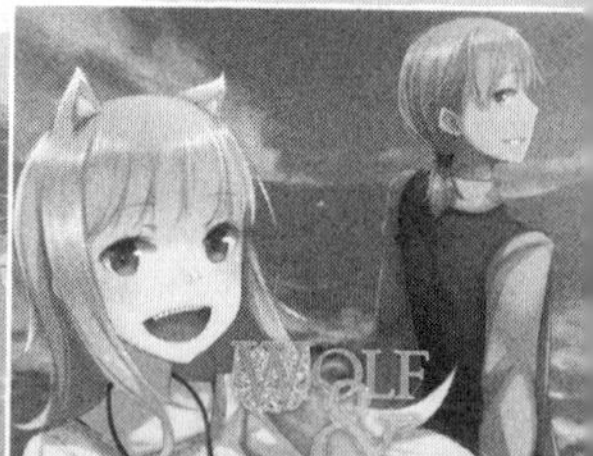
VOL. 1
ISUNA HASEKURA

WOLF & PARCHMENT, VOL. 1–9

The young man Col dreams of one day joining the holy clergy and departs on a journey from the bathhouse, Spice and Wolf. Winfiel Kingdom's prince has invited him to help correct the sins of the Church. But as his travels begin, Col discovers in his luggage a young girl with a wolf's ears and tail named Myuri, who stowed away for the ride!

Manga adaptation available now!

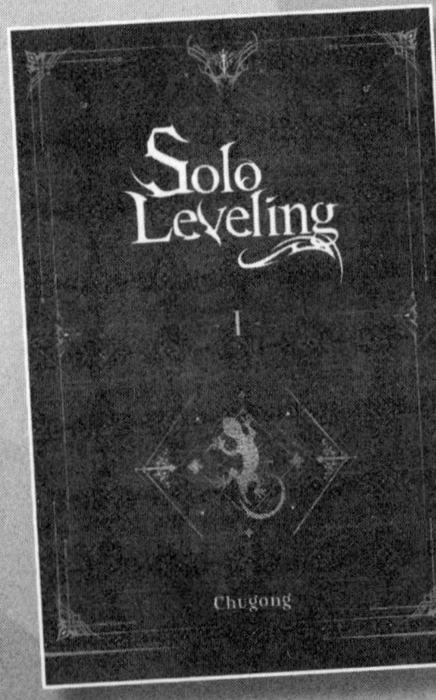
Solo Leveling
I
Chugong

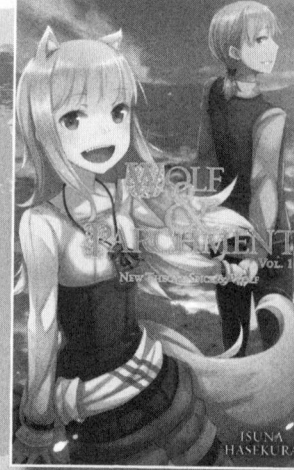

SOLO LEVELING, VOL. 1–8

E-rank hunter Jinwoo Sung has no money, no talent, and no prospects to speak of—and apparently, no luck, either! When he enters a hidden double dungeon one fateful day, he's abandoned by his party and left to die at the hands of some of the most horrific monsters he's ever encountered.

Comic adaptation available now!

THE SAGA OF TANYA THE EVIL, VOL. 1-13

Reborn as a destitute orphaned girl with nothing to her name but memories of a previous life, Tanya will do whatever it takes to survive, even if it means living life behind the barrel of a gun!

Manga adaptation available now!

SO I'M A SPIDER, SO WHAT?, VOL. 1-16

I used to be a normal high school girl, but in the blink of an eye, I woke up in a place I've never seen before and—and I was reborn as a spider?!

Manga adaptation available now!

OVERLORD, VOL. 1-16

When Momonga logs in one last time just to be there when the servers go dark, something happens—and suddenly, fantasy is reality. A rogues' gallery of fanatically devoted NPCs is ready to obey his every order, but the world Momonga now inhabits is not the one he remembers.

Manga adaptation available now!

VISIT YENPRESS.COM TO CHECK OUT ALL OUR TITLES AND...

GET YOUR YEN ON!